THE MISSING DIAMOND MURDER

Recent titles by Diane Janes

The Black and Dod mysteries

THE MAGIC CHAIR MURDER *
THE POISONED CHALICE MURDER *
THE MISSING DIAMOND MURDER *

Fiction

THE PULL OF THE MOON
WHY DON'T YOU COME FOR ME?
SWIMMING IN THE SHADOWS *
STICK OR TWIST *
A STROKE OF BAD LUCK

Non-fiction

EDWARDIAN MURDER: IGHTHAM &
THE MORPETH TRAIN ROBBERY
POISONOUS LIES: THE CROYDON ARSENIC MYSTERY
THE CASE OF THE POISONED PARTRIDGE
DEATH AT WOLF'S NICK

* *available from Severn House*

THE MISSING DIAMOND MURDER

Diane Janes

This first world edition published 2019
in Great Britain and the USA by
SEVERN HOUSE PUBLISHERS LTD of
Eardley House, 4 Uxbridge Street, London W8 7SY.
Trade paperback edition first published
in Great Britain and the USA 2020 by
SEVERN HOUSE PUBLISHERS LTD.

British Library Cataloguing in Publication Data
A CIP catalogue record for this title is available from the British Library.

ISBN-13: 978-0-7278-8954-6 (cased)
ISBN-13: 978-1-78029-630-2 (trade paper)
ISBN-13: 978-1-4483-0323-6 (e-book)

All Severn House titles are printed on acid-free paper.

Severn House Publishers support the Forest Stewardship Council™ [FSC™],
the leading international forest certification organisation. All our titles that
are printed on FSC certified paper carry the FSC logo.

MIX
Paper from
responsible sources
FSC
www.fsc.org   FSC® C013056

Typeset by Palimpsest Book Production Ltd.,
Falkirk, Stirlingshire, Scotland.
Printed and bound in Great Britain by
TJ International, Padstow, Cornwall.

ONE

'**M**r Long will see you now.'

'Thank you.' Fran took a firmer grip of her handbag and entered her solicitor's inner office, feeling absurdly nervous. She could not help suspecting that the letter she had received the day before, requesting her to make an appointment, was not going to be good news.

'Good morning, Mrs Black. Very good weather we're having for the time of the year, don't you think?'

Mr Long always remarked on the weather. It was his standard form of introduction, while holding out the high-backed chair, with its rather worn leather seat, one of the pair that stood before the enormous desk which took up most of the space in the room. You could almost have had a game of billiards on it, Fran thought, as Mr Long moved in a sedate half-circle in order to gain his own side of the giant fixture. The second chair on her side of the desk was always empty during these consultations regarding her divorce. It felt symbolic.

'Now, you will be wondering, I am sure, why I have asked you to come in.' Mr Long settled himself into his own, rather more comfortable-looking chair as he spoke. 'I have received notification that the court is in receipt of a letter which suggests that you, the petitioner, may be . . . ahem . . . enjoying some kind of liaison with a man. Now as you are aware, the court must be absolutely convinced that you do not have an ulterior motive for ending your marriage. Divorces cannot be granted for the mutual convenience of both parties. There has to be one guilty party and another who is completely innocent.'

Though he had spoken gently, Mr Long's eyes were on her face and Fran was conscious of the colour rising in her cheeks at the slight emphasis on *completely*. She hoped he would interpret it for the annoyance she undoubtedly felt.

'Mr Long, it is an incontrovertible fact that my husband left me for another woman almost three years ago and has been living with her ever since. The woman is now expecting his child. I, in the meantime, have lived alone. There has not been any impropriety with another man. May I ask the name of this other man, with whom I am supposed to be enjoying a liaison?'

'Of course. The man's name is Tom Dod – I see it is spelled with only one d at the end – probably a mistake on the correspondent's part. The authors of this type of anonymous missive are often barely literate. Please don't think that I am accusing you of any inappropriate conduct at all. It is simply that we are asked to respond to the allegation, and a simple statement to the effect that you are not even acquainted with a Mr Dod – with or without the double d – will no doubt suffice.

'In all likelihood the letter will not be taken seriously,' he went on, adopting his most reassuring tone. 'It is extremely brief and offers no particulars, merely saying . . .' He paused to glance down at the relevant sheet of paper on his blotter. *In the matter of Black v Black, someone might care to ask Mrs Black about her friendship with Mr Tom Dod.*'

Fran knew that her cheeks were positively burning. 'I do have an acquaintance called Mr Dod,' she said. 'And as it happens he does spell his name with only one d at the end, so the author of the letter must know him reasonably well. However, there has never been anything improper between myself and Mr Dod.'

'I see.' Mr Long hesitated for a moment. 'Again, you must understand, Mrs Black, that I do not doubt you for a moment, but we might have to exercise . . . shall we say, a certain amount of discretion in presenting this friendship to the court. May I ask you how well you know Mr Dod? Is he a close friend? Have you ever been in a situation with him which is open to misconstruction? We must choose our words very carefully.'

Fran thought quickly. The letter to the court had evidently been sent out of spite. Apart from her best friend, Mo, who was above suspicion, the people most likely to know both herself and Tom, and to be aware that Tom's name was spelled with a single d at the end, were probably fellow members of the Robert Barnaby Society, where she and Tom had certainly made one or two enemies in the course of the Linda Dexter affair. Fortunately their involvement in neither that case nor the more recent murders at Durley Dean had made the papers.

Mr Long took advantage of the pause to speak again. 'We must be careful not to make any statement which is open to challenge. For example, saying that Mr Dod has never spent the night at your home – however innocently – if in fact he has. The court is rather good at digging out the facts, you see, if they decide to take an interest. And, of course, you could be called into court and questioned on oath.'

'I can assure you, Mr Long, that Mr Dod has never spent the night in my home, or even eaten a meal there. I became acquainted with him because we are both members of a literary society which celebrates the life and work of the author Robert Barnaby. At one time we were both on the committee which manages the society and Mr Dod has sometimes been kind enough to give me a lift in his motor car, as I do not have a motor myself. However, I have not seen Mr Dod, or had any communication with him whatsoever for three . . . no, almost four months, because he has not been at any of the recent Barnaby Society meetings.'

Mr Long, who had been scribbling on his pad, looked up and said, 'Excellent, excellent. Would you describe Mr Dod as a friend?'

'A friend? Yes, I would. But he isn't what you would call a close family friend.' Though conscious of the little stab in her heart, she did not pause. 'I have never met his wife, for example, though I believe her name is Veronica. They have a boy.'

'Does he live in this area?'

'No. I can obtain his exact address from the Barnaby Society handbook, if it is needed, but I hope he won't get dragged into this. That would be most unfair, since he is an entirely innocent party.'

'Of course, of course.' Mr Long was at his soothing best. 'The court is very often satisfied by the response of the petitioner in cases where the allegations are as vague as this. Now let me see' – he was still writing as he spoke – 'suppose we say, "I, Frances Black, am acquainted with Mr Tom Dod owing to our mutual membership of the Robert Barnaby Society. I have, therefore, often been in Mr Dod's company at society meetings and we were at one time simultaneously serving members of the society's management committee, but as of today, I have not seen or communicated with Mr Dod for almost four months.'"

'Yes,' Fran said. 'That is all absolutely true.'

'Very good, very good. In that case I will incorporate this into my response and my secretary will type this up for you to sign. No need to do it now. We will keep it ready for the next time you come in, so that we can have it on file, in case of need.'

'The court doesn't require an actual copy of a signed statement immediately?'

'No, no. It hasn't come to that yet, and it probably won't – don't trouble yourself about it, my dear Mrs Black. A great many of these cases go through without any trouble at all. The sheer volume of divorce cases coming before the courts these days prevents them from giving too great a scrutiny to the vast majority.'

But it would be just my luck for them to pick on me, Fran thought, as she made her way back to the bus stop. It was not that there had ever been any adulterous carryings-on between herself and Tom, or even that she was obtaining a divorce in order to be free to marry him, but sometimes it was hard to prove a negative and there had been occasions, particularly last autumn, when she and Tom could have behaved badly if they had chosen to do so. If the court began to suspect that there was something going on between her and Tom, they might refuse to grant her divorce and she would end up shackled to Michael for all eternity. How very fortunate that she had broken off all communication back in November, when Tom had sent her a letter about a possible investigation for them down in Devon and she had written back with a polite but firm refusal. Since then she had been to a couple of Barnaby Society meetings, but Tom had not been at either of them – perhaps because he was avoiding her, or more likely because he was genuinely otherwise engaged elsewhere – and this had now proved most fortuitous as it had enabled her to state in all honesty that she had not had any communication with him for several months.

After the whirlwind events of the previous year, when they had been in almost constant touch with one another, it had been very difficult to come to terms with the fact that this would be the way of things from now on. Of course, there would be nothing to stop them from picking up the threads of their old friendship when she had her decree absolute, but perhaps by then Tom would have decided that it was better not to do so.

She glanced at her wristwatch, which confirmed that it was another five minutes before the bus was due. Too little time to usefully accomplish anything in town, but a bit too long to stand about in the February chill. She adjusted her gloves to ensure that they met the ends of her jersey sleeves.

She missed Tom horribly. Missed his cheery voice on the telephone, his kind brown eyes meeting hers to share a joke. Of course, the whole situation was made far worse by the absence of her best friend, Mo, who had given in to the imprecations of her mother-in-law and her husband, Terence, and gone out to spend a couple of months with him in Malaya. Letters with exotic postmarks had been arriving from each of the ports where her ship had called, full of Mo's exploits playing bridge and deck quoits, coupled with hilarious descriptions of her fellow passengers. As she read them, Fran could hear Mo's distinctive voice and hearty laugher. She had written back, so that replies awaited Mo's arrival each time the ship docked, but the time lag between their receipt meant that it was necessarily two one-sided conversations and, worse still, reading about her friend's adventures only tended to increase Fran's sense that life was passing her by.

The grim little ritual of Christmas with her mother had come and gone, with its Christmas Day visit to lay a wreath of evergreens on the village War Memorial, *because not one day can ever go by*, Fran thought bitterly, *when I am allowed to forget that my brothers are gone, while I, the second-rate daughter, am all that is left of our family.* As she stood at the bus stop, joined now by a ruddy-cheeked woman carrying a wicker basket and an upright old gentleman with a bowler hat that had seen better days, Fran reflected that perhaps she and Tom had even more in common than they thought. Poor Tom who must, she supposed, be reminded of his own dead brother every day. He too must feel second best. The younger son, who had married his dead brother's sweetheart out of duty, knowing all the time that she had really wanted his older brother.

Tom who had once told her that if they were both free . . . but she must not think about that. She could not think about it, because thinking about it only broke her heart all over again. She might be free of Michael soon, but Tom would never be free of Veronica and her son. *I have to make a new life for myself somehow*, Fran thought. *A different life which doesn't involve hankering over what I can never have.*

TWO

The Robert Barnaby Society were holding a regional meeting in Liverpool the following Saturday, where it had been arranged that Professor Cyril Draper, who was an authority on poetry in the modern era, had agreed to address them. Fran had already written a note to the organizer, signalling her intention to attend, but thanks to her interview with Mr Long she spent a good deal of time during the intervening days agonizing over it. Ought she to go along, with this thinly veiled accusation regarding herself and Tom hanging over her head? If Tom turned up, she might be able to tip him off about the anonymous letter, which she felt almost duty-bound to do. Then again, if some spiteful person saw them talking privately together, that might generate a second letter to the court, which would surely be taken more seriously than the first? On the other hand, if she cried off unexpectedly, might that not be open to accusations of a guilty conscience? Of course, if Tom did not attend, then her being there without him could be taken as another sign of their complete innocence? Oh dear! If only Mo had been there to advise her. Though of course Mo would probably say to heck with it and go to the meeting anyway – that was her style.

She could have telephoned Tom and asked whether or not he was going, but they had agreed that there should be no more telephone calls, for trunk calls were far too easily remembered by the operators, particularly operators who worked in small exchanges like Newby Bridge. Goodness, last year there had been dozens of phone calls to and from Tom Dod. Suddenly one's perfectly innocent actions could be thrown in one's face and all sorts of misconstructions put upon them. She would just have to pray that the nasty prying court officers never became interested in her telephone calls. Sending Tom a letter was also out, because that would have to be admitted if there were further questions about any recent communications between them.

Fran eventually decided to attend. She wanted to hear the professor and it was absolutely ridiculous to shut oneself away like a hermit on the strength of one anonymous letter. She took the early train from Haverthwaite, which meant two changes and got her to Lime Street Station a good hour before the meeting was due to start. She had originally planned to walk to the venue, but a chilly wind combined with thin, slanting rain soon decided her otherwise and pushing the expense to one side she took a cab, which delivered her to the church hall where the meeting was to be held rather earlier than expected. However, Miss Winterton, the organizer of the day, was extremely pleased to see her, particularly when Fran volunteered to help with setting out chairs.

'Vivian Blakemore promised to come early, but now he has cried off with the flu. It's probably no more than a cold in the head,' Miss Winterton sniffed, 'but you know what men are like.'

Having something to do was good, Fran thought, because it took her mind off the Tom problem, and for once she did not even mind that Ruth Winterton, the retired headmistress of a rather prestigious girls' school, tended to order one around as if dealing with a recalcitrant member of the lower fourth.

After the chairs had been positioned exactly as Miss Winterton had decreed they should be, there was a display of books to be arranged on the special tablecloth which a member of the society had embroidered with scenes from Robert Barnaby's books. Fran was just adjusting the final couple of volumes when she heard a distinctive burst of laughter from the other side of the room and realized that Tom had arrived. There had been a time last year when they'd felt so out of sorts with the Barnaby Society that both of them had decided not to continue as members, but in the end they had gone back on the decision and the sound of that hearty laugh made Fran glad of it. Whatever problems were facing her, the prospect of Tom's company could not help but lift her spirits. She realized too that he had instinctively avoided the trap of coming across to greet her immediately. *Good*, she thought. If they *were* being watched by someone with malicious intentions, then that person had been given nothing to fuel their accusations. It would, however, be equally suspicious if two people who had always been friendly at meetings suddenly began to ignore each other, so Fran waited until there were two other three other society members standing with Tom before she strolled across and joined the group.

'Hello, Mr Wheaton, Miss Snell. Hello, Tom,' she said. 'We missed you at the Christmas meeting.'

'Competing commitments, I'm afraid,' he said. 'I nearly didn't make it today, but I particularly wanted to hear this chap Draper.'

'I'm afraid the weather may put some people off,' Miss Snell put in, and this of course was a signal for everyone to comment on the way the temperatures had plummeted again and whether or not they could expect more snow.

'Can people begin to take their seats, please?' Ruth Winterton called fussily from the platform. Fran carefully managed not to be sitting immediately adjacent to Tom, instead sitting nearby and starting up a conversation with someone else. Tom, she noticed, had similarly engaged one of his immediate neighbours. How horrid it was that they could not even sit next to one another as they had done so often in the past. Even small pleasures were to be denied her, thanks to the nasty, suspicious minds of others.

The professor was extremely interesting on the subject of recent trends in poetry, even if he had relatively little to add to their knowledge of Robert Barnaby himself, so there was a good deal to talk about when the luncheon interval arrived. Some members had brought sandwiches to consume in the hall, but quite a group were heading out to find sustenance at nearby tearooms and a local hotel and Fran managed to tag along with the group which included Tom. As they entered the Quality Tea Rooms she found herself momentarily right next to him. Seizing her opportunity, she stopped as if suddenly recalling something to mind and said, 'Oh, I almost forgot. Here is that book which I promised to lend you ages ago. I popped it into my bag on the off-chance that you would be here.' As she was speaking, she unclipped her handbag and produced a slender volume of Fitzgerald's essays, which she had brought to read on the journey, and held it out in his direction.

To her considerable relief Tom accepted the book without question, just as if he had been expecting it, saying, 'How kind of you to have remembered. Thank you so much.' He slipped the book into the capacious right-hand pocket of his jacket, without even glancing at the cover. Though they sat down together, their lunch of ham and tomato sandwiches was chaperoned by the quartet who shared their table and when it was time to return to the hall for the afternoon section of the programme, Tom excused himself on some pretext or another and instead of returning with the rest of the group hastened away in the opposite direction.

Back at the hall, where Miss Winterton had press-ganged some of those who had remained for a picnic lunch into rearranging the chairs into groups, everyone was invited to participate in an elaborate parlour game, in which teams calling themselves by different character names from the Barnaby books competed with one another by performing mimes and answering questions about Barnaby's works. Tom arrived back just in time to join the team calling itself Dr Gruffbluster, which was soon in hot competition with the Black Shadows, led by Richard and Julia Finney, and the Hugo Hegginbottoms, which included Fran. After an hour or so of lively rivalry and a not inconsiderable numbers of disputes about the accuracy or otherwise of one or two of the answers, the Black Shadows were declared the winners amid much laughter and cheering from the livelier element in the room. With the day's programme completed, the meeting began to break up. Fran was in the act of donning her coat when Tom crossed the hall and, thrusting his hand into his pocket, produced what was obviously a book encased in a brown paper bag. 'While we were eating lunch I remembered that I had the latest Christie in my car,' he said. 'I think you said at lunch that you haven't read it yet, so I thought you might like to borrow it?'

'Oh – thank you.' Fran took the book and popped it into her handbag without looking at it. As she did so, she noticed Sarah Ingoldsby was watching them with a sour look on her face. There had been no love lost between themselves and Sarah Ingoldsby since the Magic Chair affair. Might she be the source of the anonymous communication to the court?

Only when she was safely back on the train and had put several miles between herself and the nearest member of the society did she dare to investigate the package further. When she opened the bag – as gingerly as if it contained a bomb – her suspicions were immediately confirmed, for the paper bag did not contain a brand-new edition of *The Seven Dials Mystery* but instead her own, slightly worn, second-hand copy of *Tales of the Jazz Age*. She opened the book at the title page and found folded inside the same piece of paper that she had inserted earlier that morning. It had been a risk, but fortunately Tom had caught on immediately. He must have gone off by himself after lunch and read her brief note.

Someone has sent a letter to the court suggesting that there is a close friendship between us. I felt you should know. Please forgive any apparent unfriendliness on my part, but I cannot afford to give rise to any rumours whatsoever. I am afraid the court probably has the power to question even fellow members of the society. For this reason I think it best if I do not attend any meetings in the foreseeable future.

Tom had written his own message on the back of the same sheet.

The Edgertons have been in touch again, asking for help with their family mystery. Why don't you go down to Devon and have a go at solving it? It would be the ideal excuse for you to absent yourself from the next couple of Barnaby events. I will stay right out of it and turn up at Barnaby meetings as usual. Their telephone number is Frencombe 29.

As she read the note, Fran went hot and cold at the thought of how easily they might have been caught out. Suppose that note had fallen out of the book and been discovered by someone else? On the other hand, she could not help smiling at the cheek of it. They hadn't spent so much as a moment completely alone together, and yet they had still managed to engage in some private communication. She experienced a brief thrill of guilty pleasure, cut short when she imagined attempting to explain such apparently childish antics to Mr Long if they were ever found out. She must burn the note as soon as she got home. It would not do to leave it lying around where her daily help, Ada, might see it, for Ada would naturally have to answer honestly if she was ever faced with questions about her mistress's private life.

If push came to shove and she herself were to be questioned about any recent communications between herself and Tom Dod, she had already come up with a formula which would enable her not to break an oath – she would answer by saying that she had only spoken with Tom Dod at the Liverpool meeting and had neither telephoned him nor sent him any letters through the post. A court interrogator would surely not think to ask specifically about any notes handed over in a tearoom under the very noses of independent witnesses.

In the meantime, what about the Edgertons and their 'family mystery'? They had already approached Tom once, several months before, having heard via the chief constable of Nottinghamshire something of his and Fran's success in resolving the case in Durley Dean. Tom had first written to her about it last year, but she had immediately rejected any suggestion of becoming involved. Confronted with the question afresh, she found herself hesitating. First of all, she could not deny that a 'family mystery' sounded intriguing, particularly to someone who was pretty desperate for any kind of interesting diversion, but secondly there was Tom's point about having an excuse for missing Barnaby Society meetings. It would soon be time to commit to the annual Barnaby Society weekend gathering at Furnival Towers – an event that both she and Tom had always attended in the past. If she could arrange a trip to Devon to coincide with that weekend . . . Now she came to consider it, the Furnival Towers get-together was taking place earlier than usual this year to allow for Easter, so it would be easy to plead confusion over the dates . . . Did she really need an excuse for not being at a Barnaby Society event? On the other hand, said a voice in her head, did she really need an excuse to accept an invitation to spend a few days at a nice country house in Devon?

THREE

By the time Fran had changed trains four times, snagged a stocking on a stray packing case which some fool of a porter had left lying about on the platform at Birmingham New Street and almost missed the connection at Newton Abbot altogether, excitement at the prospect of a trip down to Devon had evaporated somewhat. For much of the journey, the carriage windows had been almost entirely obscured by drizzle, but as they left Newton Abbot station and steamed south-west, following the river valley away from the town, the train emerged from under the rainclouds and shafts of sunlight lit up the lush green countryside, which looked quite unlike the pale, wintry fields at home where spring had still scarcely arrived.

Making arrangements for the visit had been simple, because she soon discovered that Tom had already been in touch with the Edgertons and paved the way for her. When she telephoned Frencombe 29, she had spoken with someone called Roland Edgerton, who seemed only too eager for her to travel down at her earliest convenience, promising, once a time and date had been agreed, that someone would be there to meet her at the station.

She wished that she had felt able to speak with Tom directly, so that she could have asked him more about the Edgertons. Roland Edgerton sounded very well spoken on the telephone and his family were acquainted with a chief constable in another county, so it could be safely assumed that they had money and moved in good circles. She hoped that they were not frightfully grand. Their address gave nothing away. Sunnyside House, Frencombe, Devon, might turn out to be anything from a castle to a Victorian brick semi-detached. She would probably get a clue, she thought, from whoever turned up to meet her. Roland Edgerton had implied a third party – which might be because he didn't drive, of course. Perhaps they had a chauffeur, or maybe it would be the village taxi service?

Now that the sun had come out, the air was noticeably warmer as Fran stepped on to the platform and began to wend her way between a group of milk churns and a couple of flat-capped old men, who seemed to be in no apparent hurry to make their way on or off the train. As she passed them she heard the unfamiliar Devon burr, so very different from the accents she was accustomed to hearing at home.

'Mrs Black?' The tall, young man who stepped forward to address her was wearing a cap too, but it was one of the broad, fashionable ones and, in contrast to the two older men on the platform, his voice was suggestive of privilege and a private education.

'Yes,' she said. 'I'm Frances Black.'

'Eddie Edgerton, at your service.' He extended a hand, and on receiving hers in return pumped it up and down so enthusiastically that she was quite relieved when he let go.

'I say,' he said, 'you're not at all as I imagined. I've never met a lady detective before. I was expecting some sort of old boot or blue stocking.'

'I'm not really a detective,' Fran said hastily. 'I've just been a bit lucky at solving a couple of puzzles, I suppose.'

'Balderdash! Roly – I'm his younger brother, by the way – says that Claude Foxton told him you were fearfully clever over that business in Nottinghamshire. Saved a fellow from the gallows when the police had got it all wrong. And were frightfully modest and discreet about it all, too! Is this the only luggage you've brought? Travelling light, eh? Well, jolly good, hand it over and we'll hop along to my motor.'

Relieved of her suitcase, Fran found herself being swept along at a pace which did not much lend itself to talking. 'I'm sorry,' she managed to say. 'But I'm afraid I don't know who Claude Foxton is.'

'Claude Foxton? Involves himself a bit in motor racing these days, I believe. He also happens to be the nephew of Lieutenant Colonel Lemon, the chief constable of Nottinghamshire, and he was at school with Roly – Claude, that is, not old Lemon. The two of them were at some sort of old boys' dinner back in the autumn and Claude was telling Roly all about that poisoning business . . . or, hang on, was it something to do with an old lady getting bonked on the head? Well, anyway, there was skulduggery involved somewhere along the line. We gathered that you'd had a hand in sorting it all out, and naturally that set Roly thinking about our own situation. Here we are . . . in you get.'

He held open the passenger door of a bright red, highly polished Riley for her. 'Hope you don't mind driving with the roof down. In my opinion, it's the only way to travel if it isn't raining.'

Once Fran had climbed in, Eddie Edgerton closed the door, placed her suitcase behind the front seats, walked around the back of the car and rather startled her by vaulting straight over the driver's door without bothering to open it. 'Hang on to your hat,' he said cheerfully as he gunned the engine into life – an exhortation which would definitely have been necessary if she had not been foresighted enough to anchor it in advance with a couple of sturdy hatpins. The car took off from the station at high speed and within less than half a minute they had left all signs of habitation behind and were hurtling along narrow, winding lanes between high Devon banks covered with primroses. Fortunately they met no other vehicles on the road.

'Perhaps you could tell me something about the mystery which you want my help with,' Fran ventured. 'You see, my friend, Mr Dod, was able to tell me nothing except that it involved circumstances which had not been reported to the police and required the utmost discretion. When I spoke with your brother, Roland, he just concentrated on the arrangements for my getting here.'

She saw Eddie Edgerton hesitate. 'I know all about it, of course,' he said. 'But I rather feel that I should leave the explanations to my brother, Roly – him being the head of the family and all that.'

'I see,' said Fran – who of course did not. 'Then perhaps you could at least tell me a little bit about your family? Unless you are the youngest by some considerable margin, then your brother, Roland, must be quite young to be the head of the family.'

'Roly is thirty-two next month – which reminds me, I must get the old chap a present. You don't happen to have any suggestions, do you? I'm a completely hopeless fellow when it comes to things of that kind. I have absolutely no imagination.'

Though slightly taken aback to be asked for advice regarding a gift for someone she had never met, Fran could not help but like Eddie Edgerton, who had a winning smile and the kind of direct manner which appealed to her. She judged him to be somewhat younger than herself: in his middle twenties probably. His fair hair was rather longer than the fashionable norm and his face was tanned. He looked like someone who enjoyed plenty of fresh air and exercise in a warm climate.

'You were telling me about your family,' she said.

'Yes, righty-ho. I suppose the family starts off with my grandfather – the one who died last year. He was Frederick Edgerton. My father was also Frederick, but everyone called him Frank, so as not to confuse him with my grandfather. Father has been dead for several years so Roly was Grandfather's immediate heir. Roly is actually Frederick Roland, named after Father and Grandfather . . . well, not the Roland part. I think Mother just liked that name. Anyway, he's always been called Roly.'

'In order to distinguish him from your father and grandfather,' Fran prompted.

'That's right. Roly is Mother and Father's eldest.'

'What about your mother? Is she dead too?'

'Good Lord, no. She's still very much with us; you'll meet her this evening. You'll like Mother. Everyone does. Where was I? Ah, yes. After Roly they had Henrietta, known to everyone as Hen. Then finally they had me – the runt of the litter.'

'What happened to your father and your grandfather?'

The question seemed to delight Eddie, who lifted his hands clear off the steering wheel and brought them down again with a slap which caused them to swerve briefly towards a solid-looking oak tree. 'By George, you are a sharp one! You knew at once, didn't you, that all this has something to do with Grandfather's death?'

'Not at all,' Fran protested. 'I was just trying to build up a picture of your family.'

'Ah, you don't fool me, Mrs Black. I could tell you were

frightfully clever the first minute I saw you. I say, do you like jazz? You don't happen to play piano, do you?'

'I'm sorry?' Fran was completely thrown off by the question. 'The assignment isn't musical in any way, is it?'

Eddie laughed again. 'Not at all. I just thought that if you played – well, anything really, a trumpet or a ukulele, we could have some jolly sessions together. In the evenings, you know. When you're not sleuthing.'

'I'm afraid I'm not a great success on the piano. I never got much past five-finger exercises and the 'Old Folks at Home'. I certainly never graduated to the trumpet or the ukulele.'

'Ah, well, not to worry. Here we are – these are our gates.'

Eddie swung the car expertly between a pair of tall metal gates which had been opened to their widest extent, simultaneously slowing the engine to a muted roar for their cruise down a drive which descended gently between trees, beyond which Fran caught occasional glimpses of the sea.

'Gosh,' she said. 'You live right on the coast.'

'We do indeed. There are sea views from most of the main rooms in the house. It's a pity that you've come so early in the year, for there's really no chance of bathing here until at least the end of May.'

'Do you have to walk far to get to a beach?'

'It's only ten minutes through the garden. Of course, it's much better now that the beach hut has been built. When we first lived here we used to have to carry all the picnic chairs and shrimping nets and so on, up and down from the house whenever we wanted them, whereas now we can keep all manner of kit down there.'

'It must be very nice to live so close. Does it get crowded down there in the holiday season?'

'Oh, it's our own private beach,' Eddie assured her, just as if having one's own private beach was the most normal thing in the world. 'Our land runs well to either side, so it isn't overlooked or anything tiresome like that.'

He slowed the car for another steep bend and seconds later Fran found herself looking up at a large, modern house with grey stone walls and a grey-tiled roof.

'Welcome to Sunnyside House,' he said.

FOUR

Someone must have been watching for their arrival, because the front door was opened before Fran had time to unlatch the car door and three strides brought a uniformed butler to a position where he could open it for her, while a maid simultaneously reached into the back of the car and hoisted out the suitcase, which suddenly looked shabby in these rather grand, modern surroundings.

A moment later a slim young woman of about Fran's own age, who she guessed immediately must be Eddie Edgerton's sister, Henrietta, appeared on the doorstep and extended her hand. 'Hello, Mrs Black, do come in. Tea is already laid out in the drawing room and you must be dying for a cup.' She drew Fran into the hall as she spoke, adding, 'Let Jamieson take your hat and coat and I will show you where you can wash your hands.'

Though Eddie seemed to have handed her on to Henrietta, Fran's sense of being swept along by a whirlwind in no way decreased. After divesting herself of coat and hat she followed her hostess a short way along a broad passage to where Henrietta indicated the downstairs cloakroom, which was twice the size of her bathroom at Beehive Cottage, though it only contained a water closet and a basin. She noticed also the electric light switch on the wall. *They must have their own generator*, she thought.

'When you are done,' Henrietta said, 'just turn right, follow the passage to the end and you'll come to the drawing room. You can't go wrong.'

Oh dear, thought Fran, who had already decided that one could very easily go wrong in the home of people who owned their own beach and enjoyed the services of a butler. She fervently wished that Tom had accompanied her. It had been a mistake to come here alone.

After washing and drying her hands, she obeyed Henrietta's

instructions, following the passage back the way she had come until it doglegged beyond the front porch and ended in a pair of double doors. Taking a deep breath, she opened them. She found herself looking into a lovely room, flooded with sunlight thanks to its having windows on three sides, which faced north and west into the garden and south towards the point where the land sloped away to the sea. The drawing room itself was most unusual, for the doors opened on to a raised area, from which a trio of polished steps descended into the main body of the room, making it feel rather as if one were making an entrance in the theatre.

Fortunately there was only an audience of four: Henrietta and another young woman, who remained seated on the comfortable modern sofas, while Eddie and a young man Fran correctly assumed to be his brother, Roland, naturally sprang to their feet the moment she came into the room. All of them smiled in a welcoming fashion as Eddie Edgerton took the lead in making introductions.

'Mrs Black, this is my brother, Roly – the two of you have already spoken on the telephone. This is his wife, Mellie, and of course you have already met my sister, Hen. My mother, needless to say, is out in the garden somewhere and will probably not grace the gathering with her presence until dinner.'

Fran took each of the extended hands in turn, saying, 'Mr Edgerton, Mrs Edgerton, Miss Edgerton,' as appropriate.

'Oh, I say,' Eddie protested. 'Do let's drop the formality.' He turned to his siblings, as if seeking agreement. 'Mrs Black is here as our guest and I'm sure we're all going to become terrific friends.'

'Perhaps Mrs Black prefers formality.' Mellie Edgerton spoke for the first time. Just as well spoken as the rest, her voice was a tone higher than Henrietta's and Fran marked her down as being possibly the nervous type.

'Oh no, not at all,' Fran said quickly. 'Please, do call me Fran.'

'Fran it is.' Eddie looked extremely pleased. 'Do take a seat and have some tea, Fran. Mellie is playing mother, in the usual absence of the real thing.'

'Please don't think that my mother is snubbing you by not

being here,' Roly put in, as his wife leaned forward to reach for the teapot. 'It's just that she tends to get wrapped up in whatever she is doing, whether it be her painting, or her gardening, or even if she is just reading a book.'

'That's perfectly all right,' Fran said.

'Do you have some more luggage coming on from the station?' Henrietta enquired.

'No, there's only the suitcase I arrived with. I will have to go and unpack when we've finished tea.'

'Oh, I expect Jane will have unpacked for you by then. You know, Mellie,' Henrietta turned towards her sister-in-law, 'Fran has had a fearfully long journey today. Why don't we skip dressing for dinner this evening?'

'Oh.' Mellie Edgerton seemed slightly surprised. 'Well, yes, I suppose so.'

She doesn't get it, Fran thought, whereas kindly Henrietta had observed the size of her case and guessed correctly that she had not brought the right kind of frocks for formal dining, it probably had not occurred to Mellie that anyone would arrive without an appropriate wardrobe.

'We'll have to get word to your mother,' Mellie said to Roland.

'Leave a note on her dressing table, where she can't help but see it,' Henrietta said briskly. 'Mother won't mind anyway. Not having to fag about getting into her finery suits her down to the ground.'

'Actually,' Eddie put in, 'I'm a bit surprised that Mother isn't here. I mean, it isn't every day that one gets to meet a lady detective.'

'Quite so.' Mellie nodded. 'We have all been frightfully curious, ever since Roly told us that you had agreed to come down. I expect you have had a great many adventures.'

'Oh no,' Fran said, pushing aside a memory of one particular adventure, which had led to her almost being murdered in her own front parlour. 'I am not really a detective at all. As I have tried to explain to . . . Eddie . . .' she hesitated to use the first name of someone she had barely known an hour, in spite of the demand for informality, '. . . it's only that I have been lucky enough to work out the solution to a couple of mysteries recently. And in those cases I was helped a great deal by my friend Mr Dod and a little bit by another friend, Mrs Gallimore. I do hope you are not expecting too much.'

'We can only ask that you do your best for us, Fran,' Roland Edgerton said. 'If you cannot get to the bottom of our little mystery, at least you will have tried. We will offer you every possible assistance, of course. Ask whatever you need, question whomsoever you wish.'

'We only ask for your discretion,' Mellie put in.

'Perhaps,' Fran said, 'you can tell me what it is that you are hoping I will find out. You see, at the moment, no one has told me anything at all about this mystery.'

'Straight down to business!' Eddie exclaimed approvingly.

'Are you sure you want to be burdened with the details now?' Mellie asked. 'You have only just arrived and must be very tired after your journey.'

'Oh, don't be wet, Mellie,' Henrietta said. 'Anyone can see that Mrs Black – I mean Fran – isn't one of those soppy women who has a fit of the vapours at the slightest obstacle or exertion.'

'Well, you were the one who cried everyone off from dressing for dinner.' Mellie looked petulant.

Fran pretended not to notice the slight spat as she retrieved her small notebook and pencil from out of her handbag.

'Aha.' Eddie looked almost childishly pleased. 'Equipped to take notes, eh? Anything you say may be taken down and used in evidence and all that.'

'So,' said Henrietta. 'Who is going to begin? Roly?'

'Very well then.' The eldest brother inclined his head in assent. 'I will do my best to explain, but if I'm to do the talking, then everyone else had better shut up and not keep on interrupting, otherwise Fran will get completely confused and we'll never get the story straight.'

'I'll be quiet as a mouse,' said Eddie.

'We'll only need to interrupt if you get anything wrong,' said Henrietta, earning herself a pulled face from her older brother.

'Silent as the grave,' Eddie intoned in a deep voice. 'Ne'er a word shall be uttered . . .'

'Just ignore them, Roly,' Mellie said. 'Do go on, darling.'

'Very well then.' Roland took a breath. 'My late grandfather was a man named Frederick Edgerton. His origins are a bit obscure to tell the truth. He never spoke much about his early life, but we do know that he went out to Africa as a young man and got involved with some sort of mining expedition, with the upshot that he did rather well for himself and returned to Europe a rich man. He dabbled in various things and, before he was forty, he'd done so well that he was able to buy his way into society – to a certain extent at least – and bag himself a jolly good class of bride.'

'Really, Roly!' Mellie was the first to interrupt. 'That is hardly a nice way of putting things.'

'Come now, sweetheart, we all know how these things work. It is most unlikely that my grandmother would have been allowed to marry him if he hadn't had a fortune to lay at her feet. Anyway, he and my grandmother were married and they had a family. Poor old Grandmother died giving birth to their fifth child, so none of us ever knew her, though there's a portrait on the stairs and she looks jolly sweet.'

'Did your grandfather remarry?' asked Fran.

Roly hesitated. 'No,' he said. 'But there was—'

'There's really no need to go into that,' Mellie interposed firmly. 'It's not a nice story and I can't see that it can possibly be relevant.'

Roly hesitated again and then continued. 'Grandfather naturally employed staff to look after the household and take care of the children while he continued to bolster his business empire. In due course Father and his younger brother, our uncle Charles, went away to school while our aunts, Lettie, Catriona and Sybil, were all tutored at home. In time, they all made pretty good marriages.'

'Everyone knew that the Edgertons were only trade,' Eddie put in, 'but money talks and Grandfather ensured that his offspring were all well provided for.'

'The family were based in London for many years,' Roly continued, ignoring the interruption. 'But Grandfather's dream was to build his own place, down here in Devon, which was where he'd got into the habit of taking a house for the summer, year after year. He was familiar with Lutyens' work at Castle Drogo and Bailie Scott's house at Blackwell, up in your neck of the woods, Fran, and he had some very clear ideas about what he wanted for himself. He eventually found the right piece of land, and as soon as the war was over he commissioned Oswald Milne and Sunnyside House is the result. It only took three years from start to finish. Of course, by now Grandfather was getting on a bit and it had always been his intention that the house should go to his eldest son, our father, so as soon as it was ready not only Grandfather but also all of us moved in here.'

'Which meant that Mother was effectively the lady of the house from the very beginning and was able to have a free hand in designing the garden,' Henrietta put in.

'As I said before, Grandfather was getting on a bit.' Roly resumed his story. 'And it wasn't too long before he had the first of his strokes. He recovered quite well from that, but by the summer of 'twenty-six he was needing a wheelchair to get around the grounds and before too long he decided that he'd like to have a nurse. Initially he got a strong young fellow who could wheel him about – Grandfather was a tall man and quite heavy. The first young chap stayed for a while, but I don't think he liked it much – we're quite out of the way here, you know – so he gave notice and another nurse, Monica, was engaged. She was a funny old thing, but Grandfather seemed to like her – well, initially at least – and she soon worked out how to manage his moods.

'He got to the stage where he couldn't really walk anywhere at all, although he still had enough strength in his arms to push himself about in the chair when Monica wasn't around. Then the summer before last . . .'

'You've missed out Father's death.'

'Nonsense, Hen, Father doesn't really come into this at all.'

'Of course he does. Otherwise how is Fran to understand why you inherited? You've got us all moving here with Grandfather, then suddenly Grandfather dies and you inherit. I mean, obviously she needs to know about Father, otherwise that doesn't make sense.'

'Fair point. Very well, just to backtrack a moment, our father was most awfully keen on motors and he liked to drive rather fast, which is hardly a problem around here, because apart from the Baddeleys no one but ourselves has a car on the peninsula. Unfortunately Father was out in the motor one evening when he came round a bend and went slap bang into the back of some fellow driving a horse and cart, loaded with logs.'

'It was Nicholas Cload,' Eddie supplied.

'Father's car ended up in the ditch, with him pinned under it. He was dead by the time they got him out. That was back in September 1923, which as my sister evidently wants me to explain, is how I came to be Grandfather's principal heir.'

'Very helpful. Thank you,' said Fran, who was still wondering where on earth all this could possibly be going.

'Righty-ho. So then, after we'd all got over the shock of Father's death, life went on much as it had before. The three of us were finished with school, so we were all living here most of the time, apart from odd trips away and a week here and there in London—'

'The family still has a house up there but that doesn't really come into this either,' said Eddie.

'Darling, do shut up or Roly is never going to get to the meat of things,' protested Henrietta.

'So anyway' – Roly shot his siblings a look – 'by that final summer, Grandfather was getting a bit frail and the old boy's mind was starting to wander occasionally. He was pretty much totally reliant on his wheelchair by then.'

'That must have made life rather difficult,' Fran said, eyeing the steps which were a feature of the drawing room.

'Oh, Grandfather never came in here,' Henrietta said, picking up on Fran's point. 'After his strokes he used the library as a sort of sitting room and bedroom combined into one. From there you have a level passage into the dining room, or out on to the terrace and the upper lawn and even along the path to the cliffs. The rest of the garden is full of slopes and steps, but that particular path runs pretty level for its full length. By the last year of his life, he had stopped eating with us in the dining room too. He said the meals went on too long and there was always too much noise for him, so he used to have his meals on a tray in his room.'

'He did sometimes come out for tea on the terrace,' Mellie reminded them.

'Mellie's right.' Roland nodded. 'He still occasionally came out for a piece of cake and a cup of tea, but he never stayed long. I think he found it too much. Too many people, too much noise. He much preferred to be quiet towards the end.'

'You see, the thing is,' Eddie explained, 'it's always been rather open house here in the summer. Grandfather started it himself. He liked to have his other children – our uncle Charles and our aunts – come to stay here with *their* children. And of course everyone is always very keen to come because it's such a jolly spot and we've always had a lively time.'

'It was much quieter, the summer after Father died,' Henrietta said, having, like her younger brother, apparently forgotten that it was Roland who was supposed to be telling the story. 'You know, out of respect for Mother's feelings and everything, but by 1926 things had got pretty much back to normal again, the place full of relatives, cousins and friends all summer long, and it was much the same the year that Grandfather died.'

'Do I take it,' asked Fran, 'that the mystery you would like me to resolve is in some way associated with your grandfather's death?'

'Oh, bravo!' exclaimed Eddie. 'What a capital detective you are, Fran. There, you see.' He turned triumphantly towards his siblings. 'Didn't I say, the moment I set eyes on her that she was a clever woman?'

'Really, Eddie,' Mellie chided. 'Please don't mind him, Mrs Black. He doesn't mean to be rude, talking about one as if one wasn't in the room.'

'Sorry, sorry, Mellie's right, of course. I'm just an idiot, first class. Please forgive me.' Eddie sounded genuinely contrite.

Fran could not help but laugh at the sorrowful countenance he affected. 'So perhaps you could tell me the circumstances of your grandfather's death?' she prompted.

Roland Edgerton took up the tale again. 'You see, Fran, that's possibly the crux of it. Grandfather went over the edge of the cliff in his wheelchair and was killed by the fall. No one saw it happen.'

'I . . . I see. There must have been an inquest?'

'Oh, naturally, yes. The coroner, Doctor Vereker, was very good about it. Scotched any suggestion of foul play or suicide pretty firmly and went for accidental death.'

'Which it could easily have been,' put in Mellie.

'But perhaps you have different ideas to the coroner,' Fran probed gently.

'Well no . . . no. Not immediately.' Roland sounded uncertain. 'You see, it could have been an accident. Grandfather had lost a lot of the strength in his arms, but he might easily have got it into his head to wheel himself out of the house and along the path, but then somehow lost control of the wheelchair and gone over the top. Even if he'd shouted for help, he wouldn't necessarily have been heard. You know what it's like when people are playing games and of course anyone down by the shore has to contend with the shingle and the noise of the sea. It was a lovely day and pretty much everyone was out of doors, enjoying themselves.'

'What about his nurse?'

'It was her half day.'

'So you initially thought that it could have been an accident, but then something happened which made you change your minds?'

'It wasn't exactly that something happened. You see, it was only when we realized that the diamond was missing that we really began to suspect there was something wrong.'

FIVE

'The diamond?' Fran repeated. As she spoke, it seemed as if a sunbeam caught the top of a distant wave and a tiny sparkle of light gleamed momentarily in one pane of the drawing-room windows.

Though Roland had been appointed storyteller, it was Henrietta Edgerton who took up the tale. 'From what we can understand, when Grandfather came home from Africa, he brought some of his newly acquired fortune in hard cash, some in gold and some of it in diamonds. As far as we know, he hadn't actually discovered a diamond mine himself, but he set himself up as a provider of equipment to the actual prospectors and he had traded successfully and sometimes been paid in diamonds. He converted pretty much all those diamonds into other assets of one sort or another, but he kept a few, one of which was made into an engagement ring for our grandmother.'

'How romantic,' said Fran, feeling that some such remark was required.

'Over the years he gradually disposed of all the other diamonds,' Henrietta continued.

'They weren't particularly big stones,' Eddie put in. 'Most of them weren't *hugely* valuable.'

'But he kept this one back.' Henrietta continued as if her brother hadn't spoken. 'He used to keep it in the safe in the room which he used as his bedsitting room. He kept one or two other bits and pieces in there too. Some rather nice rubies that had belonged to our grandmother – oh, yes – and a little diamond-and-pearl tiara that belonged to Mother. Anyway, after his funeral, when things had to be sorted out, we realized that although nothing else was missing, the diamond wasn't there any more.'

'So . . . let me get this straight.' Fran's pencil was poised above her notebook. 'The diamond was just a single stone? It wasn't part of a piece of jewellery?'

'That's right. It had been cut, but it had never been set in anything.'

'How was it kept? Was it in some kind of case?'

'No. It was actually in a little black bag.'

'It was a black velvet bag,' Mellie put in. 'The bag was a little bit worn. I remember noticing that when he showed me the stone, because it made me wonder if the edges of the stone would cause the bag to eventually wear out.'

'He showed it to you?' Fran turned to Mellie with interest.

'He showed it to pretty much everyone,' Roly said. 'At some point or another.'

'So lots of people knew about the stone and knew where it was kept?'

'Not exactly lots of people. When I said everyone, what I meant was all of the family. Grandfather wasn't a complete fool. He wouldn't have just got the thing out and flashed it under the nose of any old visitor, but we all knew about it, yes.'

'How about the servants?'

'That's difficult to say. I suppose they may have known it was there. The location of the safe certainly wasn't a secret. It's the sort one often finds, built into the wall of a house, slightly masked by the panelling. I suppose some people might have hung a picture in front of it too, but Grandfather didn't bother.'

'And you say that the safe was in his bedroom?'

'It was eventually.' Henrietta took up the narrator's role again. 'But that almost came about by accident, because when Grandfather couldn't manage the stairs any more, he had his bed down in the library, and that's where the safe had been built in.'

At that moment they were interrupted by the doors bursting open. An oversized child, wearing a large hat with a feather waving from it, and a mustard-coloured cloak, which had clearly once seen service as a curtain, burst into the room brandishing a poker. 'Ha ha!' she yelled. 'I've got you cornered now.'

'Imogen! Do be careful or you will do yourself a damage with that thing,' Henrietta protested.

'Or damage the ornaments,' said Mellie. 'Where on earth is Miss Billington?'

The question was answered immediately as a small, nervous-looking woman hastened into the room in the wake of the child, gasping, 'So sorry. Come on now, Imogen. The family has a guest. Let's get back to the playroom, shall we?'

'No, no,' the girl protested. 'They are all my prisoners.'

'Do get a grip on the situation, Miss Billington.' Mellie Edgerton spoke quite sharply, and Fran decided that she was perhaps not so frail or nervy as she had initially appeared.

'Now then, Imogen.' Eddie had risen to his feet and spoke in a much more kindly voice than his sister-in-law. 'You know that it isn't cricket to come bursting into the drawing room like this. Go along with Billie, old thing; otherwise, Cook may forget where she has put the chocolate biscuits again, and we none of us want that, now, do we?' His hand was resting on the girl's shoulder and as he spoke he began to guide her gently back in the direction of the drawing-room door. Miss Billington looked noticeably grateful.

'Can we go and see Cook now?' Fran heard the girl ask as Eddie and Miss Billington steered her out into the passage.

'No doubt you are wondering about the intrusion.' Henrietta turned back to Fran. 'That was our cousin, Imogen. She has lived with us since her mother died in 1919, so we look on her as a sort of younger sister.'

'How old is she?' asked Fran, who was somewhat puzzled by the childish clothes and actions, which clearly did not fit the sheer size of the child.

'Imogen will be fourteen this year. She's a sweet girl really, but I'm afraid she is a little bit backward, which means that she tends to indulge in some rather silly antics. I'm sure she will grow out of it all eventually.'

'Some of us,' said Mellie, 'believe that she would have grown out of it long ago, if there had been less emphasis on chocolate biscuits and more emphasis on a few good spankings.'

Fran took a moment to consult her notebook in order to avoid noticing the way the other two women had turned to glare at one another.

'Don't be unkind, Mellie.' Roland had adopted a pleading tone. 'Imogen can't help the way she is.'

'Don't be ridiculous, Roly,' snapped his wife. 'The only

thing wrong with that child is that she has been thoroughly spoiled. If my mother had had charge of her from the age of three, she would have been minding her Ps and Qs and almost ready to go off to finishing school by now, not racing about the house like a dervish with a poker in her hand.'

'Perhaps,' Fran ventured rather nervously, 'we might return to the question of the diamond that has gone missing? Tell me, Mr Edgerton . . .'

'Roly, please.'

Fran inclined her head. 'Roly, did you report the disappearance of the diamond to the police?'

'We did not.'

'But it must be tremendously valuable . . . and surely, if you thought that it had been stolen . . .'

'This is where you come in,' Roland began, just as his brother re-entered the room. 'We decided on discretion, you see.'

'There were quite a lot of factors in play,' Henrietta put in.

'To begin with, we simply didn't know whether the diamond had been stolen. You see, Grandfather was in the habit of periodically getting it out, either to have a look at it himself, or else to show it to someone else, so no one was quite sure when it might have last been taken out of the safe. Grandfather had been growing rather absent-minded . . .'

'What my husband means to say,' Mellie said, 'is that the old man had been going a bit dotty.'

'So at first you thought that he might have just put it down somewhere and forgotten it,' suggested Fran.

'Exactly.'

'But when you cleared out his room, it wasn't there.'

'Right again.' Eddie resumed the role of spokesman. 'The diamond isn't insured and we hardly wanted to advertise to every Tom, Dick and Harry that it might be lying somewhere about the place, then having burglars turning up from far and wide to see what other swag might be available.'

'Then there is the matter of Grandfather's death, you see,' Roly put in. 'Right from the beginning, the whole business seemed a bit odd. No one could remember the last time that he'd wheeled himself all the way along that path, right as far as the point where he went over the edge. But since no one had admitted to taking him up there that afternoon, we assumed that he must have got there himself. As I've said before, old Vereker was jolly good at the inquest and he didn't give any credence at all to suicide or foul play . . .'

'It isn't as if there was actually any evidence of either.' This from Henrietta.

'But that didn't stop some impudent pup of a reporter, trying to sneak into the grounds and talk to some of the servants,' said Mellie. 'Obviously he got nothing out of any of them and Marshall – that's the head gardener – soon chucked him out, but you can just imagine all the speculation there would have been if the sudden death of Frederick Edgerton had been coupled with news of a suspected jewellery theft.'

'I may need to speak with all the staff myself,' Fran ventured.

'Of course,' said Roly. 'They will be instructed to offer you every cooperation.'

'*Your* speaking to them is entirely different,' Mellie said. 'What we don't want is some idiot like Constable Dunn coming up here and asking questions. I can see him now, standing there in his great big boots and licking his pencil, the way he always does before he writes anything down. And the next thing you know, the story would be all over the village and spreading like wildfire.'

'But surely . . .' Fran hesitated. 'I understood that one of you is acquainted with the chief constable in another county. Wouldn't it be possible to use those connections in order to have the matter investigated by a senior officer?'

'Oh dear.' Mellie sighed. 'You don't really understand, do you?'

Roland silenced her with a look. 'We would much prefer not to involve the police, Fran. You see, what we would like you to do, if possible, is to track down the diamond, but along with that there is inevitably the question of whether its disappearance is in any way linked to our grandfather's death. You see, if it turns out that our grandfather's death was not the accident which we all believed in at the beginning . . . well, that could become a very delicate situation indeed.'

SIX

F ran sat at the dressing table which stood before the bedroom window, looking out into the gathering dusk. The sun had disappeared below the western headland and the garden was already swathed in shadows. Most of the room behind her was reflected in the dressing-table mirror; it was a comfortable room, immaculately decorated in shades of russet and pink, with the electric lamps already lit at either side of a large bed, which looked very inviting to someone who had spent most of the day travelling. Fran rather wished that she could undress and climb into that bed instead of having to go downstairs and eat dinner with the Edgertons.

Not only was she by now too tired to relish the prospect of keeping up polite conversation during dinner, but she was also experiencing a growing sense of unease. It was perfectly obvious that if old Frederick Edgerton's death had not been accident or suicide then suspicion would fall on the surviving members of the family. No wonder they had no desire to involve the police. Yet if she did turn up some evidence of suspicious circumstances, the Edgertons would surely not expect her to collude with them in some kind of cover-up. Supposing she discovered that there had been foul play? The house suddenly felt a long way from any kind of civilization. *Tom, Tom what have you got me into?* A pheasant somewhere in the grounds chose that moment to emit a screech, startling her horribly.

Silly, silly . . . The Edgertons were perfectly nice, hospitable people who just wanted their grandfather's missing diamond found with a minimum of fuss – and so far they had shown her nothing but kindness.

After tea Henrietta and Mellie had escorted her up to her room, indicating the bathroom which was just across the corridor from her bedroom and the discreet bell push alongside the bed, which she was exhorted to use if she needed anything at all.

'Now if you have travelled light – which is always the most sensible way – there is nothing in the way of clothes or cosmetics that Mellie and I can't lend you,' Henrietta had said.

Fran privately thought that fragile-looking Mellie's frocks would be much too small for her, while the tall, relatively slender Henrietta's would probably be overlong, but she appreciated the gesture and realized that if they normally dressed for dinner then she would probably need to take up the offer.

The maid, Jane, had unpacked all her things. This operation had included laying out Fran's hairbrushes and small collection of cosmetics on the dressing table, which gave her very little excuse to hang around upstairs. She took rather longer than was necessary to freshen up her Geranium Charm lipstick and brush her hair before heading back across the thick pile rug towards the bedroom door. The doors were well-made and a good fit, which made it impossible to hear if there was anyone approaching along the corridor, so it was only as Fran opened the door that she realized someone was passing by. Not wishing to encounter anyone on their way to or from the bathroom, she paused with the door barely an inch ajar, in order to allow the unseen person time to get out of the way.

In the same moment she heard the click of a door opening further along the passage and Mellie's voice saying, 'There you are, Roly. I was wondering where on earth you'd got to.'

Roly's reply was unintelligible, but Mellie immediately came back at him, her higher voice clearly audible. 'What do you think of her – your lady detective?'

Fran felt her cheeks burning crimson. She could not possibly walk out into the passage now, but nor did she dare to draw attention to her presence by shutting the door. She would just have to pray that neither of them was in a position to notice the way her door was open a tiny crack.

Roly's brief assessment was again too low for her to hear, and Fran guessed that, unlike Mellie, he was probably facing away from her and into their room. Though she could not hear Roly, her mother's voice sounded clearly in her head. 'Eavesdroppers never hear well of themselves.' And her mother was right, of course. One ought not to go around listening at doors.

'And have you decided whether to tell her – about you know what?'

Fran immediately pricked up her ears. Eavesdropping might have its uses after all. It was probably what proper detectives did all the time. She suspected that Tom would have had no scruples about it whatsoever, if in pursuit of what might be an important clue.

However, Mellie's question was greeted by another mumble from Roland, cut short by the distinct sound of a door closing.

Fran waited for a moment or two, but there was nothing else to be heard. *Hmm*, she thought, pursing her lips in an expression, which her friend Mo would have recognized at once. *If there's one thing I'm determined to find out about before I leave Sunnyside House, it's what 'you know what' is all about.*

She swung the door open and stepped out into the deserted upstairs corridor. 'Drinks in the drawing room before dinner,' had been Henrietta's parting words, and when Fran arrived downstairs, making her entrance through those rather theatrical double doors and descending the steps into the main part of the drawing room, she found that Henrietta was already perched on a sofa, glass in hand, next to a much older woman, her grey hair swept up into an almost Edwardian style, whose kind grey eyes made a swift assessment of Fran, even as she smiled in what appeared to be a genuine welcome.

Eddie Edgerton was also in the room, and he, of course, leapt to his feet and performed introductions. 'Mrs Black, my mother, Lady Louisa Edgerton. Mother, this is Mrs Black, who has kindly agreed to let us call her Fran.'

Lady Louisa inclined her head, offered a hand and said, 'Welcome to Sunnyside House, Mrs Black.'

'Oh, Mother, don't be so stuffy!' exclaimed Eddie. 'I'm afraid my mother simply cannot get on first-name terms with anyone until they've been acquainted for about thirty years. It's her upbringing, I'm afraid.'

'Oh, do leave Mother alone, Eddie.' Henrietta was laughing as she spoke – in fact, all three family members were taking the exchange in good part. 'Mother cannot help having been properly brung up, as Jane would say, instead of being allowed to run wild as we were.'

'Stop fussing about form, Eddie, and offer our guest a drink,' his mother said. 'Tell me, Mrs Black, did you have a very trying journey?'

The conversation moved swiftly on to the subject of railway travel, the journey times between Devon and London, and from there it moved logically to a West End play which Henrietta was hoping to see. The quartet were soon joined by Roland and Mellie and at the stroke of eight o'clock a gong sounded somewhere in the distance and Eddie sprang to Fran's side in order to escort her along to the dining room, where they were served dinner by the butler who had overseen her arrival.

Fran found the butler's attentions slightly unnerving. He kept appearing at her shoulder with wine bottles and dishes of vegetables and she was unsure how she ought to address him. He was much more of a presence than a waiter in a restaurant, and yet in another way much less obviously demanding of her attention. She tried to watch what everyone else was doing, nervous of putting a foot wrong. The others all appeared to be perfectly at their ease, but of course they were used to eating in this rather lovely house with a butler in attendance. This room would have seen much grander occasions, she guessed, involving considerably greater numbers. For them, it was just a normal family dinner, encompassing the presence of a single guest with cheerful conversation ebbing to and fro. If any of them was worrying about the mystery which had brought their guest to Sunnyside House, they were certainly not showing it just then.

Only when they had finished their dinner and Jamieson had carried all the necessary constituents along the corridor so that they could enjoy their coffee in the drawing room did the object of Fran's visit raise its head again.

'I suppose you will begin your investigations in the morning,' Eddie said. 'I hope you will allow me to be your guide around the estate and your driver, if you need to check on anything further afield. I have nothing on at all and can put myself completely at your disposal.'

'Eddie never has anything on,' Henrietta said. 'He is the laziest fellow in the county.'

'Oh, I say! Don't blacken my name immediately.'

'No indeed, Hen. You really ought to have given Fran at least forty-eight hours in order to observe Eddie's phenomenal lack of useful activity for herself.' Roland was laughing, his words clearly not unkindly meant.

Eddie took it in good part. 'This is absolutely typical of my family. I offer to make myself useful and all I meet with is abuse and ridicule.'

'Seriously, Fran.' Roland adopted a much more sober tone. 'We really do want to get to the bottom of this business if we can, so please feel free to go wherever you like in the house, or out in the grounds. Ask anything you want; speak with anyone you wish to speak with. Jamieson is going to have a word with the staff this evening, so they will be prepared to answer any questions which you may have for them and of course the rest of us are all similarly at your disposal.'

'Thank you,' Fran said. 'I will, as you suggest, begin in the morning, and' – she turned to Eddie – 'I will naturally be very glad of the initial assistance of a guide. However, I have had rather a long day and I'm feeling awfully tired, so if you will excuse me, I'd very much like to make an early night of it.'

SEVEN

F ran awoke in a much better frame of mind. Her concerns of the night before seemed doubly foolish on this morning of bright spring sunshine, and when she got down to the dining room she again encountered an atmosphere of easy friendliness, with Roland Edgerton reading out snippets from his newspaper between eating bites of brown toast, while Mellie picked at some scrambled eggs and Henrietta teased their younger brother about an invitation to a twenty-first birthday party which had arrived in the post.

'Mabel Trenchard has her eye on you, Eddie. You only have to say the word and her mother will be booking the church.'

'Don't talk tosh, Hen.'

'I tell you, she's a one-man woman. Ever since that game of musical chairs, when she ended up sitting in your lap . . .'

'Mabel has a face like a horse and a laugh to match. I can assure you that if she was the last woman on earth—'

'Do stop it, you two,' Mellie chided. 'You are both being total bores. I'm sure poor Fran neither knows nor cares who Mabel Trenchard is.'

'Quite so,' Eddie agreed. 'Do shut up, Hen. Now, please don't forget,' he said, turning to Fran, 'that I am entirely at your disposal.'

'Fran may not require your assistance,' his older brother said. Addressing Fran in his turn, he added: 'Please don't think that you have to put up with Eddie breathing down your neck the whole time. Do feel free to tell him to push off and leave you alone.'

'Luncheon is at one,' Mellie said. 'And it is entirely up to you how you fill your time between then and now, of course.'

'Thank you,' said Fran. 'But I should be glad of a guide – initially, at least – because I thought that I should start by walking along the path to the place where your grandfather fell from the cliffs, and naturally I will need someone to show me the way.'

Half an hour later, after she had finished her breakfast and been upstairs to change into her outdoor shoes and put on a cardigan (it was so much warmer down here in Devon than it had been back at home where she would most certainly have needed a coat), she met Eddie in the downstairs corridor and he showed her into the room known as the library, which had at one time become a bedsitting room for his grandfather.

The wall safe in which the diamond had been kept, she decided, was not particularly obvious unless you knew where to look for it. 'There's no handle on the outside,' she commented, and Eddie explained that the key activated a spring, so that when it was unlocked the door would automatically swing out from the wall.

'I suppose there is only one key?'

'So far as I know.'

'And where was it kept?'

'Oh, it's just here.' Eddie approached a small table, which stood against the wall and opened the little drawer which was set in it. 'Here we are. Let me open it for you.' Without waiting for her reaction one way or the other, he walked across, inserted the key into a discreet keyhole and gave it a full turn. The safe door swung ajar, just as he had said that it would.

'Where was the key kept before?'

'Oh, the same place. The table always stood here and the safe key has been kept there as long as I can remember.'

'So . . . did everyone know where it was kept?' Fran found it rather a struggle not to laugh.

'I expect so.' Eddie paused, perhaps considering the contradiction of locking something in a safe to which anyone who wished could gain access. 'I suppose Grandfather always felt that burglars would never come down here. I mean, we are quite out of the way. And, of course, he would never have thought that anyone within the household would open it up and take something without permission.'

'Very well,' Fran said. 'You had better lock up the safe again and then perhaps you can show me the route that your grandfather would have taken to reach the cliff edge.'

Eddie locked the safe, replaced the key in the drawer of the table and then held the door open for her. 'This way,' he said. 'Just along this corridor there's a door which opens on to the loggia. In the summer,' he continued as he led the way, 'this door almost always stands open, which means that even propelling himself in the wheelchair, Grandfather would have had no difficulty in getting outside.'

'And it was nice that day? The door would have been open?'

'It was an absolute scorcher.'

He held the door open and Fran stepped out on to the covered end of a long terrace, paved with the sort of large flat stone slabs which would have been easily negotiable for a wheelchair. For the first time since her arrival, she could hear the sound of the sea, faint though it was, breaking on the beach which lay out of sight at the foot of the valley. There was even a slight tang of salt in the air. She stood for a moment, breathing it in.

'The garden is very lovely, isn't it?' Eddie said. 'It will look even better in a few weeks, when the azaleas are out. All Mother's handiwork, of course. She designed the whole thing. It was just a blank canvas when we first came, but Mother knows all about gardening, so Grandfather gave her a free hand and of course now that we've been here for almost a decade the trees and shrubs are growing up and really coming into their own.'

'I noticed that your mother didn't join us for breakfast.'

'No, Mother has taken toast and lemon tea in her room for as long as I can remember.'

'And your cousin, Imogen? She didn't appear either?'

'Imogen has all her meals with Miss Billington. Mother and Mellie don't think she is civilized enough to join us in the dining room.'

'Is it true . . .' Fran hesitated. Everyone had assured her that she should ask whatever she liked, but the question seemed somewhat indelicate. 'That Imogen is a little . . . backward?'

To her relief, Eddie did not seem in the least offended.

'Imogen is a good-hearted kid, but she has always been rather slow, I believe, when it comes to her lessons, and very childish in her ways.'

'Your sister-in-law seemed to think that what she needed was . . . er . . . firmer handling.'

'There's probably a degree of truth in what Mellie says,' Eddie conceded. 'Imogen has always been rather indulged. You see, her father didn't make it back from the war and then her mother, our aunt Sybil, went and died too. Sybil was Grandfather's favourite, according to Father, so he naturally wanted to take Imogen in and give her a home. We three were all away at school by then, so Imogen was mostly being brought up as an only child and I suppose she became rather a pet with everyone. When we finally moved into Sunnyside House and the family started to get together here during the summer, Imogen was always the youngest of the cousins, and naturally everyone was specially kind to her, on account of losing her parents, and I suppose it became a bit of a habit to allow her more licence than everyone else. It perhaps took Mellie, a relative outsider, to see it. Of course,' he added quickly, 'it wasn't just a question of letting Imogen have her own way about things. Grandfather used to make her feel special in other ways – letting her be the one to put out the mince pies for Santa Claus, always leaving a special thing for her to find when we had a treasure hunt, all that sort of thing.'

'Treasure hunts? That sounds fun.'

'Oh, we used to have excellent times – particularly when we were all a bit younger and Grandfather was still active. To tell you the truth, we all used to run a bit wild – not just Imogen. Father was forever across at the garage block, tinkering with his engines – he always fancied himself as a bit of an inventor – and Mother was perpetually focused on the garden. While they were neglecting us in the nicest possible way, Grandfather used to encourage us to play at pirates and treasure hunters and sometimes we divided into teams for games of cops and robbers, which involved chasing one another all over the grounds. We were allowed to get disgracefully dirty and fall out of trees and pretty much get up to anything short of drowning one another. Poor old Mellie doesn't really understand that sort of childhood, because her mother is absolutely terrifying and utterly strait-laced.'

By now they had left the terrace and were following a path

wide enough for them to walk comfortably two abreast, which took a fairly level course between the trees and bushes. On their left a grassy bank rose, almost to head height, while to their right the garden fell away steeply. Glancing over her shoulder, Fran saw that they were already out of sight of the house. If old Mr Edgerton had come this way, no one would have been able to see him, unless they happened to look up at just the right moment from the right place in the garden, ever-changing glimpses of which were briefly visible between the trees – here a pond with gunnera, there a corner of the tennis court with last season's lines still faintly visible, though it was far too early in the year to put up the net.

'There is a very slight incline as we get further away from the house,' Fran noted. 'I suppose that would make it harder for an elderly person to get up here by themselves, propelling their own wheelchair.'

'The thing is' – Eddie took a breath and hesitated a moment before continuing – 'I don't see that Grandfather would have come all this way on his own. Not then. What I mean is that if it had happened a couple of years earlier I could easily have believed it, but by that final summer Grandfather hardly ever moved himself about in the chair – he always had someone pushing him.'

'So you were a bit suspicious about what had happened from the very first?'

'Well . . . yes . . . no . . . I don't know. It was a huge shock, of course. The awful thing was that no one had checked on him that afternoon. It wasn't until Monica, Grandfather's nurse, came back from her afternoon out that he was properly missed. For some reason there had been a mix up between the servants over taking him a cup of tea that afternoon. It was all perfectly innocent, I'm sure, but it turned out that no one had seen him after Jamieson collected his luncheon tray at around two o'clock, at which point Grandfather had been napping in his chair.'

'So Jamieson, the butler, was the last person to see him?'

'Yes. Then Monica came back at around six and found that Grandfather wasn't in his room. So she came out on to the terrace – there was a group of us sitting out there – and asked where he was and, of course, no one knew.'

'Did you begin to look for him right away?'

'Oh, yes. I think some of us were a bit worried right off, because it was so singular for him to just disappear, though one or two people said that someone must have taken him off into the grounds for a walk . . . that is to say, they would be pushing him in the chair, of course.'

'Of course.'

'Well, as you can imagine it took a while to round everyone up and establish that no one had taken him off somewhere, then once we realized that he hadn't been seen for hours, everyone began to hunt. It was rather horrid actually.' Eddie paused for a moment, as if to gather himself. 'People all over the house and grounds, calling out "Grandfather, Grandfather, where are you?" Eventually, after getting on for maybe half an hour of searching, Monica came up to Roly and told him that she had spotted something which looked like Grandfather's chair in among the rocks below the point. His body wasn't visible from the top, but we got a boatman from Avemouth to take us round and he was wedged between some rocks at the foot of the cliff. Luckily it wasn't the spring tides, when the water would have risen high enough to wash him away completely, but those rocks don't get completely covered at high tide in the summer.'

'Can you walk to the place where he was found, from your beach?'

'No. You can't walk to it from anywhere. You would always need a boat to get there.'

'So there's no question of his getting there any other way than by falling from the top?'

Eddie considered the question. 'Well,' he said. 'Obviously you could take the chair and the body round in a boat but the damage that both the chair and the poor old boy himself had suffered were entirely consistent with a fall from the top, so the doctor said.'

'And everyone but you assumed that he had got up there himself and fallen by accident?'

'Not at all. I think it probably went through everyone's mind that Grandfather might not have been strong enough, but the thing is that he *had* got up there, d'you see? And just as one couldn't see any reason why he would have deliberately chucked himself over the edge, nor did anyone have any reason to shove him off there either. For the last few months of his life, it was Monica who had spent the most time with him, helping him in and out of the chair and so forth, and when the coroner asked her if she thought that he could have got out of the house and along the path by himself, she said that he had quite recently pushed himself out on to the terrace when she was busy with something else, so she did not believe it was beyond him to have got that far by himself, if he'd put his mind to it.'

'But you didn't agree?'

'I don't think any of us really disagreed. You see, it wasn't impossible. He wouldn't necessarily have had to go the whole way along the path all at once. As the coroner said, no one had seen him for at least four hours. He could easily have done it a few yards at a time, I suppose. Anyway, here we are, at the place where we think he went over.'

EIGHT

While listening to Eddie, Fran had hardly noticed how much louder the sound of the breakers was getting, but now as they stood at the point where the path turned abruptly eastwards, she realized that they had almost reached the edge of the cliff and the sea must be directly below them.

'Be careful,' Eddie cautioned. 'It isn't really safe to go right to the edge. Everyone knows to stay on the path.'

'Tell me, how could Monica have known what had happened unless she left the path? You can't see over the edge from here.'

'The wheelchair had left marks in the grass. When Monica spotted them, she got down on all fours and crawled across until she could see the rocks. It's only a matter of about six or eight feet to the edge. That's why you have to be so jolly careful.'

'I see. Did you see the marks yourself?'

'Oh, yes. When Roly and I got here the place was obvious. It was the only spot along the whole length of the path where the grass was flattened.' Seeing Fran hesitating, he added, 'I really wouldn't attempt to look over the edge if I were you. It's far too damp to get down and crawl, and it may be slippery. We could always hire a motor boat and show you the spot from the water, if you really need to see it.'

'I probably don't. I assume it's a sheer drop.'

'Oh, yes. One step down, as it were.'

'You mentioned that some of you were sitting on the terrace,' Fran said, as they turned by unspoken consent and began to retrace their steps. 'And yet no one had seen your grandfather come by.'

'It was late afternoon by the time the alarm was raised. As it happened, the terrace had not been occupied for most of the earlier part of the afternoon. Some people had been playing tennis; some were down on the beach. Mother, I seem to recall, had spent some of the latter part of the afternoon out on the terrace reading, but she had also spent some time lying down in her room.'

'Would there normally have been anyone on the terrace during the afternoon?'

'Not necessarily. It would just depend how everyone was spending the day. Tell me, what would you like to see next?'

'Since we are already out of doors, I think it would be useful if you could show me around the gardens, specifically the places where you remember people being that afternoon.'

'Good show. Now we can either take a steep little path just along here which is a much shorter way to the beach, or we can go right back to the house and you can see which way people would normally have gone when they went down to the beach.'

'Back to the house, I think,' said Fran. 'I'd much rather get a full picture.'

'I say, I hope you won't think it frightfully impertinent, but . . . well . . . may I ask you a personal question?'

Fran laughed. 'That rather depends what it is.'

'Well, you were introduced to us as Mrs Black and you wear a wedding ring, but you have travelled down here alone and you never mentioned your husband. Is there still a Mr Black?'

'Barely. That is to say that Mr Black is alive and well, but once our divorce has gone through – assuming that it does – he will be looking to bestow the title of Mrs Black elsewhere.'

'Oh.' Eddie was silent for a moment, as if considering her response. 'And . . . if I may be even more impertinent, is there someone else waiting in the wings, ready for you to be free?'

For a fleeting moment she heard Tom's words again: *You do know that if things had been different, I would have asked you to marry me once you are free?* 'No,' she said quietly. 'There is no one.'

A slightly awkward silence ensued. She was not accustomed to being quizzed about her private affairs and divorce was such a touchy social subject.

Abruptly Eddie said, 'Well, all I can say is that if Mr Black left someone as lovely as you, then he's a damn fool.'

Glancing sideways, she saw that he had gone slightly pink under his suntan.

'That's a very nice compliment.' Fran smiled, to show that far from being offended by his curiosity she appreciated the gallant way in which he had tried to alleviate her possible embarrassment. 'Now,' she said, adopting a smooth, business-like tone to indicate that any potential awkwardness was behind them, 'it would be really helpful if you could tell me, as far as possible, who was staying here, where they all were and what they were doing on the afternoon of your grandfather's death.'

'Easier said than done, I'm afraid. Mother was definitely at home and so was Mellie and Roly, and Hen and myself. Uncle Charles and his wife, Aunt Dolly, were staying here at the time, and so were the two younger Dereham cousins. We'd also got some visitors that day. Rhona and Frank Baddeley had walked across from Baddeley Court, and a couple of the Trenchards had turned up for a game of tennis. They'd telephoned ahead, I seem to recall, to check that it was convenient—'

'Oh my goodness,' Fran interrupted. 'This is far more complicated than I thought. I'm going to need to write all this down.'

'Better see the lie of the land first and make your list of suspects later,' Eddie suggested. 'I think you should make the most of the morning, because according to the forecast in Roly's paper, there may be rain later.'

Though Fran did her best to keep her mind on the matter in hand, it was impossible not to enjoy their tour of the gardens for its own sake, with the spring bulbs blooming everywhere and the long, carefully configured stream sparkling as it tumbled down a series of realistic-looking waterfalls. There was a new and pleasant vista at every twist and turn of the path and Eddie proved an excellent guide, ensuring that she missed nothing – not the thatched pavilion which provided shade alongside the tennis court, nor the croquet lawn ('Father was rather keen on croquet, but no one has played much since his accident') and eventually taking her arm to help her over the band of shingle which ran across the top of the private beach before they strolled across an exposed strip of sand where line after line of little wavelets were breaking at the water's edge.

He showed her the changing hut which had been built on a solid stone base, well above the high-water line, opening its door to reveal the family's store of shrimping nets, buckets and spades. 'There's usually a lot more gear down here,' he explained. 'But the chairs and windbreaks are all taken up to the house at the end of the season because the canvas tends to rot if they're left down here over winter.'

How very nice it must be, she thought, *to live this kind of life, or even to be invited down to stay for a few days as a guest.*

'Do you like to bathe? You must come down and stay in the summer.'

It was almost as if he had read her mind. Fran felt her cheeks growing a degree warmer. Had her envious expression been so blatant?

She looked back up to the place where she guessed the clifftop path, which they had explored earlier, must be hidden behind the trees.

Again, Eddie seemed to understand what was in her mind. 'The rocks where Grandfather was found are literally just around that corner.' He pointed to the eastern end of the bay. 'You can't get round there without a boat, because the sea always comes right to the foot of the cliffs at that side.'

'And you can't see the path which runs above the garden from here.'

'No. Though it isn't actually all that far away. If someone was up there now and we shouted, they would probably hear us, though it would be almost impossible to hear them if they shouted back in return, because of the sea.'

'But if someone really screamed?'

'I'm not sure. You see, we can be such a noisy mob, and you might just mistake a single cry for one of the kids playing, or even something to do with a tennis match.'

'You know, I think your brother's paper may have been

right about the weather. There are some awfully dark clouds coming in.'

Eddie glanced westward. 'We'll get back to the house before it starts,' he said. 'Providing we put our best feet forward.'

NINE

They were just in time to avoid the rain. On their way back to the house, Eddie suggested that she should use the library as her 'HQ', as he described it. 'It's hardly ever used,' he said. 'I suppose people became accustomed to thinking of it as Grandfather's room and so we all got into the way of using the drawing room and the morning room, but you will need somewhere private to conduct your interviews and make your notes, and the library would be just the ticket for that.'

By the time Fran had changed her shoes and collected her notebook, Eddie had already rung for coffee, which arrived on a silver tray, accompanied by delicious homemade biscuits, and he had settled himself in one of the easy chairs 'so that you can interview me first'.

'Don't mind if I dunk, do you?' he asked, a biscuit poised above his china coffee cup.

'Not in the least,' said Fran, who had been brought up to believe that it was extremely vulgar but was melted by Eddie's cheerful familiarity.

'Jolly good, then.' As he dipped the bottom curve of his biscuit into his coffee, he said cheerfully, 'Let the interrogation begin.'

'I think it would be helpful if I could get a firm idea of your extended family . . . various aunts and uncles and cousins have been mentioned and I'm not at all clear where they fit in.'

'Fair enough. We don't need to worry about Mother's side. Her brother is Lord Curnow. He lives in Italy with a mistress. His first wife was an American and when they parted she took the children back over there, so we never see the cousins on that side from one year's end to the next.'

'Does your mother have any other siblings?'

'None. Poor dear Mother only has us – although she

probably thinks that's quite enough family to worry about, one way or another.'

'So how about your father's side?'

'Much more numerous. Grandfather came back from Africa around 1870 and was married a few years later. Father was his oldest child, then came Lettie, Charles, Catriona and lastly Sybil. His wife – my grandmother – died when she was fairly young and he never married again. As his children grew up and started families of their own, Grandfather got into the habit of renting a house by the seaside – usually in Devonshire – so that he could have them all to stay for the summer and eventually he had this place built, so they could come here.

'All his children married rather well. Grandfather was a nobody, but the gentry were inclined to overlook that on account of his money. Mother's family can trace their roots back to Edward IV . . . or is it Edward III? I never can remember, and anyway it doesn't matter a fig. It's the same with Mellie. Her family think that they are fearfully grand, but they also happen to be frightfully impoverished. Our aunt Catriona's husband claims some distant kinship with King George, I believe. Personally I don't give a damn about any of it. Marry for love, I say, and never mind money or social ambition.'

Fran smiled. 'Hear, hear,' she said. 'So you were saying that as well as your father there were four younger brothers and sisters in that generation?'

'That's right. Father married Mother and had the three of us. Aunt Lettie married Maurice Dereham and they had four children, Susanna, George, Helena and Cecilia. Susie and George are around the same ages as us and we've been spending our summers together for years and years.'

'And were these people staying here when your grandfather died?'

'Not all of them. Susie is married now and George only came down for a few days in early summer that year, but Helly and Ceccie – that is Helena and Cecilia – were still here when Grandfather died. Uncle Maurice had taken Aunt Lettie on a sea voyage in the latter part of the school holidays – she hadn't been too well, so the quacks had recommended it – and George had gone off to stay with some friend of his in Norfolk while his younger sisters stayed on with us.'

'So . . .' Fran made a note. 'Helena and Cecilia Dereham were here. How old are they?'

'Helly has just turned seventeen. Ceccie is fourteen so not too much older than Imogen.'

'Imogen was here, of course?'

'Imogen is always here. She has lived with Grandfather and the rest of us since her mother, Aunt Sybil, died.'

'How about your uncle Charles and aunt Catriona?'

'Uncle Charles was here with his new wife, Dolly. She's a rather common sort of woman and none of us likes her very much,' said Eddie, clearly forgetting the noble sentiments he had expressed a moment or two earlier about marrying solely for love.

'With their children?'

'They don't have any. As for Aunt Catriona, she had been here with her family earlier in the summer, but by the time Grandfather died they had all decamped up to Northumberland to stay with her in-laws.'

'So the only people actually staying at the house were the usual family – that's your mother, Roland, Mellie, Henrietta, yourself and Imogen, plus your uncle Charles and his wife and your two teenage cousins, Helena and Cecilia.'

'Spot on.'

'But you mentioned some other visitors – people who had come just for the day?'

'That's right. Rhona and Frank had walked over from Baddeley Court. It's only about a mile across the fields and they often pop across if they fancy a dip on a hot day. Rhona is the same age as Cecilia and Frank is a couple of years younger, so when Aunt Catriona's gang are here, they just add to the merry throng. They're all nice kids and they generally get along fine together.'

'Anyone else?'

'Just two of the Trenchard sisters, Mabel and Victoria. They had telephoned that morning, to see if anyone would be playing tennis. They have their own court at home of course, but it's not so much fun with only the two of them.'

'Are they also children?' asked Fran, who half remembered the name Mabel Trenchard from a conversation over breakfast.

'Oh no. Mabel is twenty-one next month and Victoria is a year younger, I think.'

'Anyone else?'

Eddie considered for a moment. 'No . . . I'm pretty sure that's everyone. Well, except for the servants, of course.'

'I'm going to need a list of their names too.'

'Of course.' Eddie began his recitation at once, staring with Jamieson the butler, Imogen's governess, Miss Billington, Monica Roche, who had been employed as his grandfather's nurse, working his way through the ranks of indoor staff in order of precedence, before turning his attention to the outdoor staff, staring with Marshall, the head gardener and ending with Max and Joe, the apprentices.

Fran was quite taken aback at the sheer number of people who apparently needed to be employed in order to take proper care of Sunnyside House and its half-dozen occupants. Goodness, she would probably have to talk to all of them. It was going to take ages. For now, though, she needed to focus on the principal players, starting with Eddie.

'Can you tell me what you remember about the day that your grandfather died? Starting right at the beginning, before it became clear that there was something wrong?'

Again Eddie adopted a look of intense concentration as he marshalled his thoughts. 'It's rather difficult,' he said at last. 'To begin with it was just another ordinary day. We'd been enjoying a splendid run of good weather, so one day tended to be pretty much like another, though of course in another way, no two days were exactly alike.'

Fran waited patiently, confident that an explanation would be forthcoming.

'When the weather is good we often have our lunch out of doors. That sort of thing is usually decided upon at breakfast, so that Jamiseon and Cook know well in advance what's wanted. Sometimes we would have picnic hampers brought down to the beach, or else taken somewhere in the grounds. Some days there would be visitors, either unexpected callers who stayed for lunch or tea, or people we'd invited to spend the day. Some days someone would get up a treasure hunt, or the kids would play hide-and-seek or Hare and Hounds. Other times people would just drift through the day, reading and sunbathing, swimming or looking for crabs in the rock pools at low tide. Most days someone would suggest a game of tennis. Hen is really keen and actually rather good, and our cousin, Helly, is another sporty girl, so they were always up for a few sets.'

'So on this particular day,' Fran said, 'can you remember where it was decided that you would eat lunch, for example?'

'Oh, yes. Mother and Uncle Charles preferred to eat up here at the house, so naturally Uncle Charles' wife, Dolly, came up here for luncheon too. Grandfather's was laid on a tray and taken into his room. The rest of us had a picnic down on the beach. I can't recall exactly what we ate, but I seem to remember that there was some salad, because Cecilia's tomato rolled off her plate on to the sand and that made everyone laugh. Of course, then Imogen got a bit silly and rolled her tomato on to the sand deliberately and Miss Billington had to tell her to calm down. I'm afraid she gets rather overexcited at times and it gets her into trouble.'

'Had the Baddeleys and the Trenchards arrived by lunchtime?'

'Mabel and Victoria Trenchard were definitely here by then. I'm not sure about young Rhona and Frank. I'm afraid it's terribly difficult to recall every detail.'

'You're doing very well,' Fran assured him. 'I want to concentrate on lunchtime, because we know that your grandfather was still in his room at that point. I think you said that he was in there, asleep, at around two p.m. when Jamieson came to collect his tray. Where would everyone else have been by then?'

'I can't speak for Mother, because I didn't see her again until we all went back up to the house much later, though I believe she went to lie down after lunch. By two o'clock most of us would still have been hogging down on the beach. Uncle Charles and Aunt Dolly came back down there after they'd eaten and we were all still sitting about. I don't think we even started unpacking the hampers until well after one that day.'

'So everyone else was eating together, down on the beach – even the people who'd been playing tennis?'

'That's right. I think they may have been the reason for the delay. We were waiting for them to come and join us.'

'And after lunch was finished, what did people do then?'

'Oh, various things. Hen changed into her bathers and went for a swim. So did Roly, I think. Imogen, Cecilia and some of the others started to play cricket. It was low tide around three o'clock that day so there was plenty of flat sand. Mellie was lying under her parasol – she doesn't like to get burned – pretending to read but probably just dozing. Anything to get out of ball games.'

'And what were you doing?'

'Me? Actually, I think I helped dear old Billie collect everything up and put it back into the hampers. Poor Miss Billington, she often gets lumbered with that kind of thing. Then I sat on one of the rugs and after a minute or two Mabel Trenchard came over and sat next to me and we chatted for a bit. It was just local gossip, you know, nothing at all significant. Then I went to play cricket with the kids for a while and after that I cooled off in the sea. Later a group of us went up for tennis – first to six games and the winners stay on, that kind of thing.'

'And from there?'

'We played until about five. In summer, tea is always laid out on the terrace from about half past four – or in the drawing room of course, if it's raining – and Roly was complaining that he would die if he didn't have something to drink soon, so we strolled up through the garden together. Mother and Uncle Charles were already there, and it wasn't too long before the people who'd stayed on the beach started to appear. By the time Grandfather was missed, I'm pretty sure that everyone was back up at the house.'

'Who played tennis and who stayed on the beach?'

Eddie looked thoughtful. 'I must get this right, mustn't I, because I suppose it's all a question of who could have slipped away on their own? Initially only four of us walked up to the courts. Helly, Mabel and Victoria were already in their tennis kit and I had slipped back into a pair of shorts so we were ready to set off, but Hen had to change out of her wet bathing dress. It's much more complicated for girls, isn't it? Anyway, she said she would catch us up and so did Roly. I think that he was probably still hoping to persuade Mellie to play. Dolly said that she was going to come and join us, but she didn't come right away either.'

'What about your uncle Charles? You said he got back to the house ahead of you.'

'He'd already gone off for a walk by the time we went to play tennis.'

'A walk? On his own?'

'Yes. He said that sitting about wasn't good for his digestion.'

Fran made a swift note on her pad.

'The four of us got to the court and started to play. I don't think we'd played much more than a couple of games by the time Hen and Roly joined us. Dolly arrived last. Dolly was a bit odd, actually.' He hesitated.

'In what way?'

'Well, Dolly is a pretty hopeless player. Serves underarm and mostly just flails at the ball. It's very much hit and hope for the best. I partnered her because I know she gets on Hen's nerves dreadfully. Usually she just bumbles along and laughs at herself and gets the score all wrong, but that afternoon, not long after she'd joined us, she missed a ball and when she went over to pick it up, instead of tossing it back to me so that I could serve again, she thrashed the ball away into the bushes. Then, when she turned to face me, she was quite red in the face and I thought she was about to cry.'

'I suppose it can get very frustrating, playing with a lot of people who are better than you.'

'The thing is I don't believe it was anything to do with the game at all. Dolly doesn't care a fig about the game or how bad she is. She's not competitive like Hen. It's just a way of passing the time to her. I'm sure it was something else. To tell the truth, I wondered if she and Uncle Charles had had a row.'

'And have you any idea whether they had?'

'Well, nothing happened on the beach so far as I'm aware, but it did seem a bit funny, him going off like that for a walk on his own and later on, that evening, things seemed to be a bit frosty between them.'

'In what way?'

'There was nothing specific. It was just a feeling I had.'

'So . . . if I've got this right, the people who stayed on the beach right up until teatime were Mellie, Imogen, Miss Billington, Cecilia and the two Baddeley children.'

'That sounds about right.'

'Did the Baddeley children stay for tea?'

'No, they must have walked home. The footpath leading back to their place goes up through the western coppice, so they don't need to come past the house.'

'So everyone had their tea . . .' Fran prompted.

'Some people were lingering outside. It was still gloriously warm and no one was in a rush because we never dress for dinner in high summer if it's only family. I remember someone asking if it wasn't time for cocktails and Hen saying that it was never too early, and just then Grandfather's nurse appeared and of course that put paid to any talk of cocktails for the rest of the evening.'

'This nurse, Monica Roche. You say that it was her afternoon off?'

'That's right. She went off-duty at one. She was asked about all that at the inquest of course. Apparently Grandfather was eating his lunch when she left. He'd been grumbling a bit, she said, but he did sometimes complain – mostly about trivial things – particularly towards the end. Apart from the grumbling – which wasn't really out of the ordinary – he was just as usual.'

'Do we know where the nurse went, or how she spent her afternoon?'

'We do. As I mentioned before, we're a bit out of the way here, and when she first came to us, sometimes Monica didn't go anywhere on her half day. She would just have a stroll around the grounds or take her book into a quiet part of the garden. But I gather that when she was down in Frencombe on one occasion she bumped into the Baddeleys' chauffeur, Moncrieff, and they seem to have become friendly and got into the habit of spending some of their afternoons off together.

Moncrieff's a thoroughly reliable sort – he'd been with the Baddeleys for years and years. In fact, I believe that he'd been working for them for a long time before we came here. He's retired now, but I understand they're letting him have a cottage on the estate. Hen seemed to be under the impression that there might have been some sort of romance in the air between him and Monica, but if there ever was – which I doubt – then nothing came of it. Anyway, the point is that this chap, Moncrieff, was sometimes allowed the use of Colonel Baddeley's motor, and on this particular afternoon he'd picked Monica up and taken her for a spin along the coast road. Afterwards they had tea at the Palace Hotel in Torquay. It was all above board. He had the colonel's permission to use the car and I believe the police confirmed that they'd been seen by the staff at the Palace. It's quite a pricey sort of place for a chauffeur to take a lady friend, which is probably why Hen dreamed up a possible love affair. I never saw Monica as the romantic type myself – she was a confirmed spinster, in my opinion – so I think it was probably just that they fancied a bit of a treat and decided to splash out. Anyway, Moncrieff dropped her back here at just before six p.m.'

'And I suppose she must have gone to her room, removed her hat, probably changed her shoes and come straight back downstairs?'

'And found the old man gone.'

TEN

Fran stood considering her reflection in the dressing-table mirror. Her dress, loaned by Henrietta, was a pink silk number, the colour of old-fashioned roses, made up in a loose-fitting, drop-waisted style, and it therefore worked perfectly, falling just a little lower down her calves than it would have done on its owner. Luckily she had brought a string of pearls, and with her hair brushed and her lipstick applied she decided that she looked 'not half bad', as Mo would have said.

The plain gold band on her wedding finger caught her eye. If everything went through smoothly, she would soon be granted her decree nisi, with the decree absolute following before the year was out. She would still call herself Mrs Black, she supposed, but she would not be married. It already felt vaguely wrong to be wearing Michael's ring. With her right finger and thumb, she eased it up as far as her nail, but the finger looked oddly naked without it, so she slid it back into position for the time being. Anyway, it might jinx things if she jumped the gun.

She had spent a good deal of the afternoon quizzing the Edgertons' various household servants and was rather afraid that she in turn would be quizzed over dinner about what she had found out (which was very little), so she was very relieved when she joined her hosts for cocktails, to find the talk was mostly of plays and musical entertainments, and the unlikely suggestion reported in the newspaper that there might soon be a tunnel linking England to France. Dinner passed off in the same easy manner and when they eventually withdrew into the drawing room, Lady Louisa was persuaded to play for them, which she did with considerable skill, offering them some Chopin, Bach and then the lovely Salut D'Amor.

'And now,' Lady Louisa said, when they had applauded her final effort, 'I am leaving you young people to your own devices. Come along, Eddie, it's your turn now.'

'Mother can't bear jazz,' Eddie confided to Fran as he took his mother's place on the piano stool.

'Since there are four of us,' said Mellie, 'why don't we roll back the rug and dance? You do like to dance, don't you, Fran?'

Fran confirmed that she did and noted, from the alacrity with which Roly and Hen exposed the parquet floor, that this must be a regular pastime at Sunnyside House. Like his mother, Eddie proved to be a talented pianist, belting out a series of jolly ragtime numbers, while his brother took turns to partner his wife, sister and their guest, while the two spare women danced together. Sometimes Eddie sang along, sounding, Fran thought, surprisingly professional and when the dancers ran out of energy, he continued to entertain them for some time, working through a wide repertoire of popular music, as well as some less well-known jazz and blues numbers, all played flawlessly by ear.

Only as they were on the point of parting for bed did anyone mention the purpose behind Fran's visit, when Mellie said, 'Eddie says we are not to bother you, and to let you get on with the investigation in your own way, but I just wanted to let you know that if I am needed for – well – questioning, I suppose, it would be much better if we could get it done in the morning as I have an appointment with my hairdresser tomorrow afternoon.'

'Thank you for letting me know,' Fran said. 'I will need to speak to everyone, of course. Perhaps if we were to meet in the library, immediately after breakfast?'

'Splendid,' said Mellie. 'That's settled then. Do sleep well, won't you. People mostly do here. It's a lovely peaceful house at night.'

Up in her bedroom Fran found that, just as had happened the night before, someone had been in to turn down the bed and lay out her nightgown. The modern electric bulbs in the bedside lights were shrouded by cream shades that wreathed everything in a warm, steady light, quite different to the spooky undulating shadows made by the candles one found in many homes. Mellie was right, Fran thought. The earlier, slightly frenetic energy of the drawing room had been overtaken by a sense of tranquillity and peace. It was rather hard to believe that something as nasty as the murder of an elderly man, confined to a wheelchair, might have intruded into this place.

She removed the borrowed dress and hung it in the wardrobe, among half a dozen other gowns, which Henrietta had generously provided from her own bulging closets. Some people would have made one feel like a poor relation, Fran thought, but Henrietta had affected to believe that Fran had simply travelled light, rather than that she was not the sort of woman who possessed a different evening frock for every day of the week. Tomorrow night she might wear the dark green velvet . . . or perhaps the black taffeta . . .

She pulled herself together firmly. She really must not forget the real reason she was here. Who had taken that diamond? How had Frederick Edgerton ended up dead at the bottom of the cliffs? Were the Edgertons really as nice as they seemed? Then again, why would they have invited her at all if one of their number was guilty? Perhaps she needed to look beyond the immediate family for her suspects? In the past, she had always had Tom or Mo, and often both of them, available to chew things over and discuss possible clues, but Mo was in Malaya and Tom was just as far out of bounds in a way. She realized that she had been having such fun she had hardly thought about either of them all evening. Perhaps Tom had been right to insist that she come down here after all.

ELEVEN

Mellie sat neatly on one of the library chairs, back straight, knees and ankles together, looking so much as though she were about to be interviewed for a responsible post as a governess, that Fran almost felt like asking if she had brought references. Instead she began by saying, 'Just so that I can get a little bit of context, can you tell me how long you have known the Edgerton family and how long you have been married to Roly?'

'Of course.' Mellie's face broke into a warm smile, as if she was relieved at the simple nature of the question. 'I first met Roly at a dance given by the Bruce-Forsters. I had just come out and the Edgertons had not long moved into the district. After that we came across one another on a fairly regular basis. I don't know how things are with you in the north, but down here it is mostly the same group of families at the lord lieutenant's bash and the hunt balls and so forth, and my father's place is only about twenty miles away from here, so it was inevitable that we would keep on bumping into one another.

'It wasn't love at first sight, but I think we both noticed each other, if you know what I mean. I did have a bit of a thing going with one of the young officers stationed at Devonport for a while, but luckily we realized that we didn't have that much in common and called it a day before Mother could start ordering the invitations for an engagement.' Mellie laughed and Fran joined in politely.

'Then one day the Edgertons invited a crowd of us for a party on the beach. Swimming and ball games, followed by a supper of bangers and potatoes, all cooked on a great big bonfire of driftwood. It was lots of fun as you can imagine and after supper, Roly took me off into the garden. We stood there, just the two of us in the moonlight, surrounded by the scent of roses, and he proposed. It was terribly romantic.

Unbeknown to me, he'd already been to speak with my father, so when I said "yes" we were able to go back down on to the beach and announce it to all our friends at once. You should have heard the cheers! And, of course, Jamieson had been teed up in advance and right on cue he began to pop the champagne corks. They'd got the bottles hidden somewhere nearby, all kept on ice.'

'And that was when?'

'The second of September 1928,' said Mellie promptly. 'We were married the following spring.'

'So you had only been married for a few months when Roly's grandfather died.'

'That's right.'

'Can I ask what you remember about the day it happened?'

'You can ask . . .' Mellie gave her little laugh again. 'But I'm afraid the truth is that I don't remember anything very much about it at all. It was terribly hot, I do know that. I remember having to hunt about when we realized the old man was missing, but hardly anything before that. We all spent most of the day on the beach.'

'But not everyone spent the whole day there,' Fran prompted.

'Oh no. Some people went to play tennis. Those Trenchard girls had come over for the day and they are frightfully jolly hockey sticks and forever wanting to chase about at some game or other. Roly wanted me to play too, but it was far too warm.'

'Do you remember who else went to play?'

'Not really. Oh, wait, though – I'm sure that frightful woman who has married Roly's uncle was one of them, because I was so relieved when she buzzed off. She gets on my nerves I'm afraid, chattering all the time in that affected voice, trying to disguise her shop girl's accent – as if anyone is going to be fooled.'

Fran tried a different tack. 'Can you remember who definitely stayed on the beach all afternoon?'

'Not really. You see, I was lying under one of the big para-sols with my eyes closed for some of the time. I may even have dozed off. I'm not being much of a help, am I? Oh, wait, though . . . I do remember one thing. Some of the kids were playing cricket or rounders on the sand and there was a row about it. I lifted my head off the cushions and I could see that Imogen was quarrelling with the others and then she screamed at them and stormed off. Poor old Miss Billington, who had been sitting in the shade with me, had to put down her book and go after her. She called out, of course, but Imogen was in one of her rages and took no notice. Quite honestly that child needs a zookeeper, not a governess.'

'Did you see Miss Billington catch up with her?'

'No, but then one couldn't see much from where I was lying. I think I heard Miss Billington call her name a couple of times, but I don't know whether or not she caught up with her.'

'They didn't come straight back together?'

'I don't recollect that they came back on to the beach at all. Imogen probably hid somewhere and refused to come out. She's quite smart at disappearing when she wants to. Or she may have gone straight back to the house in search of cake. The servants all indulge her to a ridiculous degree. But . . . now I think about it, Miss Billington must have come back to the beach, because I remember her walking ahead of me when we eventually came back up to the house for tea. She was carrying a bag with some towels and things. I don't recall seeing Imogen, though.'

'When you found out what had happened to old Mr Edgerton, did you suspect that it mightn't have been an accident?'

Mellie inclined her head to one side. 'That depends what you mean by an accident. I suppose I can speak in confidence?'

'Of course.'

'Well then, personally I suspected that he had done it on purpose.'

'Committed suicide, you mean?'

'I think that's a rather distasteful way of describing it. My great-uncle Chetwyn took his own life but everyone was perfectly happy to call it an accident. Gun went off accidentally, that kind of idea. It's such an embarrassment for the family to have it put about that it was suicide while of unsound mind. My eldest sister was about to come out when Uncle Chetwyn died. Rumours like that can seriously impair a girl's chances.'

'But surely . . .'

'Come now, you know how it is. Engagements have been broken off at the whiff of anything like that in the girl's family.'

Fran paused to consider this. In the village where she had grown up there had been a family with an idiot son whose sisters had never married. One always hoped that this was coincidence rather than active prejudice.

'It's bad enough that Roly and the others are saddled with Imogen,' Mellie continued. 'Without it being suggested that their grandfather was losing his mind.'

'And was he?' Fran enquired.

'Not in the sense that he was raving or anything like that,' Mellie said quickly. 'I wouldn't want you to get the idea that he was an out-and-out loony, but he had started to get a bit confused.'

'In what way?'

'Well . . . he used to get a bit muddled. Sometimes he forgot names, things like that. And sometimes he got funny ideas about things. He wanted to sack the cook, because he said she was trying to poison him. That was a couple of months before he died and it all blew over. He also got a bit of a thing about Monica, his nurse. He wanted to sack her too, at one stage. He said she was looking at him in a funny way.'

'No one considered sacking the cook or the nurse?'

'Of course not. Mrs Remington has been with the family for years and Monica was an excellent nurse and very good with old Mr Edgerton.'

'Why did he think he was being poisoned?'

'Oh, it was just his fancy. He said his food tasted funny one day. Monica said she tasted it and there was nothing wrong with it at all, but she humoured him anyway and threw the food away, I believe.'

'So it was only one occasion?'

'Yes, just once.'

'And what did he mean? When he said that his nurse was looking at him in a funny way?'

'Oh, heaven only knows! It was just his fancy, you know.'

'But these things made you think that he might have become confused and pushed himself up the path and over the edge of the cliffs?'

'Well, it seemed the obvious solution.'

'Until someone realized that the diamond was missing?'

'Oh, but I don't see that makes any difference at all,' Mellie said. 'I think he'd just taken it out of the safe and then put it somewhere and forgotten about it. He may even have hidden it, thinking it was for safekeeping. I wouldn't be a bit surprised if it isn't somewhere in the house.'

'The house has been searched?'

'Of course. But it's a big house and a small stone. It could be anywhere. In the back of a cupboard, or behind some books or, heaven forefend, stuffed into the soil of a pot plant. Even in a modern house like this there are a thousand and one nooks and crannies.'

TWELVE

Roly was the next interviewee. Like Mellie, his recollections about everyone's precise whereabouts on the afternoon of his grandfather's demise were far from certain. 'The thing I remember most clearly was the moment when Monica told me that she'd spotted Grandfather's chair at the foot of the cliffs. The rest of the afternoon is a bit of a blur, but that stands out.'

'Can you tell me about it?'

'I remember Monica's face. She was very calm, but I could see it was bad news. I went cold, even as she began to speak. We were on the terrace at the time. Everyone had split up to search, but Eddie and I had just got back when we saw Monica coming down the path from the east cliff. She told us what she'd seen and we both followed her back up there – I think Eddie has showed you the spot. I walked towards the edge and Eddie said, "Take care, old man!" After Eddie's warning I dropped down on all fours and inched across the last bit to look over. It was easy to see where he'd gone over. The grass grows quite high just there, but it was pretty much flattened where Monica had already crawled over to take a look. It's dangerous at the edge – bits have been known to drop off.'

'Did it look as if there had been a recent fall? Could it have happened that your grandfather simply went too near the edge and the cliff crumbled under his weight?'

'No. There was no evidence of that.'

'So there's no chance that the cliff gave way?'

Roly shook his head. 'After a fall there's always quite a pile of earth and stuff sitting on the rocks until it gets washed away by the high tides.'

'You said Monica was calm. Wasn't she upset?'

'I expect she was, but she didn't show it. After all, she's a trained nurse, isn't she? She's probably used to breaking bad news.'

'Can you remember how everyone else reacted when they heard the news?'

'I thought Mellie was going to faint. She went white, poor darling. Dolly had a fit of hysterics and had to be taken upstairs. Typical of that type – hardly knew my grandfather but made a great drama over how upset she was.'

'Your brother mentioned that he thought Dolly had been behaving rather oddly that afternoon.'

'Did he? I can't say that I remember. I never take much notice of Dolly, to tell you the truth.'

'He wondered if she and your uncle Charles had fallen out with one another.' Fran pursued the point.

'Well, I wouldn't be at all surprised. It can't be a success, a marriage like that. Dolly's a gold-digger of the first order. She was working as a waitress or something of the sort when they met. The wedding was a hole-in-the-corner affair, some-where abroad. Excuse my frankness, but she must be an embarrassment to him, wherever they go.'

'Do you recall what your uncle Charles was doing that afternoon?'

'I don't. He wasn't with Dolly on the tennis court. Maybe he'd stayed on the beach with Miss Billington and the kids.'

Fran decided not to beat about the bush. 'Can you tell me whether your uncle benefitted in any way under your grandfather's will?'

'Yes, I suppose he did to a degree. There were legacies for the whole family.'

Fran noticed that although Roly answered readily enough, the colour had risen in his cheeks. Perhaps it was only natural, as he had benefitted most of all.

'I trust you don't find my question offensive?'

'Not in the least,' said Roly. 'Money is usually the motive, isn't it? Let me see . . . I'm the number one suspect in this respect, because I got the house and the major part of the estate. Eddie and Hen both got modest lump sums. Grandfather had already set them up for life – all in trust funds, of course, so income, rather than capital, they could actually get at.'

Fran wondered what represented a 'modest lump sum' to someone like Roland Edgerton, but before she had time to speculate Roly helped her out, explaining, 'Grandfather had seen to it that we were all well provided for. The only reason anyone might have wanted to get their hands on a legacy any sooner was if they happened to be temporarily embarrassed, but even then, the old man was notoriously generous. I – I once ran up some gambling debts, but Grandfather settled them for me when I went to him and confessed. So you see, even if any one of us had been in a bit of bother, we needn't have bumped the old fellow off.'

'Did anyone else receive anything?'

Again, there was a moment's hesitation. 'All our aunts got a few hundred pounds and Uncle Charles did slightly better. The other grandchildren were treated pretty well and several of the staff were remembered. I'm sure I can obtain a copy of the will, if you think it would be helpful.'

'I think you've probably told me all I need to know,' Fran said, thinking that a list of recipients would be very little use without also being able to see their bank statements in order to ascertain how much they had actually needed a legacy. Just then she was struck by another idea. 'How about your grandfather's nurse, Monica? Did she benefit?'

'I don't believe so. She'd only been with us about eighteen months. It was people like Jamieson and Mrs Remington, those who'd served the family over a number of years, you know? There wasn't anything for Billie or Monica.'

'What happened to her after your grandfather's death?'

'Monica?' For a moment Roly seemed surprised by the question. 'Oh, well, she obtained another post, I expect. Obviously there was nothing more for her to do here. I expect Mother would know more about it. No doubt she would have wanted references and so forth. Technically, of course, Mellie is the lady of the house, but she's more than happy to leave all that kind of thing to Mother.'

Lady Louisa was the next interviewee, but she could give no more assistance than Roland when it came to everyone else's whereabouts on the critical afternoon.

'You see, after lunch I felt one of my heads coming on, so I went up to my room to lie down. I drew the curtains to darken the room and I must have fallen asleep, because I remember waking up briefly and hearing someone laugh on the landing, and someone else shushing them. They must have been right outside my door, because the house is very well made, so one is hardly ever disturbed by noise. The next time I woke, I glanced at the clock and realized that it was past teatime. I straightened my dress, brushed my hair and went straight down on to the terrace. I took my book, but I hardly had time to open it before the first of the family arrived for tea. I'm afraid I can't quite recall in what order they got there, though Roly and Eddie were most definitely among the first. Henrietta and the Trenchard girls arrived soon after them, I think.'

'And did everyone seem . . . perfectly ordinary?'

'I'm not sure that I understand quite what you mean, my dear.'

'Did anyone seem a bit preoccupied or out of sorts?'

Lady Louisa took a moment to consider. 'Not that I noticed,' she said. 'But then I wasn't paying much attention. I had just spotted that the *symphytum variegatum* was drooping and I made a mental note to remind Marshall – he is our head gardener – that it would need regular watering if the spell of hot dry weather continued.'

The conversation proved more fruitful when Fran turned the subject to Monica.

'She was splendid with my father-in-law. Endlessly patient. And she was no trouble at all. It can be such a trial to the other staff, having a nurse in residence. One hears of them creating absolute ructions in some households, making extra demands on the servants and causing no end of tiresome rows . . . which of course the mistress of the house then has to sort out and smooth over. These days it is so hard to keep good servants, even in country districts like this where employment prospects are generally so poor. Of course, Monica came with excellent references. She had been with old Lady Aberlithney up until she died and there had been a spell with a family in the south of France before that. The other thing is that she was a rather hefty sort of woman, which meant that she had no difficulties when it came to helping my father-in-law to move about, pushing him in his wheelchair and so forth.'

'Do you know where she is working now?'

'I do not. Naturally I provided a reference when she left, but no one has contacted me to take it up.'

'How long did she stay on after old Mr Edgerton died?'

'Oh, a week or two, I think. We didn't actually give her notice, you understand. She left of her own accord, so I assume that she either had a post to go to, or else that she had decided to take some time off before finding a position elsewhere.'

'Do you have a forwarding address for her?'

'I believe I do. It's in my desk, with the household accounts. I will let you have it. I should have thought of it, because of course you will want to question her as well.' Lady Louisa smiled. 'You know,' she said, 'I think my father-in-law would have enjoyed this. He loved games and puzzles and treasure hunts and the like. If you are finished with me, Mrs Black, shall I ask Henrietta to come in?'

Henrietta added very little to Fran's knowledge of the afternoon. She recalled the picnic on the beach, the tennis which had followed, and that it had been 'fearfully hot'. She did not particularly remember anything about Dolly Edgerton's mood ('she has the most hopeless backhand you've ever seen, and doesn't even attempt to serve properly') but she did recall that 'Mabel Trenchard was in rather a sulk because Eddie offered to play with Dolly instead of her. Poor Mabel has a terrible pash for Eddie and I don't believe he cares for her a bit.'

She knew nothing of the discovery of the body. 'I'd gone down the lane in the direction of the garages and the gardener's cottages. We all split up, you see, going off in different directions. I asked at the cottages, but of course no one had seen anything of Grandfather that afternoon, and by the time I got back to the house Monica had reported what she'd found to Roly, and Roly had been to see for himself.'

'Everyone must have been terribly shocked.'

'Oh, yes. When I got back the boys were debating what to do. Whether we ought to call the police and how we could get hold of a boat to get round there. Someone said he might have survived the fall, but Roly just said, "Don't be ridiculous." Dolly was in hysterics – I remember wanting to slap her.'

Poor Dolly, Fran thought. No one seemed to have any time for her at all, except Eddie, who had at least tried to be kind, by offering to partner her on the tennis court.

THIRTEEN

When Fran joined the family for lunch in the dining room, she was feeling somewhat dispirited. To be sure, there were some loose ends to be tied up – there was Mellie's mysterious reference to 'you know what' which she had overheard in the hall. 'Uncle Charles' was definitely of interest, for he appeared to have spent at least some of the afternoon of his father's death unaccounted for. She still needed to speak with Miss Billington, who might perhaps have seen something useful, when she had been forced to pursue Imogen after the latter fled from the beach. And then there was Imogen herself. Fran wondered whether it would be possible to keep her still long enough to get any sense out of her.

As they tucked in to Scotch eggs and salad, Eddie said, 'I do hope you are going to take some time off from sleuthing this afternoon. All work and no play makes Jill a dull girl – not that you could ever be dull of course,' he added hastily. 'But it's shaping up to be a splendid day and I was going to take a walk up through the woods and across to the west cliff. Do say you'll accompany me. It might be useful too, because it's the way the Baddeley kids would have walked the day Grandfather died.'

'That would be delightful,' Fran said. 'And as you say, it might be useful.'

'And I promise not to pump you for information,' Eddie added. 'We are all agreed among ourselves that you must be left to get on with your investigation, without any interference or undue curiosity . . . though I for one am dying of curiosity, as you must know.'

As a result of Eddie's invitation, the two of them set out together about half an hour later, initially taking the main path which led through the garden to the shore, then striking off to the right after a few minutes to follow a much steeper, narrower path through the belt of trees which edged the western side of the valley. The branches were still bare, but Fran could imagine how dim and shady it would have been on a summer's day. Pausing for a moment, to look back the way she had come, she realized that even when shorn of their canopy of leaves, the trees ensured that the house and garden were completely out of sight. It would have been most unlikely that the Baddeley children would have seen anyone or anything useful on their walk to and from Sunnyside's garden.

'Do these woods belong to your family?' she asked.

'Oh, yes. The Edgerton land goes on for ages yet. We – or rather Roly – owns all this woodland and the grazing on top. The Baddeley estate doesn't start until you get down into the Ave valley.'

'It's beautiful countryside round here. You're very fortunate.'

'Aren't we, though? Spring and summer are the best times here. I blame Sunnyside for my own lack of industry. If it wasn't for this glorious place, I might be earning a crust, playing piano in some club or other up in London.'

'You could easily make a living as a pianist,' Fran said. 'You're awfully good.'

Eddie laughed. 'I have thought of it,' he said. 'I know Mother wouldn't be keen. It's not quite the thing, is it? Being an entertainer? And it's fearfully hard to get started. The other thing is . . .' Eddie hesitated. They had come to the edge of the trees and as he turned to hold open a gate, which led into a broad green field, she saw that his expression was unusually serious. 'It's sort of . . . Oh, I don't know . . . fraudulent, somehow. You see, I don't need the money. Thanks to Grandfather, I have enough in the way of income that anything I earned wouldn't matter, so I'd be nothing but a dilettante. And what's more, I'd be taking work from someone who really needs it. I suppose you think I'm a bit of an idiot to even care? I mean, most fellows would just think that if one wanted to do a thing, one should just grab that chance.'

'Oh, but you are so right,' Fran said. 'It does seem mean to take away a job from someone else who needs it more.'

Eddie's face broke into a much more characteristic grin. 'I knew that you would see it,' he said.

'But in the meantime,' Fran said, 'I suppose that does leave you with a lot of unfulfilled ambitions.'

'You overestimate me.' Eddie gave another, self-deprecatory laugh. 'Apart from my musical bent, I am very much suited to a life of indolence, supplemented by a private income. I'd like to travel, I suppose. I've always fancied one of those long sea voyages, where one sees something new and exotic every few days. The thing is that one needs the right companion to share it.'

'My best friend, Mo, has just sailed out to visit her husband in Malaya. It sounds as if she has had tremendous fun on the voyage.'

'The company would be everything, of course.'

'I believe she has fallen in with quite a lively crowd.'

Eddie made no reply and they walked on across the field in silence, then climbed a stile to enter another grassy expanse, where the ground continued to rise gently. When they reached the highest point, Fran saw that the land ahead of them slid into a gentle fold, where a solitary house stood in a grove of newly planted trees. 'Is that Baddeley Court?' she asked.

'Lord, no. Baddeley Court is a good half-mile further west. Grandfather had this built a couple of years after Sunnyside House was finished. He had a drive put in as well, so you can get to it via the road. It's a jolly spot, isn't it? Sea views from all the south-facing windows.'

As they continued towards the house, Fran could see that it was relatively newly built, its garden not yet enclosed or laid out. 'Who lives there?' she asked, anticipating some family retainer, perhaps holding some fresh and as yet unexpected clue.

'No one,' Eddie said. 'It was built for me.'

'But you don't live here?'

'Oh, no. Roly and Mellie don't seem to mind that Hen and I are perpetually playing gooseberry. We all rub along together pretty well, as you've probably realized. So Innominate House won't be tenanted until I've persuaded the right woman to share it with me.'

'Innominate House?'

'The house with no name. Grandfather meant that I should

name it myself, but I've no imagination to speak of, so it will be left up to my bride. Like to see around?'

'Oh, I'd love to,' said Fran, whose healthy curiosity extended to other people's houses.

'It's not furnished,' Eddie said, as he fished the front door keys from his pocket.

'Is that to be left to the future Mrs Edgerton too?' Fran asked, as he held the door open for her.

'Absolutely. Women have far better taste than men.'

It was an undeniably lovely house and Fran had no difficulty in finding complimentary things to say about it as Eddie showed her over the property. He seemed gratified by her enthusiasm. 'And no one has ever stayed here?' she asked, remembering that when it came to detection, one should always consider the unexpected.

'No one. The property will be entirely virginal, even if the bride is not.'

Fran felt herself blushing and tried not to show that she was shocked. He had spoken so casually. She had heard that the upper classes could sometimes be unexpectedly liberal in such matters. Who knew what rackety, racy lives the young Edgertons lived, getting up to all sorts of things when they went up to their house in London?

'Thank you for showing me around,' Fran said. 'I suppose we had better be getting back.'

'Of course. The days go by so quickly, don't they? You know, I really must take you out for a run down to Frencombe and into Avemouth one of these days. They're both quite pretty in a rustic sort of way. And we could pop over to Baddeley Court. Young Rhona and Frank are both away at school, but Colonel Baddeley's a fascinating chap and they always have afternoon tea in the great hall, in front of the fire. The fireplace dates from the sixteenth century or something like that. We Edgertons are far too *nouveaux* to be able to offer anything half as splendid.'

'Mmm,' said Fran, who was vaguely wondering how much longer she could usefully stay at Sunnyside House, once she had interviewed just about anyone there was to be interviewed. 'Perhaps tomorrow . . .'

'Oh, it won't be tomorrow, I'm afraid. Didn't I mention that I have to go across to Winchester for a funeral? It's my old headmaster – a splendid fellow. Roly never got to know him as he only arrived the same year that I joined the school.'

'Oh.' Fran tried not to show any disappointment. An excursion to take tea in a sixteenth-century great hall was not to be sniffed at.

'You will have to manage your sleuthing without your would-be Watson. Not that I've been any help at all. Not that you need any help. You're quite marvellously independent, aren't you? And I expect you've uncovered all the family skeletons.'

'So far as I can see, there are no family skeletons.'

'Well, only the Sidmouth business.'

'I'm afraid I don't know anything about the Sidmouth business.'

There was a moment of awkward silence. 'Oh. I thought that Roly . . . Oh, I see.' He faltered to a halt.

Fran decided to leave the matter hanging in the air. Left to his own devices, Eddie might well explain what he was talking about of his own accord.

After another few strides, Eddie said, 'You see, Roly mentioned this morning that you had asked him about Grandfather's will, so obviously, I thought . . .'

He got no further, because they were interrupted by a cheerful hail from a pair of figures, which were approaching across the field.

'It's your sister, Hen,' said Fran, recognizing the tall, slender figure on the right. 'But that isn't Mellie with her, is it?'

'No,' said Eddie, a touch grimly. 'It's Mabel Trenchard. What on earth is Hen doing, bringing her up here after us? Look here, Fran, please don't ask Mabel any direct questions about the day of Grandfather's death if you can possibly help it. I'll try to steer her on to the subject if I can, but it would be far better if she doesn't suspect why you're here. The Trenchards know everyone and Mabel's mother is the most fearful old gossip. The whole business would be all over the county by teatime tomorrow.'

'Don't worry,' Fran said quietly, for she knew how sound

tended to carry over open ground. 'Complete discretion, I promise you.'

'Here you are, Mabel,' Henrietta said cheerfully as the two pairs met. 'I told you this was where we'd find them. Mabel, this is Fran Black, who is down for a few days from the barren north. Fran, meet Mabel Trenchard, one of our oldest friends.'

The two women shook hands politely, each covertly appraising the other for entirely different reasons. Fran decided that Eddie's assessment of Mabel Trenchard's looks had been less than kind. She was a handsome, broad-shouldered girl, with dark curly hair, cut in a boyish style and a face lit up by a ready smile.

'Mabel has come over to show you her new car, Eddie. An early birthday present from her parents.'

Fran noticed that in spite of Eddie's earlier irritation, he managed to adopt a warm smile and a friendly tone to match. 'A new car? What sort is it?'

'It's a blue one, of course. My favourite colour.' Mabel grinned, while Fran tried to decide whether she was being an idiot on purpose. 'I wanted you to be one of the first to see it. Promise me that you'll come back to the house right away and look it over.'

'Of course. We were on our way back to the house in any case.'

Having paused to effect introductions, the party turned and headed back the way they had all come. In a neat sidestep, Mabel placed herself next to Eddie, looped her arm through his and started to chatter about her new car. 'It positively whizzed along the Frencombe road. I got her up to fifty on the straight bit above Rigg's Farm.'

'Actually Mabel, it's funny you should turn up just now,' Eddie interjected, when the young woman at his side paused momentarily to draw breath. 'You might be able to settle something for me. Just before you and Hen appeared I was telling Fran about the afternoon when Grandfather died and I was trying to remember exactly who was there that day. Hadn't you and Vicky come across to play tennis?'

'What a curious thing to be talking about!' exclaimed Mabel. 'Why yes, Vicky and I were certainly over here. We stayed for tea, but we'd motored home before anyone realized that anything was wrong. It was a terrible shock when we heard what had happened. To think that we were all sitting out on the terrace, munching madeleines and tea bread when the poor chap . . . well, you know . . . and to imagine him shouting for help, and no one hearing a thing.'

'What makes you think that he shouted for help?' Fran asked, trying not to sound too interested.

'Well, I supposed that he might have done. If he had realized that his bath chair was getting out of control and running away with him.'

In her mind Fran pictured the path. There was really no question of a downward slope which would have provided the necessary momentum to carry the chair over the edge, particularly as it would have met the resistance of the long grass which grew for a good foot or two between the path and the drop.

'Anyway,' Mabel said briskly, 'I'm sure no one wants to dwell on horrible things like that.'

They had reached the gate which led back into the trees and she was forced to let go of Eddie's arm while he unlatched it. 'I say, are you coming to the Lyndons' dance on Friday evening? Vicky is going as Britannia, which will be hellish difficult from the point of view of dancing, I should say, though we do so love getting ourselves up in fancy dress.'

'And what are you going as?' asked Henrietta.

'It's a secret,' Mabel declared archly. 'Wait and see. You are coming, aren't you?'

'Are we invited? I'd forgotten all about it,' Eddie said.

'Of course we're invited.' His sister sounded exasperated. 'In fact, I must ring the Lyndons and ask if we can bring Fran along. Oh, it's all right,' she added quickly, waving away Fran's attempted protest. 'The Lyndons won't mind at all and we can easily find you a costume. It's a bit late to send away for something, but we've got heaps of stuff from previous parties – or we can just adapt something.'

Eddie's attempt at drawing Mabel Trenchard into conversation about the day of his grandfather's death had been a complete failure, Fran thought, deciding that it probably didn't matter very much anyway, as Miss Trenchard was neither a suspect nor the sort of person who might have made a particularly good witness.

When they reached the house, Mabel led Eddie off towards the front of the house in a manner which did not encourage his sister and their visitor to follow. As Fran and Henrietta entered by the garden door they met Lady Louisa. 'Ah, so Henrietta and Mabel found the two of you.' She smiled. 'Mabel would have been so disappointed if she hadn't been able to show off her motor car to Eddie.'

'Poor Eddie.' Hen grinned. 'Mabel has her hooks pretty firmly into him.'

'Mabel is a very nice girl,' her mother said firmly. 'Any young man could do far worse.'

It transpired that after minutely examining the car's various features, Mabel insisted on taking Eddie for a drive in it, which on their return naturally led to her being invited to stay for tea. Fran observed the scene with well-concealed amusement, as Lady Louisa – for once in the drawing room, rather than overseeing operations in the garden or otherwise engrossed elsewhere – made polite conversation with Mabel, while her older children mischievously exhorted Eddie to pass Mabel the tea cakes, the sugar and every other possible thing which could engineer extra contact between them.

When Mabel had finally been waved off up the drive, the conversation returned to the subject of the fancy-dress party.

'Fran could wear that Pierrot costume,' Mellie suggested. 'I'm going as Ophelia. I've ordered a red wig specially, so that I'll look like the woman in the painting. The famous one that's in the National Gallery.'

'Lizzie Siddons,' said Fran.

'Who?' Mellie's brow furrowed in some confusion.

'She was the model with the red hair. The one who posed as Ophelia,' Fran explained. 'You know, I really don't feel that I should come to this party. I don't know the people and I will probably have done all I can here by then.'

A chorus of protests greeted her at once.

'Oh, but you can't possibly leave before the weekend.'

'It doesn't matter a bit you not knowing the Lyndons. Friends' houseguests are always included.'

'There's no need to be shy. We'll introduce you to everyone. You'll have a splendid time.'

Fran – who had no desire to make a fool of herself by dressing as a Pierrot – held her peace, while silently deciding that something might need to happen back at home which would call her away before the event in question took place.

FOURTEEN

The pattern of the evening diverged somewhat from the previous one. After a perfectly delicious dinner prepared by Mrs Remington and served by Jamieson, the family retired to the drawing room, where they were joined by Imogen and Miss Billington, and Roly produced a wind-up racing game which required four participants at a time to frantically rotate a handle in order to make small mechanical horses move along a metal course. The competition was enlivened by placing bets in spent matchsticks, a supply of which had been stored in a little wooden box, along with the game. Imogen was inclined to become overexcited when her horse did well, and plunged into depths of despair after failing to mark up a win, but Fran was amused to see that the other Edgertons, even Lady Louisa herself, were prone to yelling encouragement at the painted tin mounts, coupled with insults at those who failed to work their handles fast enough. Only Miss Billington remained completely calm, taking victory or defeat with equanimity.

Eventually it was decreed to be Imogen's bedtime and Miss Billington led her away, not without protest on Imogen's side and reassurance on Miss Billington's that the game was being put away and all the excitement was consequently over. Lady Louisa also retired to her room, saying that she wanted to finish a book she was reading.

'Goodness,' said Hen, collapsing on to a sofa after putting the racing game back into one of the sideboards. 'Will you play for us, Eddie, or is someone going to get some gramophone records out? I don't know about anyone else, but I'm exhausted after all that. I thought my arm would drop off during that last race.'

'I'll play if you want me to,' Eddie said, glancing around to receive general affirmation before he stood up and went across to the piano. 'Any requests, boy and girls?'

'"I Wish I Could Shimmy Like My Sister Kate",' Mellie
called out. 'And make it good and lively.'

Eddie obliged them with one tune after another, some
suggested by his listeners, some produced of his own volition.
No one suggested dancing. After the frenetic atmosphere of
the racing game, it was very pleasant to lean back against the
cushions and be entertained. Fran let the music wash over her.
It was true, she reflected, that Eddie really did have talent. He
ran his fingers across the keys, bringing out the best in the
instrument as he launched into 'If I Had You', one of the big
hits of the previous year. Fran had not asked for the song, but
he sung it as if to her, looking directly at her as he crooned,
'If I had you by my side . . .' It was nice to be flirted with
once in a while, she thought. Though, of course, Eddie was
not really flirting with her, just showing her what he could
have done for a much wider audience, if ever he had put his
mind to it.

By the time Fran joined the family at the breakfast table
next morning, Eddie had already set out for Winchester. Roly
was, as usual, reading out snippets from the newspapers to
Hen, and Mellie had yet to appear.

It was just after eight thirty when Jamieson appeared at
Roly's elbow. 'Excuse me, Mr Edgerton, but there's a
gentleman asking for you on the telephone. A Mr Dod, sir.'

Fran glanced up from her poached egg and then back down
at her plate. There was more than one Mr Dod in the world
after all. Roly carefully refolded his paper and placed it to
one side of his plate, while setting his napkin at the other and
simultaneously getting up from the table.

'I was wondering,' Fran said, once Roly had left the room,
'whether it would be possible to speak with Miss Billington
this morning?'

'Of course you can,' said Hen. 'In fact, this would be the
perfect morning, because Imogen goes for her riding lesson
at ten, isn't that right, Mellie?'

Mellie, who had just entered the room, nodded, before
asking, 'Where's Roly?'

'Called to the telephone. Pass the milk please, Roly has
been hogging it down at that end.'

'I thought I ought to speak with Imogen too, later on,' Fran said.

'Oh, I'm sure there won't be any point in doing that,' laughed Mellie. 'Imogen can't be trusted anyway. She's a dreadful fibber.'

'I'd prefer to call it imagination,' Hen said, deliberately not catching her sister-in-law's eye. 'And if Fran wants to speak with Imogen, we really must not attempt to dissuade her.' Turning to Fran, she said, 'Suppose we tell Billie to come to the library at ten and then get her to buzz Imogen along as soon as she's back from riding?'

'Thank you.' Fran sensed a slight frost in the atmosphere. Mellie was nominally the lady of the house but Hen had lived there much longer. She wondered whether Mellie was really happy to leave the running of everything to her mother-in-law, still less stand contradicted by her husband's sister.

Roly reappeared a few moments later, announcing cheerfully, 'That was your friend Mr Dod, Fran. Apparently he is in the area visiting growers and someone has told him about our Woolbrook Pippins. He's keen to pop down for a chat, so I've arranged to meet him at the orchards this morning and invited him to stay for lunch.'

'Our Woolbrook Pippins? Why on earth is he interested in those?' asked Mellie.

'Because his father is the head of a big wholesale fruit and vegetable concern, my darling. Dod and Sons may give us a far better price than we are getting locally.'

'Oh, I see.'

'And it will be nice for Fran to see her friend,' said Hen.

'Indeed.' Roly had eased back into his place at the head of the table. 'Mellie, be a dear and ring the bell for some fresh toast. This has gone cold.'

Fran didn't know what to say. It was really very naughty of Tom to engineer a visit like this when the whole object of coming down here had been to prevent any potentially suspicious meetings at all. Then again, perhaps he genuinely did have business with the Edgertons and it was not as if they would be alone together. Having a well-chaperoned lunch in the company of mutual acquaintances hardly constituted suspicious behaviour. Aloud, she said, 'Please pardon my ignorance, but what are Woolbrook Pippins?'

'They are a variety of apple, native to Devon.' Roly smiled. 'The productive orchards came as part of the estate. We also grow pears here and Tom Putt apples. The Tom Putts go for cider making, but the Woolbrook Pippins are eaters.'

'I must let Mrs Remington know that we will be one extra for lunch,' Mellie said. 'Does Mr Dod have any particular preferences, do you know?'

'Not that I know of.' Fran felt her colour rising for no particular reason. 'I don't really know him all that well.'

'Oh.' Mellie sounded surprised, almost put out. 'We were given to understand that you and Mr Dod were old friends.'

'Oh, I don't think we were Mellie,' said Hen, who seemed determined to correct her sister-in-law that morning. 'Didn't you and Mr Dod meet through your sleuthing?' she asked Fran.

'No, we met through the Robert Barnaby Society.'

'What in the world is that?' asked Mellie.

Fran explained, feeling more foolish with every word, for Mellie's social life would never have encompassed joining 'a book club', as she thereafter referred to it, where one might presumably bump into all sorts of people of the kind who might not be welcomed at the Lord Lieutenant's Ball. Nor was Mellie the sort of woman who would see the point in discussing children's literature, once one had reached the age of twelve or thirteen.

Fran was quite relieved to excuse herself from the table and go out on to the terrace for a breath of fresh air. The garden soon restored her equilibrium. *It really is lovely here*, she thought. *Far too nice a spot for anyone to commit a murder.*

After a short stroll, she returned to the library, where Miss Billington joined her soon after ten, having handed Imogen over to the visiting riding instructor for her lesson.

'Thank you for seeing me,' said Fran. 'I realize that this must be one of the few times you have to yourself.'

'Mr Edgerton asked us all to put ourselves at your disposal. He also asked for our discretion. Not, of course, that I would ever discuss any family matters with an outsider, unless I had been specifically asked to do so, as is the case with yourself.'

'Don't you find it rather lonely here?' Fran asked. 'It's quite an isolated property, isn't it?'

'When I first joined the family, they made it clear that I would be welcome to join them in the evenings, but I declined. After spending the day with Miss Imogen, I am perfectly content to read or embroider. Of course, when Miss Roche was here, we sometimes used to sit together in the evenings. We had both spent some time in France, so we had that in common.'

'You must miss her company?'

'Not especially. In the summertime, in particular, there are usually so many people about the place that it is quite a relief to have an hour or two to oneself at the end of the day.'

'But having a friend in the household . . .' Fran pursued.

'Miss Roche was a pleasant enough companion, but I would not have said there was a close friendship between us.'

'You haven't stayed in touch then?'

'Oh, no.'

Fran decided to try a different tack. 'I've been trying to piece together the events of the day when old Mr Edgerton died. Can you tell me what you remember about the day?'

Miss Billington pursed her lips. 'What sort of things do you wish me to remember?'

'Well . . . who was there, what people did, where they went, that kind of thing.'

'The usual family were in residence of course, and old Mr Edgerton's son, Mr Charles, and his wife were staying, as were two of his granddaughters, Miss Helena and Miss Cecilia. It was a nice, sunny day, so most of us went down to the beach. Two friends of the family, the Miss Trenchards, turned up at some stage and the Baddeley children had also come over to join the party. It was a very ordinary sort of day.' The governess paused, looking to Fran for a sign that she should continue.

'Did you spend the whole day on the beach?'

'Most of it. A picnic was brought down from the house.'

'But not everyone spent the entire time on the beach?'

'No. Mr Charles and his wife went up to the house for lunch with Her Ladyship. Some people went off to play tennis. I'm afraid I can't be specific about who and when. I would have been watching the children, you see. Imogen was my main concern of course, but I kept an eye on the Baddeleys and young Miss Cecilia as well.'

'Someone has suggested that there was a bit of an upset over a game and Imogen went off on her own?'

'That's quite right. I'd almost forgotten, but yes, she did. There was some silly quarrel about a game, I think. Imogen flew off the handle, as I'm afraid she is rather prone to do, and then ran off.'

'Can you remember what time it would have been when this happened?'

'Not really. Only that it was some time after lunch.'

'And you went after her?'

'Yes, I intended to bring her back and have her apologize for making such an exhibition of herself.'

'And how long did it take to find her?'

'I didn't find her. As I'm sure you know by now, there is only one path leading right down to the shore and I initially followed her back along that path, towards the garden. I caught a couple of glimpses of her some way ahead of me, but though I called her name she didn't answer. Once the shore path reaches the garden it initially branches off in three directions and from then onwards the garden becomes a positive maze of different paths, twisting here and there between the shrubs and trees, with no end of hiding places along each route. I continued to search for a while, but I couldn't find the child, so eventually I gave it up for a bad job and went back to the beach.'

'And was Imogen there?'

'She was not. I didn't see her again until much later. When we went back up to the house for tea – that would have been at about four o'clock, or perhaps rather later – Imogen was already there. I scolded her, as you can imagine, but it fell on deaf ears.'

'You weren't worried when you couldn't find her?'

'Oh no. It wasn't the first time she'd run off and it probably won't be the last. She's a rather tempestuous child. It's not as if she is likely to come to any harm. She has been playing in the gardens and the woods for years. She wouldn't go near the edge of the cliff, or anything like that.'

'Unlike old Mr Edgerton,' Fran said. When Miss Billington failed to reply, Fran said, 'Can I ask you frankly, Miss Billington – do you believe Mr Edgerton fell to his death by accident?'

'I assume my answer will go no further?'

'Please feel that you can speak freely.'

'No, Mrs Black, I do not. The idea that a wheeled chair, carrying a fairly hefty man, could defy the laws of physics by propelling itself uphill until it went over the edge has seemed preposterous to me from the first.'

'So what do you think happened?'

'I think it is fairly obvious that Mr Edgerton pushed himself over the edge on purpose. I believe he realized that his mind was going and that he did not want to be a burden to his family. Naturally the family don't want it generally known, because suicide is still considered a sin by many, is wrong in the eyes of the law and inevitably brings disgrace.'

'What did his nurse think?'

'She probably thought the same. We never discussed it in so many words.'

'But she thought that Mr Edgerton was still capable of pushing himself up the incline?'

'I believe she said so, when the police asked her. The police made some enquiries, you know, immediately after it had happened.'

'It's curious that no one saw anything at all.'

'I don't believe there was anything suspicious in that,' Miss Billington said.

It occurred to Fran that, just like other members of the household, the governess had evidently given the matter some consideration.

'You see,' Miss Billington continued, 'none of the household staff would be in the family's part of the house at that time of day. The gardeners wouldn't have been up in the woods, because there is no arboricultural work to speak of in the summer months, and the family were all out and about, except for Her Ladyship, who was apparently lying down in her room.'

'I suppose,' Fran said, 'that in those circumstances anyone might have slipped into the house, taken whatever they fancied and made off without being seen?'

'Goodness, what a fearful thought!' exclaimed Miss Billington. 'But I don't think that's very likely. You see, Mr Jamieson would be in his pantry at that time of day, so he could see anyone coming down the front drive.'

Fran did not bother to point out that burglars seldom approached via the front entrance. Instead, she asked, 'Surely with it being Monica's afternoon off, someone would usually have gone to check on Mr Edgerton?'

'The servants wouldn't generally go in unless someone rang for them, I suppose. Old Mr Edgerton was known to have a nap most afternoons, so no one would have been particularly expecting him to ring. And I believe there was some sort of mix-up between the staff as to who ought to take him a cup of tea at four o'clock.'

'Yes,' said Fran. 'According to what I have been told, two of the maids each thought the other had taken his tea to him, so neither of them actually did.'

Miss Billington sniffed. 'I imagine Jamieson had something to say to the pair of them when that came out in the wash.'

'Tell me,' Fran said. 'Do you know anything of the Sidmouth affair?'

Miss Billington stiffened in her chair. 'I most certainly do not. Will there be anything else, Mrs Black?'

'No, thank you, Miss Billington. Thank you very much for your time.'

FIFTEEN

Fran had intended to see Imogen next, her interest in what the girl had to say considerably heightened by the news that she had spent a substantial part of the crucial afternoon unsupervised. However, she was not destined to interview Imogen that morning, because no sooner had Miss Billington left the room than Hen came in, wanting her to come upstairs and try on the Pierrot costume.

Fifteen minutes later, Hen was shaking her head critically as Fran stood before the full-length mirror in her bedroom. 'It isn't really you, is it? We'll have to find something else. Not to worry. We've a whole hamper of stuff up in the attic, from when we had a big pash for amateur theatricals. Let's go up and see what we can find.'

It was the first time Fran had been up to the third floor. Hen led the way up the narrow attic stairs and then through a couple of windowless rooms lit by bare bulbs which dangled from the ceiling, leaving pools of shadow around the periphery of each space. It occurred to Fran that you might very easily be able to hide a small precious stone up here, though of course Mr Edgerton himself had not been able to manage the stairs. She was about to ask Hen how thoroughly the attics had been searched for the missing gem when Hen emitted a cry of triumph and flung open a wicker hamper, which was easily big enough for a grown man to have concealed himself inside.

'Here it is. Oh, look at this' – she held up an elaborately sequinned frock – 'you could have a card pinned to your dress with a big X painted on it and go as the Flapper Election. Oh, and here is the phantom monk's hooded robe. That would be far too long for you as it was made for Eddie . . . I suppose we could get Jane to turn it up, but it's not exactly glam, is it?'

Henrietta continued to root through the hamper, holding up an assortment of suggested costumes, each less desirable than the last, while Fran wondered what on earth she was going to get talked into.

'Has anyone searched for the diamond up here?' Fran asked at one point, but Hen only said vaguely that 'of course, we searched the whole house' before returning her attention to the contents of the trunk and eventually deciding that a medieval red velvet robe with matching beaded skull cap would be just the thing with which to transform Fran into Juliet.

'Oh no, I can't possibly be Juliet, I'm far too old,' Fran protested.

'Nonsense. No woman is ever too old to play Juliet. I'm sure you will look absolutely lovely. Come on, let's take this downstairs and you can try it on.'

By the time the costume had been pronounced 'just the thing' by Henrietta, and Fran had resumed her sensible tweed skirt and pale green jumper, washed her hands and brushed her hair, she found that Roly and Tom were already waiting in the drawing room.

'What a nice surprise to find you here,' Tom said. 'I thought you might have been back home by now.'

'Fran only arrived a couple of days ago,' said Mellie. 'She's hardly had time to talk to everyone yet.'

Fran, doing her best not to catch Tom's eye over his blatant fib, said, 'The truth is that everyone has made me so welcome here, and provided such interesting diversions, that I haven't got on as fast as I probably should.'

'Fran is a delightful house guest and we are in no hurry to see her leave,' Roly put in gallantly.

Having gathered her wits, Fran turned directly to Tom and said, 'I had no idea that your business interests brought you all the way down here.'

'Oh, we've got an increasing number of connections down here in the south-west. Yesterday I was with the grower of some of the best cauliflowers I've ever seen over at Budleigh Salterton.'

'Budleigh Salterton? Isn't that near Sidmouth?' Fran enquired and was gratified to note the way Mellie shot her husband a swift glance. She had the strongest suspicion that 'you know what' was in some way related to 'the Sidmouth affair'.

'Do you know Sidmouth?' Hen – apparently unruffled – asked Fran.

'Only that it is said to be very nice there. A friend of my mother's often used to go there for the summer, I believe.'

Roly turned to Tom. 'Devon soil is excellent for all manner of things. Though of course our high rainfall produces wonderful grazing for dairy farming.'

'Now, Roly,' his wife chided. 'No business over luncheon, if you please.'

'Hardly business, my sweet. I was really commenting on that perennial conversation filler, the weather.'

Everyone laughed politely and Jamieson temporarily curtailed conversation of any sort by banging the gong which was a summons to the dining room.

'Are you married, Mr Dod?' asked Mellie when they were all seated at the table and Jamieson was padding around, offering Russian salad to accompany the smoked fish.

'I am. My wife and I have one boy, William, who will be eleven this summer.'

'An only child?' said Mellie. 'I have always feared that an only child might want for playmates.'

'William is away at school, so he hardly wants for company.'

'Not everyone wants a great tribe of brothers and sisters,' Henrietta said firmly. 'I've often thought there would be definite advantages to not having any brothers at all.' She put her tongue out at Roly, who laughed and then turned to ask Tom if he had been following the news from Australia.

'Ponsford and Bradman are piling on the runs it seems,' Roly remarked. 'It doesn't auger well for the summer test matches.'

'Oh, I think they'll find England a very different kettle of fish to Tasmania,' Tom said cheerfully.

The diversion into cricket provided a helpful distraction and lunch proceeded without any further potentially awkward observations regarding family life. When the treacle tart was almost totally consumed, Roly said, 'I hope you won't feel the need to rush away, Mr Dod, for I'm sure you would enjoy seeing the gardens. Under normal circumstances a member of the family would be glad to show you round, but my mother, the architect of the whole affair, is away at a charity luncheon, I have an appointment with my estate manager and I believe my wife has made some arrangements to call on one of her sisters. That only leaves Henrietta and Fran.'

'Oh, I can't possibly,' said Hen. 'I simply have to write some letters in time to catch the post. Fran, would you mind very much taking charge of Mr Dod until teatime – you did say you could stay for tea, didn't you, Mr Dod? That still leaves you plenty of daylight to get back to your hotel?'

To Fran, the unavailability of the entire Edgerton clan felt somewhat contrived and she experienced a quick pang of anxiety, for surely a span of several hours alone with Tom was exactly the kind of thing she had come here to avoid? At the same time, she could not help but welcome the opportunity to talk the mystery over with him, so she said, 'Well, as it looks as if I am the only person available, then of course I would be delighted to act as guide, though I'm afraid I don't know anything much about the gardens except the little I've gained from walks with Eddie.'

'Which would be little enough,' said Henrietta. 'As Eddie probably talked nonsense, the whole time he was taking you around.'

'I will just have to run upstairs and get my jacket,' Fran said.

She met Tom again in the hall a few minutes later, where Roly seemed well pleased to hand him over, though he said, 'Wish I could come with you, old chap. Much more fun than listening to McAllister banging on about a tenant's leaking roof and the price of cattle, but there we are, duty calls and all that.'

'We'll go out via the terrace,' Fran said, leading the way. 'And then I can show you where old Mr Edgerton went over the cliff,' she added when she was sure that Roly was out of earshot.

As they followed the route to the cliff edge, which Eddie had shown her on their first walk together, Fran quickly explained the circumstances of the old man's death and the subsequent discovery regarding the loss of the diamond.

'Do you think the Edgertons suspected foul play from the first?' asked Tom.

'Maybe not. The death was unexpected and I think everyone was initially shocked and assumed that it must have been an accident, even though the old man's general condition argued against it.'

'And later on, when they began to suspect, they didn't want to involve the police, in case it turned out to be one of the family?'

'I think it goes deeper than that. Mellie, in particular, is very sensitive to the idea of scandal. Her world is based on knowing everyone who is worth knowing in the immediate locality. If the other families in their circle dropped them, there would be no socializing at all. The Edgertons too, although they pretend not to give a fig about being new money, are actually quite conscious of it. I dare say that Henrietta and Eddie hope to make good marriages among the local nobs and snobs, the way Roly has. They don't want to end up being in the newspapers for all the wrong reasons. Even coming under suspicion could be really damaging and a whiff of suicide and insanity can damage your chances of finding a partner almost as much. Mellie as good as said something of the sort the other day.'

'It's pretty difficult to believe in an accident,' Tom commented a few moments later, having reached the point where the path bent to the east, but old Mr Edgerton's wheel-chair had gone due south.

'I agree. I've narrowed down the time he must have gone over the edge to about two hours. Jamieson saw him asleep in the library at around two p.m. and there appears to have been someone on the terrace from about four p.m.'

'Can we believe Jamieson?'

'There were also people having lunch at the table on the terrace: Lady Louisa, her brother-in-law Charles Edgerton and his wife, Dolly. They would have seen Mr Edgerton, if he had gone out that way – and because it's the only level route to the cliff path, he must have gone that way, whether under his own steam, or being pushed along by a third party.'

'If lunch is generally served at one, they wouldn't finish until one thirty or one forty-five at the earliest,' Tom mused. 'What time did they leave the terrace?'

'That's a bit vague. Charles and Dolly walked back down to the beach and Lady Louisa went up to lie down, as she'd developed a headache, but at a rough guess, they probably left not much earlier than two.'

'So between those three and Jamieson we can take approximately two p.m. as the start of our window of opportunity.'

'And by about four p.m. to four thirty people had started to return to the house for tea and, according to everyone I've spoken with, the terrace was always occupied by someone or other from then onwards.'

'So the question is where was everyone during that two-hour period?'

'Some people are quite easily accounted for. Mabel and Victoria Trenchard had come over here to play tennis and they appear to have been within sight of someone else the whole time. The same thing applies to the Baddeley children. They'd come to spend the day on the beach with Imogen and they seem to have been in full view of at least one other adult, except when they were walking to and from their home.'

'Which is where, in relation to Sunnyside House?'

'They live well to the west of here and their route doesn't take them anywhere near the path to the east cliffs. I don't believe they would have seen anything useful, or even been coming and going at the relevant times. I haven't been able to question them, because they're away at school but, under the circumstances, I don't believe they can possibly have anything useful to add.'

'How old are they?'

'They were twelve and fourteen at the time.'

'And the Trenchard girls?'

'Around the twenty mark.'

'And being outsiders, there's no motive either.'

'Quite so. It's when we get to the family that things become more complicated. Lady Louisa was alone at the house all afternoon, but she has absolutely no motive, so far as I can see.'

'Unless she was after the diamond.'

'She doesn't strike me as being in want of diamonds. Firstly she has some of her own already and secondly she appears to want for nothing at all.'

'What about the others?'

'Well, Roland Edgerton is the person who stands to gain the most, except that his position doesn't seem to have changed all that much. He was living here already and had taken over most of the running of the estate and so forth, at his grandfather's instigation. He wasn't short of money before his grandfather passed on and he told me quite frankly that when he'd once got into financial difficulties, he made a clean breast of it and his grandfather paid off his debts.'

'Hmmm, that's his story. Opportunity?' asked Tom.

'None so far as I can tell. He was on the beach with everyone else and then walked up to join the tennis players, accompanied by his sister, Henrietta.'

'So he vouches for Henrietta and she for him?''

'That's right. Henrietta doesn't seem to have been on her own at all either. I mean, obviously people slipped in and out of the beach hut to get changed and things like that, but it takes a good fifteen minutes to walk from the beach to the house. Then you'd have to wheel the old man up here, that's another five or six minutes at the very least. Then you've got to get back down to the shore again, which even taking a short cut, would account for another five to ten minutes. Anyone starting from the beach would need to be absent for a minimum of half an hour, possibly more.'

'What about the tennis players?'

'Once they started to play during the afternoon, no one left the tennis court at all. According to Eddie, Roland and Henrietta, the game broke up and they all went back to the house together – including the Trenchard sisters, who stayed for tea.'

'Who vouches for the younger brother – the one who isn't here today?'

'Eddie? He's at a funeral. I think you'd like him, he's rather fun. He was one of the original four who went up to play tennis and he was there when his brother and sister arrived. Again, he simply doesn't have time. Or a motive, so far as I can tell.'

'What about this uncle of theirs?'

'Ah, now here we've got something more interesting. Uncle Charles decided to go off on his own for a walk, in spite of the fact that it was just about the hottest afternoon of the year. I've got a bad feeling about Uncle Charles. The thing is that no one has said anything about my being able to interview him, or even whether he would be agreeable to me talking with him.'

'Well, if you do interview him, you'd better not go alone,' Tom said. 'If he is the murderer he might be dangerous. Remember what happened once before.'

'Really, Tom! I'm not a complete fool. Oh dear, was that a spot of rain?'

'There's a very dodgy-looking black cloud coming our way. Perhaps we'd better hoof it back to the house.'

'We won't make it in time. Hold on, though,' said Fran. 'There's a little thatched shelter just around this corner, meant for a viewpoint. Let's go in there until the worst of it passes. It will be far easier to carry on talking than if we go back to the house, where there may be people around.'

They reached the shelter just as the rain began to fall more rapidly. It was a small, rectangular construction, with solid walls to three sides, but completely open at the front, which faced out to sea. Unfortunately the view for which the structure had been created was all but obscured by low cloud.

'Well, this is cosy,' said Tom, settling himself on the bench which had been built against the back wall.

Something in his tone abruptly reminded Fran of the danger that being alone with Tom presented to the success of her divorce petition. 'You know,' she said, standing just inside the shelter, but not sitting down, 'you really oughtn't to have come here like this. If I'm asked now, instead of saying that I haven't seen you for months and then only in the company of other people, I will have to admit to having seen you here and also that we were alone together in the grounds of Sunnyside House.'

'I'm sorry,' Tom said. 'I thought the business angle provided a perfect front. Edgerton and I have done a deal this morning to ship an initial fifty boxes of his Woolbrook Pippins up to the Midlands this season, which sounds like a genuine enough reason for my presence here to me. How was I to know that the Edgertons would send us off into the garden on our own?'

'That might not have been so bad,' Fran said, 'if we had not ended up sheltering from the rain, in a little hut, out of sight of anyone else.'

'But now, here we are alone, in romantic proximity, where the evil King's Proctor might envisage the possibility that I have taken advantage of the rain shower to make violent love to you, amid the sound of the wind and the waves.'

'Please don't joke, Tom,' she said, feeling close to tears.

'I'm sorry,' he said quickly. 'I agree that it is all my fault, but if necessary I am prepared to stand up in court and take my oath that nothing improper at all has taken place. Now please come and sit beside me and continue to expound your discoveries. You had reached the suspicious activities of Uncle Charles before rain stopped play.'

She knew that Tom was right. The situation could not be helped, and besides which she was getting cold, for the temperature had dropped a couple of degrees with the coming of the rain and it might be warmer if she sat on the bench at the back of the shelter, so she settled herself in the remaining space on the bench and took up the threads of their discussion.

'Charles and his wife, Dolly – who is despised as a common gold-digger by the rest of the family, by the way – had lunch up at the house with Lady Louisa and then rejoined the group on the beach, but soon afterwards he took himself off for a walk and wasn't seen again by anyone until teatime.'

'That's extremely suggestive,' said Tom.

'The only other people who seem to have disappeared for any length of time are Imogen, who is only a girl of fourteen. Though she's a bit odd, she doesn't seem a likely candidate for the person who pushed her grandfather off a cliff, and—'

'How big is she?' Tom interrupted.

'She's quite a lump of a girl. Why do you ask?'

'You don't suppose it's possible that she could have taken the old man up there in his wheelchair for some sort of game and either pushed him over by accident, or because she thought

it would be funny – you know – not understanding the consequences of the act?'

'I don't think she's stark staring bonkers, if that's what you
mean,' said Fran. 'And I think it would take quite an effort to
get that wheelchair off the path and over the edge, so I don't
really fancy the accident theory, but at the same time there
could be something in what you say. If it was a game of some
kind that went wrong, the girl might be frightened to admit
what had happened. I still need to talk to Imogen, though that
process is fraught with doubt, given that Henrietta suggested
she's "imaginative", while Mellie claims point blank that she's
a liar.'

'How did she come to be on her own?'

'She had a falling out with some of the other children on
the beach and ran off. Her governess, whose name is Miss
Billington, went after her, but she didn't manage to find her.'

'The girl might have seen or heard something. Especially
if she spent a while ranging around on her own, keeping out
of sight of the governess.'

'And don't forget the governess is another person who left
the beach and was therefore alone for an appreciable time.'

'Miss Billington . . .' Tom mused. 'No obvious motive, so
far as you can tell?'

'No . . . and her separation from the rest of the party was
unplanned,' Fran said. 'She had no way of knowing that Imogen
would run off, and if Imogen hadn't made a bolt for it as she
did, Miss Billington would have just stayed with the kids, on
the beach, the whole time.'

'So Uncle Charles remains the prime suspect. Who else is
still left for you to talk with?'

'Well, I've covered most of the household servants. Two
until four in the afternoon is their quiet time. They're mostly
in the servants' hall at the back of the house, though Mrs
Remington, the cook, has a little sitting room of her own and
Jamieson has a room which looks on to the turning area by
the front door. There was a mix-up between two of the maids,
who each thought the other had said she would take a cup of
tea through to old Mr Edgerton. That all sounds genuine enough.
After the lunch things had been cleared away no one answered

any bells, or went into the family's part of the house at all. And, actually, that sets up a little mystery, because Lady Louisa claims that she heard someone laugh in the upstairs hall when she was in her room, followed by someone else telling them to hush, but according to what everyone else says, there was no one else in that part of the house all afternoon.'

'She probably dreamed it. Go on.'

'Well, I'm going to try Mr Marshall and his team of gardeners, though I don't hold out much hope there, because I'm sure they would have said something to someone at the time if they'd seen anything of interest. Then there is old Mr Edgerton's nurse, Monica Roche.'

'Roach – as in the fish?'

'Pronounced roach, but actually spelled R-O-C-H-E according to the name and forwarding address provided by Lady Louisa. She was off the premises during the relevant time, but she's the one who actually spotted that the wheelchair had gone over the cliff and I'd like to ask her about that. I hope she will agree to speak with me, but of course she's not an Edgerton employee now so it is entirely her choice.'

'You're shivering,' Tom said abruptly. 'Come here, for good-ness' sake.' He put his arm around her and drew her close, saying as Fran attempted to protest, 'Damn the King's Proctor. And anyway, there's no one here to see.'

Grateful for the warmth, Fran made no further objection. 'There's one other servant I haven't spoken with – a maid called Connie – who was employed here when old Mr Edgerton died but has subsequently left. I don't suppose she will have anything else to add, but I'd like to track her down if I can, for the sake of completeness. And, of course, the other outstanding clue is the Sidmouth affair.'

'The Sidmouth affair? What on earth is that?'

Huddled against Tom's side, Fran glanced up and was amused by the expression on his face. 'I don't know – yet. But I intend to find out. It's evidently quite well known within the household, for I'm sure that Miss Billington knows perfectly well what it's all about, for all that she denied it.'

'How do you intend to find out what it is?'

'I'm going to ask Eddie Edgerton outright. You know, I'm

pretty sure he was about to tell me what it's all about when we were interrupted the other day, but I haven't really had a chance to get him on his own since then.'

Tom made no reply and they sat there in silence, watching the rain gusting across the gap against a backdrop of slate grey sea. After a while Tom rubbed his hand gently up and down the sleeve of her jacket. 'Warmer now?' he asked.

'Yes, thank you.'

He stopped rubbing and resumed his former position, still holding her protectively against his side. *If only*, Fran thought, *if only* . . . But it was no use thinking about anything at all. Better to just live in the moment, herself and Tom, shut in by the rain, with no one else in the world at all.

SIXTEEN

The rain eventually stopped long enough for them to hurry back to the house, but thanks to the dripping trees, Fran needed to go straight upstairs and exchange her damp jacket and woollen jumper for a fresh blouse and cardigan.

'Did you get soaked?' Mellie asked, as she officiated over the teapot when they were all seated in the drawing room again.

'Fortunately we were able to take shelter in the little thatched view house on the cliff path.'

'You know,' said Henrietta, 'we have really been most remiss in not inviting Tom to stay the night.'

'Absolutely,' agreed Roly. 'We won't hear of you going off to eat dinner alone and spending the night in a hotel, will we, Mellie?'

'No, indeed. Do say you'll be our guest, Tom.'

Fran held her breath. Tom calling in on a legitimate business matter and happening to find her staying here could be made to sound perfectly innocent. A walk around the garden did not, perhaps, mean all that much, but an overnight stay in the home of mutual acquaintances was most definitely open to connotations of bedroom hopping.

'That's awfully generous of you, but I have already trespassed on your hospitality quite enough for one day. Besides which, going on to Exeter this evening will considerably shorten my journey north. It would be a fearful rush to make my appointment in Gloucestershire tomorrow if I were to stay here tonight.'

'What a pity. Perhaps on another occasion?'

'That would be delightful, thank you.'

Fran had no further occasion to speak with Tom alone and she was careful to make nothing of his departure, merely wishing him a safe journey and not bothering to accompany him to the front door, as Roland and Mellie Edgerton did.

'What a nice chap,' remarked Hen, when they were left together in the drawing room.

'Yes. He's good fun, isn't he?' Fran replied, attempting to sound as if the idea had only just occurred to her.

Later on, when she was alone in her room, Fran allowed herself to think – just a little – about Tom. It would probably be much better if she tried to forget him altogether. Once this case was behind them, she would have to make a clean and final break. Give up detection (after all, there was no reason to believe that another investigation would ever come her way), and resign from the Robert Barnaby Society, leaving no excuse whatsoever to maintain contact with Tom. Mo was right: there were plenty more fish in the sea and perhaps there was someone else out there whom she could learn to care for. Someone who was available. Someone to share her life with. The plain gold band on her third finger caught her eye. Taking it between her right thumb and forefinger, she slid it off and placed it on the dressing table. She noticed that the place it had occupied was paler than the surrounding skin, creating a ghostly suggestion of a marriage soon to be dissolved. Well, that would fade and the sooner the better. From now on, she would not wear Michael's ring.

Eddie had returned in time for dinner and was keen to regale his brother with news of mutual acquaintances. 'Bozzy Fosdyke was there. He's on two sticks now, the poor old boy, he must be about a hundred years old. And, oh yes, do you remember Burns Minor?'

'Wasn't he that horrid little squirt who used to cheat at cards?'

'That's the fellow. Well, he's done tremendously well for himself in the City and he turned up in a chauffeur-driven Rolls-Royce. Chap's worth an absolute fortune, according to Gilkes-Watson.'

'A cad is always a cad,' said Roly.

'Just so. I cut him dead at the church door.'

'Does everyone have their costume sorted out for tomorrow night?' asked Mellie, who was clearly bored by all this talk of people she did not know. 'How about you, Eddie? You always do leave everything to the last minute.'

'I'm putting on my cricket whites and a false beard and going as W.G. Grace.'

'That shows a singular lack of effort,' said Henrietta.

'Thank you for your usual endorsement of my character. What are you going as, Fran?' Eddie turned to her with a smile.

'Your sister has persuaded me to go as Juliet, though I'm really not sure . . .'

'You will be perfection in the role. You must allow me to drive you. Juliet needs a winged chariot and Roly's vehicle is far too sedate.'

'Don't be silly, Eddie,' Mellie objected. 'We can all fit into Roly's car and Fran will freeze if you persist in driving with the roof down. She won't be able to wear a proper hat, as that little beaded Juliet cap is part of the costume.'

'I shall have the roof up and the heater full on. I assure you that Fran's health and costume will not be compromised in any way. Besides which, it would be a fearful crush in Roly's car. Far better for us to split up.'

'He is right,' Henrietta conceded, turning to her sister-in-law. 'Your skirt is very full and has a ton of petticoats under it.'

Mellie conceded the point immediately. Now that the auburn wig had arrived, she had decided that it did not suit her and having abandoned the idea of Ophelia, was going as Cinderella instead. There was nothing in the fairy story to suggest that Cinderella's ball gown had been crushed and creased on arrival.

SEVENTEEN

Friday morning dawned bright and sunny, which presented the perfect opportunity for Fran to seek out the head gardener, Mr Marshall, who while clearly devoted to the Edgertons and their garden, and extremely keen to assist in whatever way he could, was able to add little or nothing to the sum of Fran's knowledge, though she did ascertain that the grass which grew alongside the cliff path was never cut and that none of the outside staff had been deployed anywhere near that part of the estate on the afternoon of old Mr Edgerton's death.

'We wouldn't have wanted to be a-trimming of that grass, madam, because long grass would be less likely to tempt anyone to go too near that old cliff edge, d'ye see?' He paused for a moment or two before adding: 'Now as for anyone a-seeing of anything unusual, there was just one thing, madam, only I don't rightly know if it would be anything of interest to ee?'

'Oh, I am interested in anything at all out of the ordinary,' Fran assured him.

''Twas young Max and Joe as mentioned it and they'll be across to the sheds for their ten o'clocks any time now, if ee'd care to wait for un.'

Fran duly accompanied Mr Marshall through a door in the garden wall, which led directly into a low-roofed brick outbuilding, full of every kind of gardening implement, at the end of which was a pot-bellied stove where a rusty kettle was simmering. Right on cue two youths appeared, one wheeling a barrow, the other with a spade sloped across his shoulder like a musket.

'Now then,' said Mr Marshal. 'Look sharp. You'll recollect as what Her Ladyship said on Monday? Well, this 'ere is Mrs Black and you've to answer her questions.'

The two youths exchanged looks which conveyed a mixture of amusement and apprehension.

'Please, do get your tea first,' Fran said. 'I don't wish to intrude on your break.'

'There ain't no intrusion about it, madam. You just go ahead and do the asking and they'll do the answering. They can 'ave their tea after.'

Fran turned to the young men and said, 'Mr Marshall tells me that you saw something a bit unusual the day that old Mr Edgerton had his accident.'

The lads exchanged looks, as if deciding who was to speak.

'Well, madam,' the one with the fairer hair of the two began, 'Joe was walking down the path alongside what we call the dogwood patch. It's a bit o'the garden what runs above the back lane and he noticed a car pulled into the side of the road. It's a funny place for a motor car to be and he remarked on it to me when he got back down to the rose garden.'

'What did he say?' asked Fran and caught the swift warning look which unmistakably passed between the boys before the lad answered.

'Oh, nothing in particular. I don't rightly remember his exact words, like. Just that he'd seen a car.'

Fran turned to the boy called Joe. 'Were you able to see whether there was anyone sitting in the car?'

'No, madam. You're right above the lane on that particular path, so you can only see the roof of it. Dark blue or black, it was. There mightn't have been anyone in the car at all.'

'Folk do sometimes park in the lanes hereabouts and go for a walk,' Mr Marshall put in. 'Some on 'em try to cut through the grounds, thinking as they can get down to the sea. I've seen a few folk off meself.'

'But not on the day of Mr Edgerton's death?'

'No, madam. No strangers was actually seen on the property that particular day. We was all asked about it at the time.'

Fran got no further with the outside staff. Her final interviewee within the household was Imogen. Thinking that the girl might be intimidated by a summons to the library, Fran had arranged to see her up in the schoolroom. She knocked at the appointed time and found Miss Billington and her charge sitting at a table, with a French grammar book open in front of them.

Miss Billington welcomed Fran in French and bid Imogen do the same.

'*Bonjour*, Madame Black,' the child piped up mechanically. 'I say, you won't want to talk to me in French the whole time, will you? Billie and I haven't got much further than days of the week.'

'Imogen, *tu sais que ce n'est pas vrai.*'

'Your accent is frightfully authentic,' said Fran. 'Where did you learn?'

'In France,' the governess replied, almost as if she thought it a foolish question. 'Imogen, I am going to leave Mrs Black to talk with you a while. Please remember your manners and answer her sensibly, won't you.'

'Of co-ou-rse,' sang Imogen. 'I'm not a silly billy. Will you come and sit on the window seat, Mrs Black? It's much nicer to talk there than it will be sitting at the big desk.'

As Miss Billington left the room, Fran followed the girl across the room and sat with her on the blue-and-white-checked cushion, which had been made to fit the seat.

'Now Imogen, do you remember your grandfather?'

'Of course I do. He was nice.'

'Good. Do you remember how he used to get about?'

The girl considered a moment. 'First he used to walk with a stick and then he used to have to be pushed around in a chair.'

'And do you remember when he died?'

'Yes. His chair fell over the edge of the cliff.' The child sounded grave.

'Can you remember the day it happened?'

'Oh, yes.'

'That was the day you were playing games on the beach, wasn't it? With some other children.'

'There were lots of days on the beach. I can swim you know. I'm a good swimmer. I'm faster than Frank Baddeley and he's a boy.'

'That's very good. Frank Baddeley was there on the day I'm talking about.' Fran seized on the opportunity to get the conversation back on track. 'You and Frank and Rhona and your cousin Cecilia were playing a game on the sand, but you got cross and ran away.'

'Frank said I was out.' Imogen sounded indignant. 'I wasn't out, I'd touched the stone before he stumped me.'

'So you had a bit of a quarrel and then you ran away from the beach. Where did you go?'

'I went up the path which leads back to the garden. It was too hot to run very far, and I sat down on the grass beside the gunnera pond, but then I heard Billie shouting for me, so I got up again and headed for the woods. I knew she wouldn't come up there after me.'

'Which woods, Imogen?'

'The woods which run around the back of the house. I thought I might go into the kitchen and get Cook to give me some lemonade. I climbed up the bank, but when I reached the path which leads back to the terrace, I realized there was someone coming along it, so I hid behind the rhododendrons until they were past. I'm excellent at hiding.'

Trying hard to keep the excitement out of her voice, Fran asked, 'Did you see who was coming along the path?'

'No. I was hiding in the bushes. You don't try to see who it is, when you're hiding, because if you can see them, that probably means they can see you. Cousin Eddie taught me that ages ago, when he still used to play with us.'

'It wasn't your grandfather, was it? In his wheelchair?'

'I told you, I couldn't see. But I'm pretty sure it wasn't Grandfather, because his wheelchair makes a different noise. This was someone walking. I could hear their feet on the path, just quietly, one, two, one, two, like a person's feet go when they're walking quite fast.'

'How many pairs of feet could you hear?'

'Just one. I'm pretty sure it was just one person. I thought it was probably Billie, still looking for me.'

'Which way was the person going? Towards the cliffs or towards the house?'

'Towards the house.'

'And what did you do next? When the person had gone past? Did you follow them along the path to the house?'

'No. I didn't want Billie to find me, because I knew I'd been naughty and I thought she'd give me a scolding, or maybe send me to bed, so I decided to go back a different way. It's a longer way round, but in the end it leads back to the house, so I went the opposite way to the way the feet had gone and then cut up the little path which leads to the grotto. I wasn't going to go inside the grotto, only when I got there, I decided that I would. We sometimes used to go in there and make a wish and I thought about wishing that Billie would forget all about me running off.'

Imogen, who had been fidgeting during this last little speech, now got up and abruptly began to dance about the room, waving her arms in a manner which threatened first the vase of narcissi on the table and then the print of *And When Did You Last See Your Father?* which hung on the wall nearby.

'Look at me,' she said. 'I'm a fairy. I'm the grotto fairy who grants the wishes. Make a wish, Mrs Black.'

'I wish you would sit down, Imogen.'

'Oh no! That isn't a proper wish.' The child stopped flapping around the room and began to twirl round and round on the central rug. 'Look at me, I'm a spinning top.'

'Please sit down, Imogen.' Fran spoke a tad more firmly.

'I'm going to whirl and whirl until I fall down.'

'Nonsense,' said Fran briskly. 'That is the sort of thing a baby would do. Not a big girl like you. Now stop that, please. Come and sit down and talk to me sensibly. Otherwise I shall have to go and fetch Miss Billington to carry on with your French lessons.'

The dervish on the rug slowed and, staggering a little, made its way reluctantly back to the window seat.

'That's mean,' the child grumbled.

'Well, maybe so,' said Fran. 'But don't you realize that it's rude to start bouncing around the room when someone is trying to talk to you? Now then, you were just telling me that you'd got to the grotto and were going to make a wish.'

'Yes, but I didn't because I decided I was on a treasure hunt instead.'

'When?' Fran was confused. 'Do you mean that you just decided now, this minute? Or do you mean that you decided you were on a treasure hunt that day.'

'I was on a treasure hunt that day. And I found the pirate's treasure and took it away and kept it all to myself, because everyone else was being horrid to me. Especially Frank Baddeley and Miss Billie.' Imogen's tone had become petulant, but now she began to chant, 'Silly Billie, Billie silly,' and to Fran's irritation she jumped up and began to cavort around the room again.

Her concentration span is so short, Fran thought. *I'll never get any more sense out of her.* She decided on one more try. 'Imogen, please!' she exclaimed and, catching hold of the girl's hand as she passed, Fran managed to arrest the latest circuit in mid-skip so that Imogen paused reluctantly before her. 'Just one more question, but it's very important. When you had finished treasure hunting did you go back to the house, and did you see anyone on your way there?'

'That's two questions.'

It abruptly ran through Fran's mind that Imogen was not as slow as all that. 'Very well – it's two questions.'

'Yes and no.'

'Which answer goes with which question?'

'That's another question. You're a bigger cheat than Frank Baddeley.'

'Please, Imogen. It might be very important?'

'Yes, I went back to the house and no, I didn't see anyone on the way.' The girl pulled her hand out of Fran's and began to weave dreamily around the furniture, waving her arms, like someone casting spells.

Feeling more than slightly exasperated, Fran went off to let Miss Billington know that she was finished with her charge. After finding the governess, Fran slipped back into the garden and, after about ten minutes' exploration, she was rewarded with a glimpse of young Joe wheeling what appeared to be a barrow-load of horse manure.

'Hello there,' Fran said brightly, affecting surprise.

Joe's expression suggested that he wasn't fooled. 'Hello, madam.' He lowered the handles of the barrow, coming to a halt on the path in front of her.

Fran decided not to beat about the bush. 'I don't think your friend was being completely frank with me when he claimed that he couldn't remember what you said to him about spotting that car in the lane.'

Joe turned a little redder under his permanent sunburn. 'No, madam.'

'Didn't Her Ladyship explain that she wanted you to answer any questions as honestly as possible?'

'Yes, madam.' Joe's head drooped. 'But you see, madam, Mr Marshall . . . ee's always said you don't say nothing what's disrespectful to the family, or disrespectful in front of a lady.'

'Well, of course, Mr Marshall is absolutely right in normal circumstances. But what you said that day could turn out to be very important.'

'I don't reckon as it can be, begging your pardon, madam. Not something I've said.'

'Why don't you let me be the judge of that? You tell me what it was that you said to your friend after you'd seen the car in the lane and I'll decide whether it's important or not. In the meantime, Mr Marshall doesn't need to know anything about it at all.'

'All I said was "It be a right old day for courtin' at Sunnyside".'

'Is that because you'd seen a couple in the car? Perhaps kissing . . . or something of that sort?'

'Oh no, madam. It was as I told you. I couldn't see anything of the car, 'cept its roof. I'd seen it parked there once before, you see, in the same place, where the lane is just wide enough for summat else to pass. So I didn't reckon as it was someone what was lost and just parked up, looking at a map like.'

'So you just guessed that it was a courting couple?'

Something of the disappointment in her tone encouraged him to say more. 'Well, yes, I s'pose I did. You see there'd been another time, the summer before – a different car that one was – a little open-topped thing – when Mr Marshall had actually caught the couple in the woods. And I was just having a joke with Max, see, on account of what we'd seen earlier on.'

'Do you mean when Mr Marshall caught the couple in the woods?'

'No, madam. I meant what we'd seen earlier on that particular afternoon.'

'And what had you seen, earlier on?'

Joe looked supremely uncomfortable. 'It was Mr Charles, madam. He was round the back o' the 'ouse, having a word with one of the maids, like.'

'Having a word?'

Joe remained silent. The crimson flush beneath his sunburn had spread right to his ears.

'Could you hear what was being said?'

'No, madam.'

'But something about this . . . er . . . meeting, made you think about a courting couple.'

'Ee kissed her, madam.' Joe's voice had sunk to a mumble. 'An' after ee kissed 'er, ee smacked her on the you-know-where, just as she turned to go back inside.'

'And after that?'

'I dunno, madam. We was past the side of the 'ouse by then, so I didn't see no more.'

'I see. Thank you for telling me this, Joe.'

''Twon't get back to Mr Marshall, will it?'

'No. I promise it won't get back to Mr Marshall. Can you tell me which of the maids it was that you saw with Mr Charles?'

''Twere that Connie, madam. The one as was dismissed.'

Back at the house, Fran returned to her base in the library, where she rang for Jamieson.

'Good morning, madam, how may I be of assistance?'

'I believe you told me that there was a maid called Connie working here, when old Mr Edgerton was alive?'

'That is correct, madam.'

'I believe she was dismissed.'

'Indeed she was, madam.'

'Can you tell me why?'

Jamieson, his expression remaining impassive as ever, did not hesitate. 'She had developed a bad attitude, madam. One day she disobeyed my orders and then she cheeked Mrs Remington.'

'I see. May I ask what this act of disobedience entailed?'

'The between maid was unwell, so I instructed Connie to undertake some of her duties. Connie refused, saying that it was not her job and that she would spoil her hands if she undertook heavy work. There is no room for that kind of attitude here, madam. We must all pull together, in order to ensure the smooth running of the household.'

'And the problem with Mrs Remington?'

'Arose out of the same conversation, madam. Mrs Remington told the girl not to give herself airs above her station and the girl, Connie, insulted Mrs Remington and called her an old maid. "Mrs" is a courtesy title, of course, denoting her status as cook.'

'Oh, dear me!' said Fran, wanting to laugh, but feeling that some expression of shock was called for. 'So Connie was told to leave. Do you know where she went?'

'She is a local girl, madam. She returned to her home in Avemouth.'

'I suppose she would have found it difficult to obtain another position. I assume you didn't provide her with a good reference?'

'Certainly not.' Jamieson's tone contained unmistakable asperity. 'However, I understand that she has been employed as a waitress at the Copper Kettle Tea Rooms. There is no future in the role of course, unlike domestic service, where a good girl may rise to become a ladies' maid, or even the housekeeper of a superior establishment, assuming of course that she does not marry.'

'Well, perhaps Connie will have a better chance of marriage now,' suggested Fran. 'She will meet a great many more eligible young men, I dare say, living in Avemouth.'

Jamieson said nothing and, sensing his disapproval, Fran swiftly moved on. 'There was absolutely no question of any dishonesty on the young woman's part? No question of pilfering?'

'There was nothing at all of that nature.'

'I see. Thank you for your help, Jamieson.'

'Will that be all, madam?'

'Well, actually, there is one more thing. I believe the late Mr Edgerton's nurse was in the habit of spending her afternoons off with Colonel Baddeley's chauffeur. Do you know the man in question?'

'I do, madam. Until very recently, the position of chauffeur to Colonel Baddeley has been occupied by Mr Moncrieff and if he had driven Colonel or Mrs Baddeley over, he would generally join us in the servants' hall for a cup of tea.'

'Did you realize that he was romantically involved with old Mr Edgerton's nurse?'

'I wouldn't have put it that way myself, madam.'

'What way would you have put it?'

'I believe a friendship grew up between them, such as can easily occur between two people who have been in service a long time.' Jamieson spoke rather stiffly. 'When the family are all away, I myself have occasionally accompanied Mrs Remington out to luncheon or afternoon tea.'

'But the nurse and the chauffeur had not been a long time in service together. They did not even work in the same establishments.'

'I meant that they had each been individually a long time in service. Taking afternoon tea with an acquaintance that shares a similar outlook and similar experiences is naturally more pleasant than taking afternoon tea alone. Unfortunately the younger maids have had their heads filled with silly ideas derived from their chosen reading matter and so they tend to see romance where none exists.' Jamieson sniffed.

'So you give no credence to any suggestion of a romance?'

'None whatsoever, madam. Miss Roche and Mr Moncrieff had their war experiences in common, I believe.'

'Their war experiences?'

'She had nursed the wounded and Mr Moncrieff was among the staff from the Baddeley estate who followed the colonel into service in Belgium and France. A number of the men answered the call, I believe and two of the under gardeners did not return. Mr Moncrieff was rather too old to serve, but I expect the colonel was able to pull some strings. Mr Moncrieff was wounded and invalided out, so I have heard, and this left him unable to perform heavy duties. After the war his employment prospects would have been very poor, but naturally Colonel Baddeley reinstated him in his old position at Baddeley Court. I gather that now he is all but retired from duties, the colonel has found him a cottage on the estate.'

'So he has been with Colonel Baddeley for at least ten years.'

Jamieson inclined his head in agreement. 'I believe it is more than twenty.'

'And Colonel Baddeley clearly thinks well of him.'

'So I believe.'

'I see. Thank you, Jamieson, that will be all.'

'Thank you, madam.' The butler gave his usual stiff little bow before letting himself out of the room and latching the door with a neat click.

EIGHTEEN

When Eddie enquired over lunch whether the 'lady detective' would be available for a walk that afternoon, Fran requested instead that Eddie run her into Avemouth, if it was not too much trouble.

'No trouble at all. As I said on Day One, consider me completely at your service.'

Nothing further was said about her request until they were driving out of the main gates, when he enquired, 'May I ask if this is linked with your detective work, or merely a shopping expedition?'

'It's a little bit of detective work,' Fran said. 'I'm just tying up a loose end. There was a maid working at Sunnyside House who was dismissed, not long after your grandfather died and as I'm speaking to all the staff, I need to speak to her too.'

'Leaving no stone unturned, eh? That would be Connie, I suppose.'

'You remember her?'

'Of course. She was with us for about a year.'

'What was she like?'

'In what way?'

'Was she pretty?'

'I suppose so. She knew it too, used to simper at any passing male when she thought Jamieson wasn't looking; lowered her head and batted her eyelashes, if one met her in the corridor. Can't say I took to her.'

'I understand that she works in a tea room called the Copper Kettle now.'

'So you're going to pop in and order a pot of tea,' Eddie said. 'In that case, it will probably be better if I lose myself for half an hour. She's far more likely to open up if I'm not there, don't you think?'

'Actually I do,' Fran said. 'But I feel rather badly, leaving you to sit in the car while I drink tea.'

'Don't trouble over me. I will be perfectly able to amuse myself. I may take a walk along the quayside. There's always something to see down there.'

'That's very sporting of you.'

'Not a bit. Haven't I said that I am to be considered your willing slave in this business? Your wish is my command.'

'In that case,' Fran said, 'would you mind telling me what the Sidmouth affair is?'

'Aah.' Eddie made a sound somewhere between a laugh and a sigh.

'I thought you were going to tell me about it that day when we went to see your house, but then we met your sister and Miss Trenchard.'

'You're absolutely right – as usual. Though of course I thought that you already knew – until you told me otherwise. You see, I assumed that my brother had explained the legacy Grandfather left for Mrs Headingham.'

'I have never even heard of Mrs Headingham.'

Eddie took a deep breath. 'Mrs Headingham was the governess at Sunnyside House, when my aunts were growing up and my grandfather became very fond of her. Naturally this was all a very long time ago. Grandfather was still a young man when his wife died and Mrs Headingham came to the family as a young widow. One half wonders why they never married . . . anyway, for some reason they never did. My aunts grew up, but Mrs Headingham stayed on as part of the household. Officially I think she was like a sort of housekeeper, but essentially, I suppose . . .' Eddie hesitated. 'Well, essentially she was Grandfather's mistress. As you can imagine, when my father married my mother and she found out what the situation was with Mrs Headingham, she wasn't too amused and so Grandfather agreed to set Mrs Headingham up in a little house in Sidmouth, which was far enough out of the way to avoid any local gossip. Grandfather thought a great deal of my mother and wouldn't have wanted to embarrass her. Mother was much younger then and had led quite a sheltered life. Victoria was still on the throne, for goodness' sake . . .' Again Eddie trailed momentarily into silence. 'I suppose Mother was embarrassed or scandalized, or quite possibly both. Anyway, she didn't like Mrs Headingham mentioned by name, so it became the custom to refer to the matter – if at all – as the Sidmouth business, which was fairly ambiguous. The servants weren't supposed to know what it meant, but you can bet your life they did.'

'I seem to remember that your family told me at the outset that they wouldn't hold anything back, and yet I'm only now being told about this Mrs Headingham, who had a financial interest in your grandfather's death.'

'Oh Lord, Fran, don't be annoyed,' begged Eddie. 'I thought Roly must have told you, honestly I did. I admit there had been some discussion about it before you came and my mother and Mellie were all for keeping it quiet. Mother said that she didn't see how the Sidmouth business could have any possible relevance. Grandfather had stopped making regular visits to Sidmouth long ago and Mrs Headingham never came to Sunnyside House. Mellie took the same line. She hadn't even known about Mrs Headingham until then and when it was explained to her, she said she didn't see the point in dragging it all up and putting very old dirty linen on show. Even so, I thought Roly wouldn't have taken any notice of them.'

'Have you ever met Mrs Headingham?'

'No. She never visited Grandfather. I don't believe she's been back to Sunnyside House in my lifetime.'

'If this affair with your grandfather began when she came to look after your aunts, then she must be quite old by now.'

'I dare say she is.'

'Would you be able to get her address for me?'

'Roly will have it. I could ask him for it and can easily run you over there, without Mother or Mellie being any the wiser, if you like. Actually I'd be quite curious to meet the old girl myself.'

The Copper Kettle was situated in a prime position, over-looking the little harbour. Eddie dropped Fran a short distance away and she walked the last few yards, passing the usual assortment of village shops, which thanks to Avemouth's seaside location were leavened with a couple of emporiums containing unseasonal displays of brightly coloured tin buckets and little wooden spades. A bell above the door tinkled as Fran entered

the almost empty teashop, where the only other customers were
two generously built matrons, occupying a table in one corner.
Fran took up a position diametrically opposite and removed her
gloves, while she awaited the arrival of a waitress.

'Yes, please, what would you like?'

Fran had been concentrating on the view from the window,
through which she could see Eddie Edgerton pausing to chat
to an old fellow who was tending to some lobster pots, so she
was startled by the silent arrival of the girl who stood at her
shoulder, wearing a black dress and a spotless white apron,
complemented by a white starched cap. The girl had a small
pad, above which she held a stump of pencil expectantly. One
glance suggested to Fran that this was probably not Connie,
for the waitress, though smart in appearance, was thin and
mousy, with a pair of round spectacles, rammed well on to
the bridge of her nose.

'A pot of tea and a scone, please.'

'Will that be a Devon scone? With jam and clotted cream?'

'Oh no,' Fran said quickly, mindful that lunch was not far
behind her. 'Just a buttered scone, please.'

The girl noted this on her little pad in careful longhand, all
the time wearing an expression of one whose offer of a local
delicacy has been unreasonably scorned. Once the taking of
the order had been accomplished she disappeared behind the
beaded curtain which was suspended across a doorway which
led into the rear of the establishment, leaving Fran to contem-
plate the possibility that if it was Connie's day off she had
made a wasted journey.

The preparation of the order seemed to take rather less time
than noting it down had done, with the waitress reappearing
as silently as she had originally arrived, bearing a loaded tray.
'Tea,' she announced, placing the pot on the table. 'Hot water,'
she added unnecessarily as she placed the steaming jug next
to the pot. 'Milk . . . sugar . . . cup and saucer . . .' Fran
managed to suppress a smile, wondering whether the explanation of each article was deemed to be for her benefit and
noting the slight edge to the final 'buttered scone', which was
clearly perceived as a distinctly inferior article to a proper
Devon scone.

'Thank you. I wonder if you can help me?'

'I will if I can, madam,' the girl replied in a patient tone, which suggested to Fran that perhaps she anticipated having to explain the use of the tea strainer to this ignorant off-comer, who had foregone the opportunity of a proper cream tea.

'I have been given to understand that a young woman called Connie works here.'

'She did, madam. Up until last week.'

'Oh, I see. She doesn't work here any more?'

'No, madam.'

'Why is that?'

The girl affected an even more patient tone. 'Because she's left, madam.'

'Well, yes . . . but are you able to tell me why . . . and where she's gone?'

'She gave her notice in madam. 'Tis lucky it's our quiet time. Otherwise we'd be sorely pushed to manage.'

'Did she go to another position? Somewhere in the village perhaps?'

'I wouldn't know about that, madam.'

It occurred to Fran that Avemouth was not a particularly big place and certainly not large enough for anyone working there to be unaware of what had become of an ex-colleague in such a short space of time. She decided to pursue the point. 'I believe Connie lives here in the village?'

'That's right, madam.'

'Does she live with her parents?'

'She does.'

'And where do they live?'

Having ascertained the name of the cottage and directions on how she could find it, Fran let her reluctant informant return to the nether region of the premises, while she drank a cup of tea and sampled the scone, which was rather dry. Not even jam and clotted cream, she thought, would have greatly improved it.

As soon as she emerged into the street, she spotted Eddie lurking further along the quay. He was evidently watching for her and they met beneath the sign of the dolphin, which proclaimed the location of a public house.

'Any luck?'

'Not really,' Fran said. 'Connie gave in her notice last week and the waitress claims not to know where she is working now. She's given me the girl's address.'

'So you're going to try there? I'd better make myself scarce again. How's the tea at the Copper Kettle?'

'The tea is fine but I don't recommend the scones.'

Fran found the cottage easily, in a cobbled alley, a matter of yards above the harbour. The paint on the front door was blistered, but the front step had been holystoned within an inch of its life. Her knock was answered by a woman almost as wide as she was tall, wearing a sacking apron over a black bombazine frock, which had been out of fashion twenty years before. When Fran tentatively enquired after Connie, the woman turned back into the house and called, 'Connie, come 'ere! There's a lady wants to speak to ee.'

A moment later the plump, black-clad figure gave way to a creature who could scarcely have been more different in appearance, with her blonde, Marcel-waved curls, periwinkle blue eyes and a perfect figure beneath a cheap, but fashionable frock.

'You must be Connie.' Fran extended a gloved hand, which was accepted doubtfully, while the young woman regarded her with a suspicious expression.

'I wonder if you could spare me a few minutes? You see, I'm trying to look into something for some friends of mine and I think you might be able to help.'

'I might.' Connie tilted her head to one side and regarded Fran archly. 'Depends what's in it for me, doesn't it?'

Taken by surprise, Fran said, 'I'm not sure that I understand what you mean.'

'You want information from someone, then you expect to pay, don't you?'

'Well . . .' Fran hesitated. It would be very easy for Connie to retreat indoors and moreover her remark implied that she had something useful to impart. 'As it happens,' Fran said carefully, 'I wouldn't normally expect to pay anything. Not just to be able to talk with someone. But of course, if someone was in a position to provide me with something *very* useful, well that might be different.'

Connie nodded, as if this was precisely the kind of reaction she had in mind. 'You hang on here a minute, while I get my coat, and we'll go for a walk. You can't never be sure who's listening here,' she finished rather loudly and pointedly, precipitating the distinct sound of someone moving further into the darker recesses of the cottage.

Fran was left standing on the doorstep until Connie returned, wearing an emerald-green coat and a garishly trimmed hat. 'This way,' she said, waving an arm in the opposite direction to the quayside. 'There's a shelter up here, where we can be a bit more private.'

Sure enough, the steep alleyway gave way to a broad expanse of windswept grass, in the centre of which had been erected a large stone shelter, roofed with slate. Inside the shelter, a plaque on the back wall had been inscribed to the memory of the men of Avemouth: the list of their names coupled with the ship or regiment in which they had served. Their loyalties appeared to have been roughly divided between the Devonshires and the merchant navy, Fran noted.

'Now then,' said Connie when both women were sitting on the wooden bench and Fran was trying not to be distracted either by the memorial plaque or thoughts of another sojourn in a shelter facing the sea just twenty-four hours before. 'If I'm to be a named party, it'll be a pretty steep price. So I think we'd better talk about the money, first of all.'

'Oh, but I don't think there is any question of your name being mentioned at all,' Fran said. 'This is all in strictest confidence, I assure you.'

Connie looked dubious. 'I thought the other party always had to be named.'

'The other party?' Fran was catching up, but slowly. 'You are thinking of – of a divorce?'

'Well, what else?'

'You think I'm trying to gather information for a divorce? Oh, no, it isn't anything like that.'

'So you're not working for the major's wife?'

'The major? Major who? No, no. I can see we're at cross purposes . . . unless, unless Charles Edgerton is a major?'

'Him! It's about him, is it?' Connie sounded distinctly disparaging. 'Well, I never thought *she'd* divorce him, I must say. But the conditions are still the same. I'm saying nothing without a proper arrangement being made. I want to make a better life for myself, well away from here, and I can't do that without proper recompense for services rendered.'

Fran hardly knew what to say next. The young woman was so brazen. A vision of her mother rose unbidden in her mind, reaching for the proverbial smelling salts. She pulled herself together. 'Connie . . . may I call you Connie? I assure you that I am not here to ask you about anything with a view to anyone obtaining a divorce. I only want to know about an afternoon when you were working for the Edgerton family at Sunnyside House. It was the afternoon when old Mr Edgerton died.'

Connie regarded her warily. 'It comes down to the same thing, don't it? Asking about that afternoon?'

'Not at all.' Fran knew that she needed to avoid starting any gossip about the nature of her enquiries, but on the other hand, since Connie was clearly not about to broadcast the nature of her activities without reward, Fran decided that she had to take a risk. 'You see, I have been asked to satisfy myself that no members of the family were with old Mr Edgerton that afternoon, so if you were able to confirm that Mr Charles Edgerton spent the afternoon with you . . .'

'I reckon you're just trying to trick me into saying summat.'

'The thing is, Connie, I don't need you to confirm that something improper took place between yourself and Mr Charles, because although you may not be aware of it, you and Mr Charles were seen together in compromising circum-stances that afternoon, so if evidence were required in respect of a divorce, there is already someone else who can provide it.' Fran hoped that she sounded confident and commanding, because she really had no idea whether a glimpse of a kiss and a slap on the behind was anything like enough evidence to support an accusation of adultery, and in fact she strongly suspected that it was not.

Fortunately she was convincing enough for Connie who capitulated at last. 'Very well then,' she said sulkily. 'I know that silly wife of his saw us together in the garden, but I didn't realize she had followed us back to the house.'

'Well, there you are,' said Fran, greatly relieved. 'The thing that I need to know is how long the two of you were together – and where you were. That way I can be sure that Mr Charles was never with his father, you see.'

'I don't see as why I should do anything to help him,' grumbled Connie. 'A girl agrees to meet a gentleman and he takes advantage, well then the girl naturally expects a present or something. There's a lot of gentlemen as can be very generous, so long as a girl is discreet. The major now, he had offered me a place as his secretary. In Hampshire. That would be a step up. I made up my mind a few years back that I mean to get away from 'ere and get on in life and I thought that would definitely be a step in the right direction. That's why I gave my notice at the Copper Kettle, only then I got word that his wife is cutting up rough, you see.'

Fran could not help feeling that the less she heard about the major – whoever he might be – the better. 'Getting back to Charles Edgerton,' she said. 'I gather that you had arranged to meet him in the garden that afternoon, after lunch.'

'After lunch was the best time. It's quiet then and with old Jamieson and Mrs Remington snoozing in their rooms, it's pretty easy to slip off for an hour or so.'

Thinking that Jamieson had been absolutely correct in his assessment that Connie had the wrong attitude for domestic service, Fran prompted: 'So you met in the garden and then went back to the house together?'

'We slipped in through the tradesman's entrance and then up the back stairs. I'd never been in one of those bedrooms for anything other than dusting and tidying and the like and it tickled me, knowing what Her blooming Ladyship would think of the likes of me, up to all sorts on one of her silk counterpanes. I was giggling and we was shushing each other, though there wasn't anyone there. No one knew what was going on 'cepting for Mr Charles's wife seeing us together in the garden.'

Little do you know, Fran thought. Out loud, she said, 'Did Mr Charles realize that his wife had seen you?'

'No. He was facing me, with his back to the path and that Mrs Dolly, she just appeared for a minute between the bushes as run alongside the path. I knew she'd seen us like, but she turned and headed off the other way.'

'Didn't you tell Mr Charles that his wife was there?'

'Of course not.' Connie was openly scornful. 'If she wants to set a detective on him and they pay me to tell tales, well, that's all to the good, isn't it? She won't though, not that one. She married him for his money, they say and perhaps she'd not be sure of getting too much good out of a divorce.'

Fran found that she could imagine, all too easily, the look of surprise and pain on Dolly's face, as she glimpsed her husband, trysting with one of the maids. Poor Dolly, despised by her husband's relatives and cheated on by the man himself. 'But what about Mr Charles?' she asked. 'Didn't you think you ought to warn him that his wife knew what he was up to?'

Connie made a derisive sound verging on a snort. 'Dirty old goat,' she said. 'He deserves all the trouble he gets, if you ask me.'

'Can you tell me how long you were with him that afternoon?'

Connie tossed her blonde curls. 'Wasn't looking at my wristwatch. About an hour, maybe? I went down to meet him as we'd arranged, at three p.m. I waited for him a short while and just as I thought he wasn't coming after all, he came panting up the path. Right eager he was. We went straight back up to the house and afterwards I left him in the bedroom. I had to get back into my frock and down to the servants hall to start laying up for family tea. And he didn't take long, if you know what I mean.'

Connie made to nudge her but was thwarted when Fran stood up abruptly and ostentatiously dusted down her coat. 'Thank you for your help, Connie, you have said quite enough.' She turned on her heel and strode swiftly away, ignoring what she fancied was a call of 'Stuck up cow'.

Oh dear, she thought, as she headed back down the hill. *What on earth am I to say, if Eddie asks me whether I have found anything out?* Fortunately her chauffeur merely expressed concern that she appeared to be rather cold and insisted on putting a rug around her knees for the drive home.

NINETEEN

'Oh, bravo!' exclaimed Eddie when he saw Fran appear in the doorway of the drawing room. 'Your chariot awaits, Milady Juliet.'

'Juliet didn't have a chariot, did she?' asked Mellie.

'Didn't she say something about wanting one?' asked Henrietta. 'I'm sure I remember something about it at school. Doves drawing Cupid's chariot, or something was it?'

'It's the speech in Act II,' said Fran. '"Loves heralds should be thoughts, which ten times faster glide than the suns beams—"' She came to a halt, blushing slightly lest the Edgertons might think her a show-off or a bore.

'Good heavens!' cried Roly. 'You don't just look the part, you actually know it.'

'Do go on and give us some more,' begged Eddie, but Fran shook her head, protesting that she didn't know the rest and then Mellie asked whether they oughtn't to see if the cars had been brought down from the garage.

The party at the Lyndons' turned out to be far more fun than she had expected. Most of the costumes were considerably more elaborate than anything she had encountered at the modest fancy dress parties she remembered from childhood, with everything from teddy bears to Tutankhamun represented. Mabel Trenchard's Charlie Chaplin disguise was so successful that no one initially recognized her, though her sister's elaborate Britannia took a bit of managing, leaving Fran secretly grateful that her own outfit fitted her so well and was surprisingly comfortable, apart from the beaded skull cap, which needed a lot of well-concealed Kirby grips to keep it in place.

There was a splendid buffet supper, an endless supply of fruit punch laced with gin and a professional band had been engaged for the dancing, which took place in a real ballroom, for the Lyndons' residence was much larger and grander than Sunnyside House. Though she knew no one but the Edgertons,

Fran experienced no shortage of partners willing to take her for a turn around the dance floor, and Eddie made a point of ensuring that she was never left on her own between dances. She could hardly believe it when she realized that everyone was beginning to leave.

As they joined the line which had formed to thank their hosts, Fran took a lingering look at the portraits on the walls and the decorated plaster ceilings. It wasn't every day that she got to dance in surroundings like this – in fact, it wasn't any day and it might never happen again.

'Such a pleasure to meet you,' Emmeline Lyndon said in response to Fran's thanks. 'I do hope that we'll be seeing a lot more of you in the future.'

There wasn't time to explain that she was only in Devon temporarily and besides which it seemed impolite to respond that she would probably never see them again, so Fran just nodded and smiled and said 'thank you' again.

'Phew,' said Eddie, as he climbed into the Riley, having seen Fran safely into the passenger seat. 'At last I can take off this blasted beard. It's frightfully hot and itchy.'

'In that case, I am removing my cap too,' said Fran. 'One of those pins is sticking straight into my scalp.'

'Toss it into the back with the beard,' said Eddie. 'What say we go back via the coast road? It's not much out of our way and it's such a beautiful clear night.'

'Morning,' she corrected him. 'Goodness, but it's ages since I've stayed up so late – or had so much fun.'

The beam of the Riley's headlights sliced through the darkness of the lanes. They met nothing on the road and within about a quarter of an hour, Fran could see that they had reached the coast, for when the road emerged on to high ground, she was immediately confronted by an expanse of dark water stretching out before them, overlaid with a glittering mantle of silver, where the moonlight had made a pathway across the sea.

'Oh,' she gasped. 'How lovely!'

'There's a good place to stop here.' Eddie slowed the car as he spoke, steering it to the side of the road. 'Come out and see it properly,' he instructed. 'Hold on. Let me put this rug around you so you don't get cold.'

After draping the rug about her shoulders, he guided her a few steps away from the car, and sure enough she saw that the land fell away gently, revealing an even lovelier aspect.

'It's beautiful,' Fran said. 'I've never seen anything quite like it before.'

'The drawing room at Innominate House faces the sea. This will be the view from there every night, when the moon is in the right place.'

Fran was silent. Vistas of dancing and laughter and coming home to a beautiful view and someone who cared tremendously for one swam enticingly on a silvery ocean of moonlight and a little too much gin.

They stood in silence for a few moments before Eddie spoke. 'I know we've hardly known each other for a week yet, but sometimes that's all it takes. No, no . . . please don't say anything yet . . . You see, you are the most wonderful woman I've ever met – and I know you're probably in the same camp as everyone else, thinking I'm a complete and total idiot, and I don't mind that. Only don't say "no" just yet. Let me keep my hopes up, Fran – darling Fran – that one day, soon, you will agree to be my wife.'

Fran opened her mouth to speak but nothing came out.

'I expect you've got a string of fellows in pursuit and you must think it's jolly presumptuous of me to ask, but you see I saw that you had taken off your wedding ring and I thought that maybe you were doing it as a sign . . . to let me know that, well, you'd seen how much I care for you.'

'Oh no.' Fran managed to get a word in. 'Oh no, Eddie, I didn't mean anything by it at all. Nothing was further from my mind.'

'Of course not. Of course not,' he hastened on. 'As if you are the sort of girl who would ever encourage a man or lead him on in any way at all. I didn't mean that, of course I didn't. I'm an idiot, such an idiot. The thing is, that . . . well . . . I'd be honoured. Only . . . well . . . yes . . . as I say, please don't give me an answer now. Please think about it first. Take as long as you like. Only promise me that you won't say "no" tonight.'

Fran couldn't see his face, but she could imagine it, his

eyes looking earnestly into hers. She made no objection when he put both his arms around her and kissed her. It was very nice to be kissed, properly kissed, after such a long time. When the kiss was over, he released her, very slowly and gently, saying, 'Promise me you will think about it.'

'Very well, I promise.'

They walked back to the car in silence.

'You won't say anything to your family?' she asked.

'Not until . . . unless, you say "yes".'

'Everything just as normal tomorrow,' Fran said, firmly.

'Of course. Everything just as normal.'

TWENTY

. . . *B*ut *of course, everything is not normal at all,* Fran wrote to Mo. *I am supposed to be here on a detective mission and instead I'm attending fancy dress parties and receiving proposals of marriage. Eddie Edgerton is supposed to be one of the suspects, not a prospective suitor. He is driving me see Mrs Headingham in Sidmouth this afternoon, which means . . .*

Fran put down her pen and reread the most recently written page. What did it mean? She could just imagine Mo, could almost hear her saying, 'But you haven't said "no", have you? He's a jolly nice chap and he's obviously crazy about you. You could do a damn sight worse. In fact, you already have done, once . . .'

She picked up the last sheet of notepaper and tore it carefully into tiny pieces. She would bring Mo up to date another time about the Eddie complication. Anyway, it was time to set off for Sidmouth.

It took them almost an hour to drive to Sidmouth, but much to Fran's relief, Eddie stuck to safe, ordinary topics and made no reference to the conversation which had taken place on the coast road in the early hours. She did wonder if she ought to interpret his silence as an indication of him having thought better of it, now that the effects of the gin punch had worn off, but somehow she rather doubted that. Instead they talked about the places they drove through and he asked her about the countryside where she lived, rather in the manner of a person who intended to visit the area soon.

Mrs Headingham lived in a white-painted terraced house, a couple of streets back from the promenade. Her maid opened the door and showed them into a rather over-furnished drawing room which reminded Fran very much of her own mother's. She had been half expecting a faded femme fatale, but the woman who had once been Frederick Edgerton's mistress was disappointingly ordinary. Warned to expect them by a telephone call from Roly, Mrs Headingham appeared to be as curious about them as they were about her.

'Edward,' she said. 'Do come into the light, so that I can see you better. There now . . . very much like your grandfather, when he was younger. But you, my dear.' She turned to Fran. 'You are not like the Edgertons at all. But then you're not a member of the family, are you? Roland tried to explain it on the telephone, but I'm afraid I couldn't get the gist. You are going to have to tell me again. And do speak up, because I'm a trifle deaf.'

'Mrs Black is helping the family with a bit of a mystery,' Eddie said, probably rather too loudly. 'It's all to do with a piece of jewellery that we've lost. Grandfather was a little bit confused at times, in his last few months, and he may have put it somewhere unexpected. Mrs Black just thought that perhaps you – having known him very well at one time – might have had some ideas.'

'Did she really? So this has got absolutely nothing to do with the fact that your grandfather met his death by falling off a cliff? Now really, young man, don't look so surprised. I may be old but I'm not senile. I read the newspapers and my eyebrows hit the ceiling at that.'

'It is just possible that old Mr Edgerton's death was not an accident,' Fran said, having made a swift assessment that Mrs Headingham's unusual circumstances meant that her discretion could be relied upon. 'We don't know whether the missing jewellery is connected to his death or not.'

Mrs Headingham nodded thoughtfully. 'Old Mr Edgerton? That's what they call poor Fred now, is it? Well, well, I suppose there are probably people who call me old Mrs Headingham too. Which piece of jewellery is it that's gone missing?'

'You may not know it. It was a single diamond, which he never had made up into anything. It was kept in a black velvet pouch.'

'And you can't find it?'

'No.'

'When did you last see it?'

'No one is really sure. Just some time before he died.'

'Well, perhaps he gave it back.'

'Gave it back?' Fran asked, careful not to betray her suspicion that Mrs Headingham was also fairly well advanced in her dotage, in spite of the sentiments she had expressed a moment before.

'Gave it back to its owners.' Mrs Headingham scrutinized their faces before adding, 'I can see that you haven't the least idea of what I'm talking about. You don't know the full story of that diamond, do you?'

Fran and Eddie shook their heads in perfect unison.

'Well, what do you know about it?'

It was Eddie who answered. 'As I've always understood it, Grandfather brought it back from Africa, along with various other assets. He had the stone cut, but for some reason or other, he never had it made into a piece of jewellery. I think he used to like to keep it close by him for some reason, and he often showed it to people. I expect it was worth a good deal of money, but I don't ever remember him telling us how he got it – and certainly not that it belonged to anyone else,' Eddie added by way of an afterthought.

Mrs Headingham looked thoughtful. 'I suppose Fred told me a great many things that he would never have confided in anyone else. He wasn't a man to make close friendships and after his wife died I became the next best thing. He asked me to marry him once, but I turned him down. I was very fond of him but I never could have loved him the way I had loved my husband.' She sighed. 'I told him that it wouldn't have worked out well for him anyway, marrying his children's governess. People would have looked down on us, I said, but that wasn't the real reason. I couldn't forget that I loved my first husband more than him. I suppose it was foolish really, because I was happy enough with Fred in a way . . . and I could never have my poor dead husband back again. It may sound strange to you, but I quite enjoyed being his mistress rather than his wife. There's a lot of tiresome responsibility goes with being a wife, particularly one who is expected to participate in local society. But then, of course, your father, young Frank, married Lady Louisa and she was very shocked at the idea of living under the same roof as her father-in-law's mistress, so I was shipped off to live here and Fred could only come and visit me after that. As he got older, the gaps between those visits grew longer and longer and I admit that I missed seeing him, perhaps rather more than he missed seeing me.' She laughed softly and shook her head. 'I hadn't anticipated that and I admit I sometimes thought then that perhaps I should have settled for marriage, when it was offered, all those years before, but there, I didn't and that's all there is to it.'

'And the story of the diamond,' Fran prompted gently.

'The diamond. Of course. Fred told me the story of the diamond years ago, when his girls were still quite small. It seems that when he was travelling about, making his fortune, he fell in with a French fellow, by the name of George. He and this George became good friends, and I think they got into some scrapes together, one way and another. George had been involved in the Kimberley diamond rush, and he'd done pretty well, but that kind of thing always attracts scallywags and ne'er-do-wells and Kimberley was no exception. George was a fool when it came to gambling, Fred said. Couldn't resist a card game and had lost a great deal of his money through it. By the time he decided to return to his wife, he'd got himself into a lot of trouble with professional gamblers and card sharps and he was afraid they would find out that he was still in possession of not only quite a lot of cash, but also his one remaining diamond, so he asked Fred to take care of it for him.'

'Gosh,' said Eddie. 'He must have really trusted Grandfather to do a thing like that.'

'Indeed.' Mrs Headingham inclined her head in agreement. 'I understood that Fred and George were great friends. However, they travelled back to Europe separately, with George going on a few months ahead of Fred. When Fred returned to London, he wrote to the address which George had given him but he received no reply. He wrote again, but still nothing came. He wrote a third time and still there was nothing. He even asked the French Consulate to see if they could trace George, but they were unable to help. So he held on to the diamond, thinking that sooner or later, George would track him down and ask for it back.'

'But he never did?'

'No.'

'I wonder why not,' mused Eddie. 'And why Grandfather never told us that the diamond was sort of held in trust, for someone else. I mean to say . . . we all just assumed that it belonged to the family.'

'Eventually,' said Mrs Headingham, 'I think your grandfather operated a sort of finders-keepers policy. I sincerely believe that he made an initial attempt to track his friend down, but later on, I think a combination of factors encouraged him to – well, let us say – forget, that the diamond didn't really belong to him.'

'What factors were those?' asked Fran.

'To be candid, Fred did not like the French. His friendship with George, was, he always said, the exception which proved the rule. I believe there had been some problem, or rivalry, with a Frenchman, out in Africa, and there had always been a certain degree of suspicion about the French, among Englishmen . . . a sense that they would do an Englishman down, given half a chance . . . and of course he blamed France for dragging us into the Great War. Not that it was really France's fault at all. The final straw were the French mutinies in 1917, when our brave boys were fighting on French soil and the French just threw in the towel and gave up, so to speak.'

'But George had been his friend,' Eddie protested.

'I suppose the memory of that friendship had faded as time passed and other silly prejudices took its place.' Mrs Headingham sighed. In a different tone altogether, she said, 'I must ring for tea. It's angel cake today. I'm sure you will enjoy it. Elsie has a very light hand.'

'Tell me, Mrs Headingham,' said Fran, anxious not to become overly distracted by the refreshments. 'Can you recall George's other name?'

'Ah, now there you have me. Fred mentioned it a few times, I suppose, in the course of talking about their times together, but I have to admit that my memory is not what it was. Now when it comes to poetry I can still bring plenty of that to mind, particularly Lord Tennyson and good old Longfellow, and of course one never loses the multiplication tables . . . but names! Now let me see . . . It was a name that put you in mind of something else . . . a French name, of course . . .

Poison . . . no, but something very like it, I think . . . Poussin?'

'Poussin? Wasn't he a composer?' asked Eddie.

'A painter,' corrected Fran, as Mrs Headingham hesitated, doubt etched across her expression.

'Yes,' the old lady said at last. 'I think I must have been thinking of Poussin.'

'Well, well,' said Eddie, when they were driving back along the road towards Exeter. 'There we were, thinking that we were hunting for a missing family treasure and it turns out not to have been our family treasure at all.'

'The question of actual ownership probably wouldn't have bothered the thief – if there was one,' said Fran. 'But of course, the existence of this George – or more likely Georges – Poussin throws up another possibility.'

'Does it?' Eddie sounded surprised.

'According to Mrs Headingham, your grandfather held on to this man's diamond, when he'd promised to give it back.'

'But only by default. I mean, he intended to give it back in the first place, surely?'

'Well, yes,' said Fran. 'But suppose you were Georges Poussin and you didn't get the diamond back. Suppose your grandfather wrote to the wrong address and didn't get a reply, but all along Georges Poussin was still waiting for his old friend to get in touch with him at the right address to give him back the diamond, but he never heard a thing?'

'Umm . . . yes, I see what you mean. Old Poussin would be pretty mad.'

'Precisely. Maybe mad enough to take the diamond back and push his old friend over the cliff into the bargain.'

'Good gracious, do you really think so?'

'Oh!' Fran gasped, as the car had to swerve to avoid a couple of geese that had wandered into the road. Recovering quickly, she said, 'It's a possibility. Though this Georges Poussin must be as old as your grandfather . . .'

'Perhaps he had a brother? Or an avenging cousin?'

'A son would be more likely. Let's see, that would make it someone around the same age as your father and his siblings.'

'Someone who'd married into our family – that's what it would be in a detective yarn,' said Eddie. 'Except there's no one who's French. They've all got impeccably Anglo-Saxon heritage apart from Aunt Dolly, who's lineage is probably Anglo-Saxon, but definitely not impeccable. East Peckham, more likely. What a shame Mother doesn't employ a French lady's maid. A French maid would be the obvious suspect. She could be called Hortense.' He began to sing, 'Hortense, you're not so frightfully dense, the police just won't see sense, though we all know you're gu-i-i-lty . . .'

When Eddie had subsided again, Fran said, 'I think that my enquiries here are pretty much exhausted. After the weekend, I will have to go home.'

'Oh, but you don't have to go home at all,' Eddie protested. 'Everyone loves having you here, and besides which it's the Vyvian-Smythes' party next weekend, and I was relying on you for a partner. Do say you will at least stay for the party? It's always tremendous fun.'

'I have really trespassed on your family's hospitality quite long enough – and besides which, I have to go and see my mother and,' Fran added, rather desperately, 'my cat.'

'Do you have a cat? I'll bet your cat would enjoy life in Devon. I'm very fond of cats – you've never mentioned that before.'

'There are lots of things I've never mentioned,' Fran said. 'That's the point, you see – we hardly know anything about each other at all, and . . .'

'All the more reason for you to stay on and give us time to get to know each other better. Dearest Fran, I'm trying not to pile on the pressure, but I'm absolutely mad about you. Please don't go without giving me some hope. At least promise that you're still thinking about things.'

'Oh, I am . . . thinking about lots of things. But I simply can't stay on here indefinitely. Being away from you – from here – doesn't stop me from thinking. In fact, it will help, you know, a little bit of space and distance often puts things into perspective.'

'And I can't even persuade you to stay for the party?'

'No,' she said. 'I think I ought to leave on Monday.' *I will definitely not stay for the party*, she thought. *There must be no more lingering kisses and moonlight drives, because one's judgement could so easily get clouded . . .*

TWENTY-ONE

When Fran announced her imminent departure at dinner that evening, it was greeted with universal disappointment. Lady Louisa bemoaned the fact that she had still not found time to guide Fran through the hothouse and show her the orchids, Roly claimed that life would be much duller without her and Eddie fixed her with such a mournful look that she had to escape by focusing resolutely on the contents of her soup plate.

'But you haven't finished your investigation,' Mellie protested.

'No, but I believe I've spoken with everyone I need to speak to here. I still have to get in touch with Miss Roche and I would also like to have a chat with your uncle Charles and his wife, if that's possible.'

'And then will you know?' asked Mellie. 'What happened to the diamond, I mean?'

'Perhaps.' Fran hesitated. 'You see, after we've – I mean I've – spoken with everyone, I usually, sort of . . . think about things until everything falls into place. Only, of course,' she hurried on, 'as I said right at the start, I can't guarantee that I will manage to find out anything at all.'

'But Fran has found out heaps of things already,' Eddie said. 'Including – wait for it – the diamond doesn't belong to the Edgertons at all!'

'Whatever do you mean?' Mellie's astonishment was echoed all around the table.

'Eddie and I went to Sidmouth today,' Fran said. 'And according to Mrs Headingham, who is an old friend of your husband's grandfather, he told her years ago that the diamond belonged to a friend of his, a Frenchman called Georges Poussin.' She watched their faces for any flicker of recognition, but all that greeted her was astonishment and doubt, part of which, she thought, was probably due to her casually mentioning Mrs Headingham's name over dinner as if it were the most natural thing in the world.

'If it belonged to this friend, what was Grandfather doing with it?' asked Henrietta.

'He was supposed to have transported it back to Europe on behalf of this Georges Poussin, but when he returned to England and wrote to Monsieur Poussin, he received no reply and in fact he never heard from him again.'

'But that must have been a good fifty or sixty years ago,' said Roly. 'This other fellow's probably long since dead.'

'I don't believe anyone could come and claim something so long afterwards,' mused Mellie.

'Do you think there was ever anything in writing?' asked Roly.

'Perhaps,' said Fran. 'Who knows?'

'Well, well,' said Roly. 'That's a flanker and no mistake. I wonder why Grandfather never mentioned it to any of us.'

'Probably taking the same line as you, old man,' said his brother. 'Assumed this Poussin chap had long since snuffed it.'

'Really, Eddie!' protested his mother.

'Oh, come on, Mater, it isn't as if any of us knew the chap. And everyone at this table – with the exception of Fran – is sitting here, thinking what a dashed nuisance it would be, if the chap turned up now and claimed what we've all assumed to be a valuable family heirloom.'

'Pretty worthless at the moment, as we don't know where it is,' Roly pointed out.

'Do let's talk about something else,' said Mellie. 'Did you see in the paper that Harry Durley rode three winners at the point-to-point last week? He's having a frightfully good season.'

Dinner passed off without any further reference to the owner-ship of the diamond and as the party moved into the drawing room for coffee as usual, Henrietta linked her arm through Fran's and drawing her casually to one side, so that they were well to the rear of the group, said, 'We're all so sorry that you're leaving. It's been such fun having you here, you feel like one of the family already.' She squeezed Fran's arm gently, before relinquishing it.

'I don't know what Eddie has told you—' Fran began, in a low, hurried voice, but Henrietta cut her off.

'I assure you, darling, that Eddie hasn't said a thing. He doesn't have to. I've seen the way he looks at you. I just wanted to let you know that I'm sure we'd all be very happy for you. Mother would soon get over your being divorced, if she thought it guaranteed that Eddie would give up any silly notions about becoming an entertainer.'

'Really, Henrietta, I . . .'

'Hush,' the other woman put a finger to her lips. 'I didn't mean to embarrass you. Not another word will be said.'

The others were already in the drawing room, where Mellie was proposing a card game, while Eddie had already lifted the piano lid and was improvising a tinkling melody. Fran caught herself noticing how handsome he looked in profile before she firmly turned her attention to Mellie's query about the rules of Rummy. There was always something to do, here at Sunnyside House, she thought, as she put the prospect of lonely evenings at Beehive Cottage firmly to the back of her mind.

The family retired early that evening, as they all planned to attend morning service at the parish church the next day. Sitting up in bed, swathed in the gentle glow of the bedside lamps, Fran tried to assemble her thoughts. Nothing had been said, one way or the other, about the suitability of her going to interview Charles and Dolly Edgerton. A potentially delicate undertaking, given what she knew about the way Charles Edgerton had spent the afternoon in question. There was also old Mr Edgerton's nurse, who might have something useful to tell her, in spite of having been away from the house at the critical time. It was funny, she thought, that in all the hours she had spent talking with the household here, hardly anyone seemed to have seen or heard anything useful at all, apart from Imogen's hearing a pair of unidentified feet, walking along the path which ran between the terrace and the edge of the cliffs. That it should be Imogen, of all people, who might hold a genuine clue!

Tomorrow, Fran decided, she would attempt to speak with Imogen again, in the hope that something more might emerge.

Her opportunity arose unexpectedly, for she found herself standing next to Miss Billington and Imogen after church and Miss Billington remarked that it was looking like a nice afternoon for a walk. 'Imogen and I always have a walk on a Sunday afternoon,' she explained, for Fran's benefit.

'Always,' repeated Imogen gloomily. It was evident that she considered the weekly walk an imposition.

'Instead of going with Miss Billington,' Fran suggested, 'would you like to go for a little walk with me? You could show me the grotto and the places where you've found hidden treasure. That would be fun, wouldn't it?'

'Much more fun,' said Imogen decidedly.

Over lunch, Fran had to dissuade Eddie from accompanying her and then reassure Mellie that a half hour of the child's company would not be some kind of dreadful torment. Even when the time came for handing Imogen over in the front hall, Miss Billington asked whether Fran was 'absolutely' sure that she did not want her to go along, almost as if Imogen was some slightly dangerous creature, from whom Fran might need protection.

Imogen herself, clad in a green tweed coat and matching hood, which fastened under her chin, looked distinctly grumpy as they set out, but brightened up at once when Fran said, 'Why don't we turn our walk into a sort of game? Let's play at being detectives, shall we?'

'Yes, please! Will we be Sherlock Holmes and Dr Watson?'

'Oh no,' said Fran. 'I think we should be Sherlock Black and Dr Imogen, don't you?'

'What are we going to detect? Has there been a horrible murder like in the stories?'

'I think we should go on the trail of a real mystery. The mystery of the mysterious footsteps.'

'Ooh.' Imogen sounded impressed. 'But is that a real mystery?'

'Yes, it is. Because you heard them yourself, do you remember, up in the woods, on the same day that your grandfather died?'

'Oh, those footsteps.' Imogen sounded deflated. 'They were just ordinary footsteps. That isn't a mystery.'

'Oh, but it is,' persisted Fran. 'It's a proper mystery, because you don't know whose footsteps they were and because . . . because later on you found some treasure, and I suspect that the person who made the footsteps might have been on the trail of the treasure too.'

'But they didn't get it, because I found it first!'

'Precisely, Dr Imogen. You foiled the villain who was trying to steal your treasure. Now the first thing we have to do, is return to the scene of the crime, so I need you to take me to the place where you heard the footsteps and show me where you were hidden at the time. Can you do that?'

'Of course,' the child said, immediately picking up her pace as they headed past the drawing room windows and on to the terrace. 'Should I fetch my magnifying glass so we can look for clues?'

'Not just now,' said Fran. 'Speed is of the essence, Dr Imogen, for the game is afoot, and we don't know who else might be on the trail.'

She was relieved to see that Imogen accepted this readily and continued to lead the way along the path which took them through the edge of the east woods and towards the cliff edge where old Mr Edgerton had fallen to his death, all the while keeping up an enthusiastic commentary about bloodhounds and footmarks and a variety of other potential clues. 'Wouldn't it be useful if we found a scrap of the villain's clothing, stuck on a bramble?'

'Yes, it would, but let's not waste time looking for that just yet. Oh, where are we going now?'

'We turn off here.' Imogen paused to look over her shoulder. 'This takes us up towards the grotto.'

'And is this where you heard the villain pass by?' asked Fran, who had envisaged the encounter taking place on the path which ran directly from the terrace.

'Yes. It's up here.'

Imogen continued to follow the steep little path until it met another one, which though a little wider, was still far too rough for a wheelchair. Then Fran remembered that the person Imogen had heard had not been pushing a wheelchair. If it was 'the villain' as her young companion liked to phrase it, then by the time he or she had been heard by Imogen, the deed must have already been done, and of course it made perfect sense to leave the scene of the crime by a slightly different route, where the trees and bushes grew more thickly and there was less chance of being seen.

'Does this path lead back in the direction of the house?' asked Fran.

'If you keep going along here, it brings you to the rockery above the kitchens – you can just walk down some steps and you're at the kitchen door. Or if you carry on along the right fork, you can go in a big circle, through the woods and back round to the cliffs, or you can take the left-hand path that's a bit blocked by a big, dead tree trunk and that will take you on to the path that runs alongside the back lane. There's heaps of ways to go. It would be very easy to get lost, if you didn't know your way. I *always* know where I am. I'm like an Indian tracker.'

'Well, that's lucky for me,' said Fran.

'Here we are,' Imogen announced. 'This is the place. I know it was this bush I hid in because there's a silver birch opposite and it's the only one on this path.'

Fran glanced to her right and saw the tree which the girl was indicating, at the opposite side of the path. The bush where Imogen had hidden was actually a large rhododendron, already showing an array of buds which promised an abundant flowering later in the year.

'Do you think you could manage to show me how you were hiding that day, without getting yourself too muddy?'

'Of course.' Imogen needed no further bidding, but scrambled in behind the twisted lower branches and shiny dark green leaves.

'Now,' said Fran. 'We are going to try a detective experiment. I am going to walk away down the path and then I'm going to come back and walk past your bush. I want you to keep hidden, exactly as you did that afternoon, and listen very carefully so that you can decide if the footsteps sounded like mine or not. Do you understand?'

'All right.' The girl's voice emerged clearly from her hidey-hole. 'I'm ready.'

Fran headed back the way she had come for a few yards and then returned. Looking straight into the bush, she was soon able to make out the colour of Imogen's coat and hat. *But then I know she's in there*, Fran thought. *I probably wouldn't have noticed her if I hadn't been looking on purpose.*

'Now then,' she said, having returned to her original position and assisted Imogen in the act of dusting a few dead leaves and some strands of dry grass from her clothing. 'Do you think my feet made the same sort of noise as the feet you heard that afternoon?'

'The feet I heard were a bit quicker, I think. And the person might have been bigger, because they made more noise.'

'Thank you, Dr Imogen, that is excellent remembering,' said Fran.

'Now I have to show you the grotto.' Imogen was hurrying ahead again and just as before, she made an abrupt deviation from the main path, in order to climb an even steeper one, which ran off to their right.

'Gosh,' said Fran. 'Don't go too fast. Don't forget I need Dr Imogen, my Indian tracker, to guide me safely through the woods.'

To her relief, however, the path climbed only a short distance before it came to a halt in front of what could best be described as an artificial cave, built from large boulders, so that it affected to be part of the natural hillside. Fran judged it to have been constructed at the same time as the clifftop shelter, where she and Tom had waited in the rain. The chief architect of the gardens and grounds at Sunnyside House was evidently fond of these little resting points and follies.

'This is where I found the treasure.' Imogen waved a proprietorial hand at the structure rather as if she had conjured it into being herself. 'Would you like to see?'

'See where you found it?'

'No, silly. See the treasure itself.'

'But it isn't still here, is it? Didn't you take it back to the house?'

'I did, when I first found it,' Imogen said. 'I hid it in my tin box in the schoolroom. But at Christmas time, I wanted to make a treasure hunt for everyone else to do, so I brought it out here and hid it again in the place where I'd first found it. Only no one wanted to do an outside treasure hunt at Christmas. Instead we had lots of games and things indoors and I forgot all about it. I was meaning to bring it back inside again, but I kept on forgetting – and then I thought I might as well leave it here until it's warm enough for outdoor games again.'

As she was speaking, Imogen led the way into the grotto and Fran followed her, then watched as the girl reached up to the point where the sloping roof met the back wall. There was evidently a narrow, hidden ledge there, for Imogen produced from the shadows a small black velvet bag. Fran gave a gasp as she realized, without a shadow of a doubt, what the bag contained.

TWENTY-TWO

At the outset of her return journey, Fran had been fortunate enough to get a compartment to herself and as the train steamed steadily north and east, away from Devon, she gazed out of the window with unseeing eyes, picturing the expressions of astonishment when she had entered the drawing room the afternoon before and produced the missing diamond from behind her back.

Henrietta had gasped in wonder and clapped her hands together, like someone who has just witnessed a baffling magic trick. Roly jumped to his feet and insisted on pumping her hand up and down, as one might on encountering a winning sportsman or a famous military hero.

'I knew it!' Edie had exclaimed. 'I knew you'd solve it. Fran is an absolute genius, didn't I say so from the very first?'

Fran's protestations that she had virtually found the gem by accident were waved away by all the family except Mellie, who on learning the circumstances of the discovery had immediately stated her conviction that she'd always known 'that wretched girl would be involved in it somehow. I expect she took it and hid it there herself, to play a trick on us all.'

However, Mellie had quickly put aside her dire suspicions regarding her husband's youngest cousin, eager as she was to drop the broadest of hints about some news of her own. 'Don't you think,' she asked Roly, 'that the terrific news we had confirmed today and the discovery of the diamond are somehow linked? If we have a girl, perhaps we ought to call her Diamond.'

Roly winced slightly. 'That sort of thing might do for the Cunards, my sweet, but I'm not sure that it's quite the thing for the Edgertons.'

'I'm sure it would be OK,' Henrietta said, somewhat mischievously. 'She would be called Di, for short, so people who weren't in the know would think it was a perfectly normal name, like Diana.'

Eddie had still been full of praise for Fran when he drove her to the station next day. 'You know,' he said. 'I half think that you had solved the mystery ages ago and simply waited to produce your rabbit out of a hat on the very last evening, in order to create the maximum sensation.'

'Oh no,' Fran said quickly. 'I would never do anything like that, I assure you.'

'To think that you have managed to solve the whole thing in only seven days. You really are a marvel, you know.'

'But I haven't really solved the whole thing, have I?' said Fran. 'There is still the question of how the diamond came to be in the grotto in the first place, to say nothing of how your grandfather met his death.'

'I suppose so,' Eddie had said, sounding rather more sober. 'In all the excitement last night, I think everyone forgot about those aspects of it.'

Though Fran had tried to insist it was unnecessary, Eddie had waited with her on the platform and seen her on to the train, catching hold of her hand at the last minute and saying, 'You can't imagine how much I long to kiss you goodbye.'

'Eddie, please,' she had lowered her voice, which was entirely pointless, given the amount of noise the engine was making. The Edgertons were so fearfully modern and unconventional that she was momentarily fearful he might put desire into action, which would be horribly embarrassing, as respectable people did not go about canoodling in public places – not even if they were married to one another – and certainly not if they were potentially under observation by that terrible unseen entity the King's Proctor. (Mo was right – the name *did* put one in mind of an unpleasant medical procedure).

'You will think about what I've said, won't you?' His eyes were full of such undisguised adoration that it was impossible to remain unmoved.

'Of course,' she'd said. 'I'm thinking about it all the time, only . . . only . . . I can't rush into anything. You do under-stand, don't you, that I am still legally married to someone else?'

'I'm willing to wait.'

'All aboard.' The railway official who doubled up as guard

and porter was moving along the platform, slamming carriage doors.

'I have to go.'

He released her hand and she withdrew into the compartment, where she remained at the window, smiling and waving to him until the moving train took her out of sight.

'Tickets, please!' Her reverie was interrupted as the compartment door slid open and the train guard held out an expectant hand, while she fumbled in her handbag, blushing for no reason at all.

I'm such an idiot, she thought. *I could blush for England if we were fielding a team.*

When the guard had examined her ticket, clipped a small square gap in one side of it, and gone on his way, she turned her thoughts back to the discovery of the diamond and how it impacted on the mystery of old Mr Edgerton's fall from the cliffs.

Unlike Mellie, Fran did not subscribe to the theory that Imogen herself had been responsible for the initial presence of the diamond in the grotto. To begin with, the child apparently had no conception of the item's value or significance. On their walk back to the house, once Fran had successfully bargained with Imogen, persuading her to trade the little black bag and what it contained for a necklace of glass beads – a bargain which pleased Imogen considerably as she considered the original treasure to be 'just a sparkly stone' which wasn't nearly so much use to her as a pretty necklace would be – Fran had elicited a few further details regarding the location of the find.

Yes, Imogen had said, everyone would know about the little ledge at the back of the grotto, because it had been a regular place for leaving clues, messages and occasionally treasure – except of course that there had been no further treasure hunts or games which involved the grotto since the one which she assumed her grandfather had been organizing on the day he died.

And yet, Fran thought, 'everyone' in this context probably did not include the servants, or the gardeners, or indeed anyone else who had never participated in these family games. She herself would not have suspected the existence of the hiding pace, if Imogen had not led her to it. What was more, the grotto itself was in an out of the way place, reached by a narrow path which seemed unlikely to attract the attentions of any unauthorized explorers looking for a shortcut to the sea.

When talking with the family that evening, Fran had established that no one had thought to look in the grotto during their initial searches for the diamond (though, of course, the diamond would not have been there in any case, as Imogen had temporarily removed it) and also that nothing as valuable as the diamond would normally have been used in a family treasure hunt.

'Crumbs, no!' Henrietta had laughed at the suggestion. 'It was usually sweets or the sort of token trinkets one gets in a Christmas cracker.'

'You did say that your grandfather was becoming a little bit confused towards the end of his life . . .'

Henrietta had only looked even more doubtful. 'I'm not sure he was ever *that* confused,' she'd said.

In the general euphoria over the recovery of the diamond, nothing had really been said about continuing to explore the question of old Mr Edgerton's death. Fran sensed that both Roly's mother and Mellie would now be perfectly happy to let the matter drop. The possibility of murder, which had been suggested by a potential theft, now appeared to have receded from everyone's minds, and with the diamond found, why rake up some sort of scandal, when the matter had long since been put to bed as an unfortunate accident?

On the other hand, no one had specifically forbidden her to carry on the investigation. *And once we get started on something*, Fran thought, *we don't stop, even when we're told to. We?* Well yes, in the past it had always been 'we'. Herself and Tom and darling Mo, of course, who had generally managed to help in some inadvertent way or another. If only Mo hadn't gone off to see Terence in Malaya.

It was dangerous to initiate contact with Tom. She could not forget that wretched anonymous letter, attempting to suggest that she had an ulterior motive for wanting to divorce her husband. Until she received her decree absolute, there always remained a possibility that her petition might be denied, on the grounds that her own conduct had been just as bad as her estranged husband's. Oh, it was so ridiculous and unfair! Michael and Winnie's child must be due at any time, which was surely tangible evidence of his culpability in the matter. Damn the King's Proctor and the nasty minded suspicions of mean old judges. Had any of them the slightest idea of how difficult it was to keep unwarranted suspicions at bay? She had travelled the length of the country to avoid Tom and he had turned up anyway, on the hunt for cauliflowers, so he said. And what would these spiteful arbiters of private morality make of the admission that she had been alone on at least a dozen occasions with Eddie Edgerton, during which she had allowed him to kiss her and get as far as proposing marriage? Was any of this her fault? And anyway, what of it? It was 1930 not 1830!

So drat them all, she had written Tom a note, suggesting that if he wanted to return the book she had loaned him in Liverpool, and it happened to be convenient, then he would be able to catch her in the station refreshment rooms when she was changing trains at New Street.

TWENTY-THREE

I t was crowded in the refreshment rooms, but Tom had already secured a table and was waiting for her. He stood up as soon as he saw her approaching, doffed his hat and pulled out a chair for her.

'It's counter service, I'm afraid,' he said. 'What can I get you? The teacakes are unexpectedly good. A generous size and plenty of fruit.'

'Just tea will be lovely, thank you.'

When he returned, carrying a cup and saucer in each hand, he asked a little anxiously, 'Is everything all right? You're not in any danger, are you?'

'Goodness, no. I just wanted to bring you up to date and talk things over with you.'

'But I thought you said we weren't to meet one another?'

'This is just a brief stop for a cup of tea and the exchange of a book in a completely public place,' Fran said. 'I really don't see how somewhere as utterly unromantic as the refreshment rooms of a railway station could possibly be interpreted as an improper meeting. Who ever heard of anything romantic happening in a station refreshment room?' As she spoke she glanced around, taking in the woman who was dispensing stewed tea from a huge metal urn on the counter and the variety of travellers, sitting at the surrounding tables, some consuming the ubiquitous ham sandwiches or rock buns which were always to be had in such places, others stringing out a solitary cup of tea, glancing every now and then at their watches or at the huge black-and-white clock which hung on the wall behind the counter, above the shelves and shelves of crockery.

'Unlike a clifftop shelter,' Tom agreed. 'I'm sorry about that. It was entirely my fault. Anyway, you've got something exciting to tell me about. I can see it in your face.'

'I've found the diamond. Well, no, to be absolutely honest, it simply fell into my lap in an entirely unexpected way.'

After a single exclamation of surprise and congratulation, Tom listened intently, only occasionally interrupting with a quick question as Fran brought him completely up to date.

'So,' he said eventually, 'there is just the possibility that the old man really had lost the plot.'

'What do you mean? Why?'

'Well, he could have hidden the diamond there as Imogen thought he had, then become confused about his direction and pushed himself over the cliffs.'

'Not a chance,' said Fran emphatically. 'I've thought that through and absolutely dismissed it. If we can be sure of anything, it's that the one person who certainly did not put the diamond on that ledge was old Mr Edgerton. He couldn't have reached up to the ledge from his wheelchair, and even if he could have stood up momentarily to do it, he would never have got that far in the first place, because the path to the grotto is far too steep and narrow. I've looked at the place from all angles and there's no way it is accessible for anyone in a wheelchair.'

'I see.' Tom was silent for a moment, revising his mental picture of events. 'I suppose we can't be sure that the diamond and the death are linked at all.'

'No, strictly speaking we can't. We know that the diamond was discovered by Imogen on the same afternoon that her grandfather died, which is suggestive, but that doesn't mean it was definitely put there that day.'

'But you've also got the fact that Imogen heard someone walking along the path, coming from the direction of the cliffs, back towards the house and not so very far from the grotto. Someone whose feet sounded a little bit louder than yours.'

'We have to be careful not to read too much into that,' Fran said. 'First of all, we're expecting her to compare two sounds she heard months and months apart, and secondly, the path may have sounded different in the summer. There had been a long dry spell in the summer, but it had rained quite a bit around the time when I walked along it. That might make a difference. It's only a beaten earth path.'

'Fair enough. The key thing is that no one admits to being the person who was walking through the woods that day.'

'No. Miss Billington was looking for Imogen, but I've double checked with her and she says she didn't go into the woods.'

'Which sounds reasonable,' said Tom. 'From what I saw the other day, it's a regular rabbit warren. There would have been no point trying to follow the kid in there.'

'The trouble is that almost everyone appears to have an alibi. Though there's no one to verify that Miss Billington didn't go into the woods, or that Lady Louisa was really resting in her room. We don't know how long Charles had on his own before he met up with Connie and Dolly seems to have had quite a long period unaccounted for. I suppose it's even possible that Mellie took advantage of Miss Billington's absence to slip away from the beach for a while. I haven't interviewed any of the children apart from Imogen, so I have nothing to confirm that Mellie stayed down there the whole time.'

'There's also this business about the diamond actually being held in trust for someone else,' said Tom. 'What did the Edgertons make of that, d'you think?'

'I don't honestly know. They probably weren't too bothered. Although the diamond is obviously valuable, they're not exactly hard up.'

'They didn't much like the idea of losing it. I mean, isn't that why they called us in, or rather called you in, in the first place?'

'I think that may have been as much because the disappearance of the diamond threw doubt on the way their grandfather had died as because the thing had been lost. If someone had stolen the diamond from the old man's room, while everyone else was out enjoying themselves at the beach, and old Mr Edgerton had been found at the bottom of the cliffs that evening, that would have suggested foul play, but that scenario doesn't work so obviously if someone only *hid* the diamond in the grounds.'

'I'm not so sure,' Tom mused. 'The person who hid the diamond wouldn't have anticipated Imogen's finding and removing it that same afternoon.'

'But why would you do that? Only hide the diamond in the grounds, rather than making off with it altogether, I mean?'

'Goodness only knows.'

'I suppose there could be reasons . . .' Fran began to answer her own question. 'What if you shared a room with someone else and you didn't want them to accidentally come across the stone? By hiding it out in the woods, you could choose your own time to come back and fetch it.'

'So going back to this question of the actual ownership of the stone . . .' Tom nudged her back on track.

'The news that Mrs Headingham claims to have been told that it actually belonged to someone else didn't exactly cause a furore. Mellie did question whether anyone would have anything in writing to prove ownership, but I expect they probably all thought deep down, as I did myself, that if no one has come forward to claim the diamond by now, then they're probably never going to.'

'How long had old Edgerton been in possession of it?'

'More than fifty years, I think.'

'His friend probably didn't make it back home from Africa, or wherever they met up. I don't suppose anyone else even knows about Edgerton having the diamond. And you haven't been able to make anything of the French connection?'

'Well, there is one tiny thing. Imogen's governess, Miss Billington, speaks noticeably good French and when I asked her where she'd learned, she told me it was in France.'

'And she's one of the people who hasn't got a solid alibi for the whole afternoon.'

They both fell silent for a moment, as a woman wearing a white wrap-around overall cleared away their tea cups and rather officiously wiped a couple of invisible spots from the wooden table.

'I think we've outstayed our welcome,' said Tom with a smile. 'Unless of course, you'd like another cup?'

'No, thanks; my train is due quite soon. There is one more thing I thought I ought to tell you.' Fran hesitated. It wasn't exactly part of the investigation, but somehow, it had to be said.

'Go on.'

'Eddie Edgerton has asked me to marry him.'

She had expected Tom to express surprise or remark that it

was all rather sudden, but after a brief, excruciating silence, he attempted a smile and said, 'And are congratulations in order?'

'Of course not. I . . . I hardly know him.'

'But you haven't turned him down?'

'He asked me not to give him an immediate answer, so I've promised that I'll think about it.'

Tom momentarily looked down as if he had just discovered something of immense interest on the empty table. 'His brother seems a jolly decent chap,' he said, looking up again and meeting her eyes. 'So I'm sure Eddie is too. You were dealt a rotten hand first time around and you deserve to find someone you can be happy with. He's a very lucky man, if you'll have him.'

Fran was about to say something else, but Tom stood up and lifted her suitcase. 'Let me see you to the gate of your platform. You don't want to be late for your train.'

TWENTY-FOUR

There was quite a pile of letters awaiting Fran's return home. Ada had left the fire laid and after Fran had put a match to the kindling, hung up her coat and hat, unsuccessfully attempted to mollify Mrs Sneglington, who was sulking as she always did after one of Fran's absences, and poured herself a large gin and tonic, she sat down to read through all her correspondence, saving the envelope addressed in Mo's handwriting to the end.

Mr Long, her solicitor, had written to inform her that he was in possession of the information that the named party in her divorce petition had recently given birth to a daughter. The paternity of the child, he wrote, was not in dispute and the court had been informed. In the meantime, he had also received notice that her decree nisi had been issued. She was part way there. If everything went smoothly, then according to what Mr Long had said of the process, the divorce would be made absolute in a matter of months, leaving Michael free to make an honest woman of Winnie the Ninny, while she would be . . . free . . . and alone.

There was a bill from the grocer to be settled and an advertisement for a horticultural suppliers from whom she had once purchased some rose bushes for the back garden. Of considerably more interest was a note from Miss Roche, one-time nurse to Mr Edgerton, saying that she would be pleased to meet Fran at a mutually convenient time, if she would care to suggest a date when she was likely to be in London, where Miss Roche now lived. Bother! London was an awfully long way to go, just to interview someone who hadn't even been on the premises at the relevant time. The address Roly's mother had originally provided was in Stoke-on-Trent, which was considerably more convenient. Her letter must have been forwarded to Miss Roche's latest abode. Of course, Charles and Dolly Edgerton lived in London too, according to Eddie, but without an introduction, she could hardly just call on them and start asking questions.

Her godmother had sent a letter from Clitheroe, bringing her up to date with various family news, a charity was soliciting her support for a Manchester orphanage (how on earth did they obtain one's name and address, she wondered) and finally there was the pale blue envelope, which she had immediately singled out by Mo's distinctive sloping hand.

Mo had feigned reluctance over the trip out to Malaya, but from the contents of her letter it was perfectly obvious that she was having a jolly good time, now that she had actually arrived. Mo was naturally sociable, Fran reflected, so she would enjoy the round of parties and get-togethers which seemed to be a feature of colonial life. It was a lively letter, filled with hilarious (and not always kind) descriptions of the various people Mo had met, all written in her own irrepressible style, which made Fran smile unconsciously as she read it. It was the contents of the final paragraph however, which stopped Fran in her tracks.

Absolutely between ourselves, though it may be too early to tell, I feel as sure as I can be that my mother-in-law's determination that the family line doesn't end with Terence, is going to be satisfied by the outcome of the trip.

Fran remembered now that it had been Terence's mother, more than anyone, who had urged that Mo should go out on a visit. Mo and Terence had such an odd relationship really, one might almost have called it a marriage of convenience. But in spite of that there was going to be a baby. Fran let the hand holding the sheets of notepaper droop into her lap. Everyone – even the utterly unmaternal Mo – seemed to be producing infants, left right and centre. The bedroom which faced east at Innominate House would make such a lovely nursery. She sighed and leaned her head against the back of the armchair. It had been such a long day. So many hours on the train that her head was still ringing with the rhythm of the wheels on the rails.

The telephone at her side began to ring.

She reached over with a weary hand to lift it. 'Hello? Newby Bridge 87.'

'Ah, Frances.' It was her mother's voice. 'You are home, I see. I thought I would save you the trouble of ringing to ask me how *I* am.'

'I have been home barely an hour, Mummy. I fully intended to telephone later this evening.' As usual, Fran found herself apologizing for some filial failure, real or imagined.

'Well, I have saved you the trouble.' The tone was unrelenting. 'I trust you have been enjoying yourself with your new friends in Devon. I did think that you might have sent me a postcard.'

'I'm sorry, Mummy. Yes, of course, I should have done.'

'I have not heard a single word from you. And anything might have happened to me in the meantime.' Her mother sniffed.

'Now really, Mummy, dear, I'm sure that if there had been the least sign of anything happening to you, someone would have contacted me immediately.'

Her mother sniffed audibly again. 'Well, now that you are back from your junketing, I'm the bearer of bad tidings, I'm afraid. Cousin Alice has died. The funeral is in the parish church at ten o'clock on Wednesday. I trust you will be available to accompany me.'

Fran suppressed the desire to say that naturally she would not miss the fun of a family funeral for anything. (It was hard to feel sad about her mother's cousin, Aunt Alice, who had been ninety if she was a day and had spent the past thirty years bullying her two much younger sisters without mercy.) Instead she said, 'I have some news for you too. I have heard that my divorce seems to be going through and that Michael and the . . . the other woman have had a daughter.'

'Frances! Have you no sensibility for my feelings at all? Can you imagine how dreadful it is to have such news conveyed over *an instrument*? I thought that I had made it very clear to you that I have no wish to know *what* is occurring with regard to these terrible divorce proceedings. I fear to think what your father would have had to say if he had lived to see such goings-on.'

For once, something inside Fran snapped. 'If *a telephone* is a suitable vehicle to inform someone of a death, then it must be equally suitable for news of a birth. I assume we are meeting at the house and I will see you at nine thirty on Wednesday.' Fran did not trouble to keep the asperity from her voice.

'Frances! Frances!'

Taking up a torn envelope from beside the phone, Fran crumpled it in her free hand, so that it rustled and crackled into the receiver. 'Oh dear,' she said, keeping her mouth at a distance. 'I think we're being cut off.' She placed her finger across the rest and held it there until she was sure it had had the desired effect and then replaced the receiver, experiencing a rather satisfying sense of wickedness as she did so.

When the telephone rang again a few moments later, she was very tempted to ignore it, but trying to take a stand against her mother always ended up being more trouble than it was worth, so she lifted the receiver and said reluctantly, 'Hello, Mummy.'

'Hello? Is that Mrs Black?' It was a male voice, definitely familiar and evidently surprised by the greeting.

'Oh, yes, it is. I'm so sorry, I was expecting someone else.'

'Fran? It's Roland Edgerton here.'

'Oh.' Fran had placed the voice now and thereby felt doubly foolish. 'Yes, it's me. I'm so sorry, you rather caught me unawares.'

'Did you have a good journey?'

'Yes, thank you.'

'Fran, the family have been talking things over and, first of all, we feel most awfully remiss in not offering you any kind of reward for the recovery of the diamond. Fees were never really discussed, but naturally—'

'Oh no, I don't charge a fee,' Fran broke in. 'I have been amply repaid with your friendship and hospitality, and besides, I did nothing very much to find the diamond. It was only a question of asking the right thing of the right person, because in the end, it wasn't really lost at all.'

'Come now, you are being far too modest. Thanks to you, the family has recovered a valuable piece of lost property and you most surely deserve a reward of some kind.'

'No, really, there isn't any need. And anyway, the whole of

the mystery isn't solved yet, is it? There is still the question of your grandfather's death.'

'We have been discussing that too.' Roland paused, as if deciding how to frame his words. 'The coroner's jury decided that it was an accident, and there has always been the strongest possibility that they were right.'

Fran said nothing. She had not shared most of her discoveries with the Edgertons. Ought she to do that now? Suppose she told Roland about the footsteps that Imogen had heard in the woods that afternoon? Was it overdramatic to imagine that such information could endanger the child, if the person who actually made those sounds on the path got to hear about it?

'It has always been a delicate matter.' Roland was speaking again. 'Mother was most concerned that rumours of a private investigation might begin to circulate, but now that the diamond has been found, any speculation regarding your mission here would be easily accounted for. Something had been mislaid and you managed to recover it, as simple as that.'

'So you don't wish me to continue making enquiries on your behalf?' Fran said aloud. The voice in her head whispered: *We don't give up, do we?*

'The general consensus is that it's best to accept the coroner's verdict. It's time to put aside the past, look forward and embrace the future – especially with Mellie's wonderful news. However, we do hope that you will come down and stay with us again very soon, as a family friend, rather than a lady detective.'

'Thank you,' said Fran. 'I shall look forward to it very much.'

'And you are absolutely sure that there is nothing we can do by way of a reward?'

'Absolutely nothing.'

It would have been rather embarrassing and sordid, Fran thought, to have named a price for her services. She was suitably gratified, however, when a delivery van arrived at the gate next day, bearing an enormous basket of spring flowers and an attached card, which read, *With sincere thanks from all at Sunnyside House.*

TWENTY-FIVE

I t did feel somewhat underhand to carry on making enquiries about the Edgerton family without their knowledge and against their wishes, but Fran recalled that she and Tom had not always enjoyed the blessing of those closely associated with their previous cases, in which their persistence had undoubtedly paid off and ultimately brought to book some very dangerous individuals, who might otherwise have gone on to do even more harm.

While, on the one hand, it was not terribly convenient that Miss Roche lived in London, on the other it provided a jolly good excuse for a trip down to the capital and a stay in that little hotel just off Trafalgar Square, which she and Mo had liked so much on a previous visit. What a pity Mo wasn't around to accompany her. They could have gone to the theatre together in the evening – one could hardly go alone. Instead Fran contented herself with a couple of hours in the Victoria and Albert Museum on the afternoon of her arrival, followed by a quiet supper in her hotel.

She occupied the first part of the following morning with a little window shopping. She had a couple of hours to fill, because Miss Roche had named eleven o'clock as a convenient time and nominated the portico of St Martin-in-the-Fields as their meeting place. Fran arrived a few minutes early for the rendezvous, whereas Monica Roche approached at precisely the nominated hour. 'Mrs Black?' She extended a hand and gave a firm handshake. She was a tall, strong woman, Fran noted, qualities which were presumably extremely useful in a nurse. She was somewhat older than Fran had expected, with iron grey hair, cut in a short, modern style, which would again have been extremely practical when undertaking her professional duties.

'My apologies for not inviting you to my home,' said Miss Roche. 'My mother is somewhat frail and finds visitors a trial.

There is a very pleasant tea room just round the corner, and I thought we could talk in there.'

'Please don't apologize,' said Fran. 'It is very kind of you to see me at all.'

'I have to own to a certain amount of self-interest,' Miss Roche said, as she led the way briskly across the road. 'Lady Edgerton was somewhat vague in her letter, merely saying that you were looking into a matter which concerned the family and would be most appreciative if I could spare some time. I simply cannot imagine what this matter might be and curiosity forced me to acquiesce.'

Fran had not intended to approach the purpose of the meeting until they were sitting down somewhere, face-to-face, but the clear note of enquiry in her companion's voice forced her to come clean immediately. 'I trust that we can speak confidentially, Miss Roche?'

'I am a trained nurse, Mrs Black. Confidentiality is my watch word.'

'Very well then. The thing is that after Mr Frederick Edgerton died, the family were faced with rather a puzzle. A valuable item appeared to have gone missing and coupled with that, the circumstances of Mr Edgerton's death were, shall we say, a little bit strange. The family hoped that I might be able to recover the item which had been lost and at the same time reassure them that Mr Edgerton's death had been nothing more than a tragic accident.'

'And have you?' Miss Roche turned to ask, as she held open a teashop door and stood back, allowing Fran to precede her.

'Have I?' Fran was taken aback by the abrupt nature of the question. *Every avenue leads to a teashop*, she thought, wondering about the wisdom of a cream horn, as she glanced at the display under a glass dome on the counter.

'Have you recovered the lost item, or managed to throw any additional light on the death of Mr Edgerton?'

'In a manner of speaking,' Fran said. 'The item has certainly been recovered.'

'May one ask – confidentially, of course – what this item is and where it was discovered?'

'It was a diamond. And in a sense, it was never lost. It was recovered from a little grotto in the grounds of Sunnyside House.'

The other woman flopped so heavily into her chair that Fran thought for a moment it would give way. 'A diamond, you say! And it was found in the grotto? When? By whom?'

'Imogen found it.'

'Imogen! That little monkey.' Miss Roche shook her head angrily. 'Of course, I'm not surprised it turned out to be Imogen who took it. She was always a wilful child and a terrible trial to her poor governess. Miss Billington always said the girl was inclined to tell fibs, and it appears that she was not above stealing things either.'

'Oh no, you misunderstand me,' said Fran. 'Imogen didn't steal the diamond from the house. She found it, when she was playing in the grotto. Someone else must have put the stone there in the first place.'

'How do you know that?'

The question took Fran by surprise again. It had been asked quite sharply, Fran noted. Miss Roche was clearly in the same camp as Mellie, so far as any assessment of Imogen's truthfulness or reliability went.

'Well . . . I suppose I don't know, for sure. Though I am inclined to believe that the circumstances of the find were as Imogen described them.'

'So how did Imogen tell you that she came to find this diamond?'

'She had gone off by herself on the afternoon that her grandfather died. In fact, she had run away from the beach in a temper and eluded her governess by going up into the woods. Once she got up there, she decided to play at treasure hunting, so she went to look in the grotto, which was, I believe, one of the usual places for putting clues and so forth when the family had a treasure hunt. According to Imogen, the little bag with the diamond in it was hidden up on a ledge, at the back of the grotto. She assumed it had been put there as part of one of the usual family games and so she took it back to the playroom with her. She had no idea of its worth. Later on, before the diamond was missed and the house searched, she actually returned it to its hiding place again and it had been there ever since.'

'I see.' Miss Roche nodded. Then added after a moment: 'A likely story, I must say.'

Fran decided it was about time that she became the interrogator. 'One of the things that I thought you might be able to help me with is the question of who knew about this diamond and would have known where to find it under normal circumstances. The family say that it was always kept in a small wall safe in Mr Edgerton's room?'

'That's correct.' Turning to the waitress who had appeared at her side, Miss Roche said, 'We will have a pot of tea for two and a plate of buttered crumpets, please. And do be sure that the crumpets are piping hot. There's nothing worse than indifferent crumpets,' she added, returning her full attention to Fran. 'Where were we? Ah, yes, the little wall safe. So far as I recall there were several small pieces of jewellery in there. Mr Edgerton used to get them out to show people occasionally. I think he liked to gloat over them. The diamond was probably the most valuable item in the safe. Not that I know very much about the relative worth of jewels. The key was kept in the drawer of a table in the same room. A ridiculous arrangement, if you ask me.'

'So in your opinion, it would have been quite easy for anyone to have taken the diamond?' asked Fran, putting the thought of cream horns firmly out of her mind.

The other woman considered this before answering. 'I wouldn't say that. It would have been almost impossible for a stranger. To begin with, how would they have known that the diamond was there at all? If anyone had come to the house at night, they would have been heard breaking in, and what's more Mr Edgerton slept in that same room, so they would surely have been afraid of waking him. He spent most of his days in there too, and he wasn't often left alone.'

'Except perhaps on your afternoons off?'

'Even then, a thief would have had to count on not being seen entering the house and on finding Mr Edgerton asleep.'

'So when do you think the diamond could have been stolen?'

'I should have thought it was obvious. The theft must have occurred in the days immediately after Mr Edgerton's death. There was seldom anyone in the library then. The child, Imogen, could easily have slipped in, unlocked the safe and taken out the bag with the stone in it and no one would have been any the wiser. The house is generally deserted during the afternoons. The Edgertons are a very outdoorsy crowd. The younger ones are always at the beach or on the tennis courts and Lady Edgerton herself is generally gardening. That's why no one saw old Mr Edgerton leave the house that afternoon.'

'Did you believe he was capable of pushing himself all the way up that path?'

'Well, he must have been, mustn't he? He didn't fly there.'

Why did brusque, capable women like this always make one feel such a prize idiot? Fran wondered. She decided to return to the question of the diamond. 'Imogen thought her grandfather had put the diamond in the grotto, as part of a game, because he'd put things there in the past.'

'I dare say he had at one time,' Miss Roche agreed. 'But not since he'd been confined to his wheelchair. As a matter of fact, I seem to recall that on at least one occasion when Miss Billington and myself had been roped in to help hide the clues on his behalf, we were asked to put something in the grotto. There's a sort of shelf in the back, half hidden, close to the roof. Is that where Imogen says she found the stone?'

'That's right,' Fran said. 'I suppose there isn't any question of him asking someone to hide the diamond there on his behalf, just before he died?'

'Oh, I wouldn't have thought so. He was a bit past organizing treasure hunts by then. And although he wasn't always entirely sensible, one can't imagine him suggesting to anyone that they should hide a diamond in the grounds of the house for him, and even if he did, who on earth would be fool enough to agree to such a thing?'

'You say that old Mr Edgerton wasn't always rational towards the end of his life?'

'It's a common problem with older patients,' said Miss Roche. 'They become a little bit forgetful, a little bit confused about things. Mr Edgerton wasn't too bad, most of the time, but occasionally he would start to ramble and become a little bit muddled in his ideas.'

'Someone told me that he took an irrational dislike to you at one point.'

'I wouldn't put it as strongly as that. He said once or twice that he thought I was looking at him strangely, but there, his eyesight had been failing for some time and I'm not convinced that he was focusing properly.'

'And I was also told that he claimed Mrs Remington, the cook, was trying to poison him.'

'That was only on one occasion. I'm not sure that he specifically blamed Mrs Remington. He said that his food tasted bitter and that it must be poisoned. I tasted it myself and there was nothing wrong with it at all, but I threw it away to humour him. I think he had got it into his head that someone might be trying to do away with him. There had been an accident with a log falling out of the fire and setting the hearthrug alight and that was what started him off on that track. It was all just his fancy.'

'When was the accident with the rug?'

'Let me see . . . it must have been in the late spring of 1928. It was quite late in the year to be having a fire, but it had been a chilly sort of evening so I had asked the maids to light a fire for him in the library.'

'And what happened exactly?'

'I had settled Mr Edgerton down and gone off-duty for the night. I fancied a breath of fresh air before going up to bed, so I got my coat, unlocked the front door and went out on to the terrace. It was lucky that I did, because I was only just outside the library window when I heard him shouting that the place was on fire. I rushed back, of course, but by the time I got to the front door people were already coming from all directions. There was quite a lot of smoke, but the fire was easily quenched and I made up a bed for Mr Edgerton in the morning room that night because the smell from the smoke was still quite bad in the library. I have to admit that I blame myself entirely for what happened. The maid must have built the fire up far too much, but I ought to have noticed that she had forgotten to put the fireguard in place. She was rather rushed, I suppose, what with there being the usual houseful of people. A novice's mistake, I'm afraid, and one which could have had terrible consequences for my patient.'

'Goodness,' said Fran. 'How terrible. So old Mr Edgerton had a narrow escape.'

'I suppose so. Though as I mentioned, I was still downstairs myself when it happened and could well have noticed something amiss and given the alarm myself if Mr Edgerton had not done so when he did. The smell of smoke was quite strong and enough to alert anyone who was nearby.'

'So there was a fire which he thought might not have been an accident and then he suspected he was being poisoned – that came afterwards, I suppose?' She waited for Miss Roche's nod before continuing. 'And was there anything else?'

'Anything else?'

'That might have made Mr Edgerton think that someone was trying to harm him? Apart from your giving him funny looks, of course.' Fran smiled, but her companion didn't join her in the joke.

'I cannot bring anything to mind. Ah, good, here comes the tea.'

Fran refused to be distracted by the arrival of tea and crumpets. 'And you mentioned the way old people sometimes ramble on a bit. Did you have anything specific in mind?'

'Not really. He sometimes talked about being a boy in London, seeing Queen Victoria ride by in a carriage, that kind of thing.'

'What about his days in Africa and abroad, when he was a young man making his fortune?'

'Nothing that I can bring to mind. Do you take sugar, Mrs Black?'

'Mrs Headingham – you know perhaps that Mrs Headingham was a very old friend of Mr Edgerton – told me an interesting story. She said that according to Mr Edgerton, the diamond which went missing hadn't actually belonged to him at all.'

'Really?' Miss Roche was concentrating on the transfer of a crumpet from one plate to another, a feat which was difficult to perform without butter dripping on to the tablecloth. 'He never said anything like that to me.'

'Did he ever mention an old friend, a Frenchman, called Georges Poussin?'

'Poussin? No. Though I'm not sure I would have remembered if he had. During the course of any given day, a person may say a great many things, the vast majority of which are not worth remembering or repeating. Allow me to pass you the crumpets.'

'Tell me, Miss Roche.' Fran shifted a crumpet, still hot from the grill and oozing with butter on to her own plate as she spoke. 'And please be assured that you can speak to me entirely in confidence: did you ever entertain the slightest suspicion that some member of the household might have been attempting to harm your patient?'

'Of course not.' The nurse spoke briskly. 'If I'd had the slightest suspicion of anyone, it would naturally have been my duty to go to the police.'

'But you must have thought it strange, when Mr Edgerton appeared to have pushed himself over the cliff.'

'Life is often strange. I believed that it was an accident. A tragic accident. As did the coroner's jury.'

'It was you who first realized what had happened, wasn't it? That must have been rather horrid.'

Miss Roche considered and for a moment she half smiled. 'The idea of death is not something mysterious and fearful for those of us who have, for many years, nursed the sick and the dying. I was at a field hospital near Passchendaele, Mrs Black. Nothing will ever surpass the horror of that.'

'I wonder,' Fran ventured, 'if you could tell me what you remember of the afternoon when you last saw Mr Edgerton alive and what happened when you returned from your afternoon off and discovered that he was missing.'

'I am sure I can't tell you anything which you don't already know. When I left my charge, he was eating his lunch, which had been brought to him on a tray in the library as usual. I expect I wished him good afternoon and said that I would see him later, but I cannot honestly remember anything in particular about what was said. I often spent my free afternoons alone, but on this particular day I was collected by motor car and taken out for tea, by a friend. We went to the Palace Hotel in Torquay. I understand that the local police sought corroboration of our movements from the hotel staff.' The nurse's tone betrayed a hint of indignation and she paused momentarily before continuing: 'When my friend dropped me back at Sunnyside House it was approaching six o'clock. I seldom remained away from the house into the evening, although I would have been perfectly entitled to do so, had I wished.

'On my return I think I went straight to the library and when I saw that Mr Edgerton wasn't there I went on to the terrace, naturally assuming that he must be outside with the rest of the family. From what I can remember, they were all lounging about out there, after a day on the beach, and when I asked after my patient it became clear that no one had seen the old gentleman for several hours.

'Jamieson, the butler, was fetched, I remember, but none of the servants could throw any light on the matter, and as for the maids who should have taken in Mr Edgerton's tea that afternoon, each thought the other had done it.' Miss Roche sniffed contemptuously and took another small bite of crumpet, which she chewed and swallowed, before continuing. 'Some of us checked the downstairs rooms and then Mr Roland Edgerton instructed everyone to split up and start searching the grounds. His grandfather could not manage the stairs, so once all the ground floor rooms had been checked, it was obvious the search had to be widened.'

'Everyone must have been very concerned,' suggested Fran. 'I assume he had never gone missing before?'

'Certainly not during my time there. There was some sort of discussion between the family about who would go in which direction. I decided not to waste any time and took the path which leads straight from the terrace towards the sea. It goes along the edge of the east wood, then follows the edge of the cliffs to a viewpoint, where there is a shelter.'

'I know it,' said Fran.

'I thought it likely that Mr Edgerton had gone that way, because it was not as difficult for the wheelchair as most routes through the garden and I had often taken him that way at his request, because he enjoyed the view. I walked right along the path to a point beyond the shelter, where one can see for a considerable distance across the clifftop, but there was no sign of the old man, so I began to return by the same way and that was when I noticed the flattened grass, leading over the edge of the cliffs.'

'Can you remember what it looked like?'

'What do you mean?'

'Well, how much was the grass flattened? Could you see clear tracks, where the wheels had been? Did there appear to be any other signs of the grass being flattened?'

'I don't remember it in any kind of detail. I just noticed that the grass had been disturbed in some way and I'm afraid I immediately feared the worst. I got down on my hands and knees and crawled across to the edge and, when I put my head over, I could see that there was something on the rocks below.'

'That was very brave of you,' said Fran. 'Going right to the edge like that.'

'Not really.' Miss Roche shrugged. 'I have a pretty good head for heights and I knew the ground was not likely to give way under me. Not if it had taken the weight of Mr Edgerton and his wheelchair.'

Again Fran felt as if she had been censured as a somewhat spineless female, who could not cope with heights, or death or possibly even the sight of a drop of blood on some band-ages. A thought suddenly struck her. 'On the night when Mr Edgerton's rug caught fire, you mentioned that the maid was particularly busy because there was a houseful of people. Were there some overnight guests?'

'There were. Mr Charles Edgerton and his wife were staying that weekend, along with some cousins of Mr Roland.'

'Are these the same cousins who were staying when old Mr Edgerton died?'

'No, I don't believe so. They were grown-up cousins. They were the son and daughter-in-law of one of old Mr Edgerton's daughters.'

So no common denominator there, thought Fran, *apart from the coincidence of Charles and Dolly Edgerton's being there, which might be significant.* Aloud, she said, 'It must have been rather trying, living in a house with so many visitors coming and going.'

'It made no difference to me. In fact, it made my job easier, because it meant a change of faces and some different company for my patient. Some of my posts have involved quite lonely invalids, whereas Mr Edgerton remained surrounded by his family.'

'You must have been in lots of interesting situations,' Fran said. 'Of course, Sunnyside House is in quite an isolated position. It must be a good deal more convivial to have a position down here in London. I hope you have found a nice situation?'

'I have given up nursing professionally, in order to take care of my mother.'

'Oh, I see . . . I'm so sorry . . .'

'There is no need to be. I always intended Sunnyside House to be my final post. When I left, I spent three weeks in Stoke-on-Trent, taking care of an old friend who was convalescing after an operation and then I came home to live with Mother.'

'And of course,' Fran hastened on, feeling somehow that she had led the conversation up an awkward cul-de-sac, 'it was not so very lonely at Sunnyside House. There were always plenty of visitors and I believe you had a friend in Miss Billington.'

'Ah, yes. Poor Miss Billington, having to cope with that monster Imogen.' Miss Roche grimaced at the remembrance of the child. 'I do not envy Miss Billington one little bit.'

'Imogen is a rather difficult girl.'

'Miss Billington is trapped in an impossible situation.'

'But surely,' Fran demurred, 'if she was unhappy in her position, she could give notice?'

'She cannot possibly give notice and seek another situation, unless Lady Edgerton provides her with a good reference.'

'But why ever wouldn't she? I thought Miss Billington a most competent governess.'

'Which is why Lady Edgerton will do everything in her power to ensure that Miss Billington remains at Sunnyside House.' A note of bitterness had entered Miss Roche's voice. 'I assure you that these families have no scruples whatsoever about holding on to people who are useful to them. Firstly the Edgertons know how difficult it would be to find someone willing to take on a child like that; secondly they won't want gossip circulating, via their ex-governess, that Imogen is uncontrollable or off her head. Miss Billington is well and truly trapped. Only a complete change in her personal circumstances would facilitate an escape.'

'Oh dear, I hadn't thought of it like that,' said Fran. Deciding that a change of subject was advisable, she continued: 'And

there was another friend, wasn't there? The one with whom
you spent your afternoon, the day that Mr Edgerton died.'

'A short-lived friendship,' said Miss Roche.

'May I ask who this person was?' asked Fran, who knew
perfectly well, but was intrigued by the rumours of a possible
romance.

Miss Roche flushed. 'I rather feel like saying that you may
not, but since that might create undue suspicion, I will tell
you that it was a Mr Moncrieff, who was in service with the
family at Baddeley Court.'

'I thought you told me that the person who collected you
had a motor car.'

'Mr Moncrieff was the Baddeleys' chauffeur. He was sometimes permitted to use one of their motor cars on his day off.'

'And you became friendly with him while working at
Sunnyside House?'

Miss Roche was stony-faced. 'Mr Moncrieff and I had an
acquaintance. It is impossible, I'm afraid, to avoid gossip and
speculation in any medium-sized or large establishment. I regret
to say that the servant class are always overly interested in
everyone else's private life and I think some inaccurate assump-
tions may have been made regarding myself and Mr Moncrieff.'

'I see.' Fran again tried and failed to engage her companion
in a smile. 'I notice that you spoke of his employment with
the Baddeleys in the past tense.'

'That is correct. Like myself, Mr Moncrieff was approaching
retirement. He had been promised a small pension and a cottage
on the Baddeley estate and I believe he has now stood down
from his post and turned his hand to growing vegetables, which
seemed to be the summit of his ambitions.'

'Mr Moncrieff is single, I assume.'

'You assume correctly.'

'But perhaps he had hopes . . .' Fran left the statement
hanging in the air.

'If you are trying to suggest that something of a romance
existed between myself and Mr Moncrieff, then I can assure
you that it most definitely did not.'

TWENTY-SIX

After her tea and crumpets with Miss Roche, Fran took herself for a brisk walk along the Embankment, towards Cleopatra's Needle and the extravagant bulk of the Hotel Cecil. Miss Roche's story of the fire had given her pause for thought. Suppose old Mr Edgerton had been right about someone trying to kill him? Was it just a coincidence that his son Charles had been staying at Sunnyside House both at the time of the fire and when the wheelchair went over the cliff?

Charles and Dolly Edgerton remained a missing link in the investigation. She had already looked up their address in the London telephone directory, but what possible pretext could she use for calling on them? Whatever excuse she managed to invent, any visit would be sure to get back to the Edgertons, which was potentially embarrassing. After all, the Edgertons had taken her into their home and treated her as a friend and Eddie . . . well, Eddie would be justifiably upset by any deception on her part.

On the other hand, what if she was open with Eddie? Eddie had declared himself willing to do anything for her and if she took him into her confidence, might he not be able to organize an introduction to his uncle? She paused to allow for the passage of a tram, before crossing the road and turning purposefully back to her hotel. Then she remembered that the hotel would mark up the cost of any trunk call on her bill and decided to use a public telephone box instead. It would be quicker too.

The call, when it was eventually connected, was answered by Jamieson. 'Oh no, Mrs Black. I'm afraid that Mr Edward is not at home. Miss Henrietta is at home, if you wish me to fetch her to the telephone?'

'Oh . . . er . . . no . . . please don't trouble her. Can you tell me when he will be back?'

'Not until the day after tomorrow, madam. He is staying at his club in London.'

'I see. I am in London myself. Can you tell me which is his club?'

'It's the Bath Club, madam.'

'Oh dear, I don't know where that is.'

'It's in Dover Street, madam. Just off Piccadilly.'

'Oh, thank you, Jamieson. You've been most helpful.'

The Bath Club was only a short walk away. *I can leave him a note*, she thought, *and he can call me at my hotel. I can tear a page out of my notebook.* Then again, they were sure to have some notepaper available at the desk.

Only as she turned the corner and approached the front door of Eddie's club did it occur to Fran that they probably did not admit women – perhaps not even to leave messages. She had slowed her pace in anticipation of this problem when none other than Eddie himself appeared, bowling down the front steps in his usual exuberant fashion. He saw her at once. 'Fran!'

'Hello, Eddie.'

'What are you doing here? Don't say you were coming to see me?'

'Actually I was.'

'How absolutely splendid! No point in asking my favourite lady detective how she tracked me down.'

'There's no mystery about it.' Fran laughed. 'I telephoned Sunnyside House and Jamieson told me where you were.'

'Did you want to speak to me about something special? Well, yes – damn silly question – of course you must have done, or you wouldn't have telephoned. Is it – dare I ask – your answer . . . ?'

'No, no,' she said quickly. 'It's nothing like that. You see, well . . . It's like this . . . Once I'm on the trail of a mystery, I don't . . . can't . . . just give up. And . . . and I don't believe your grandfather fell accidentally.'

'So you are still investigating,' Eddie finished for her, his expression giving away nothing.

'I went to see Miss Roche this morning,' she confessed. 'I want to talk with your uncle Charles and his wife too, and I need your help in getting to speak with them, but also, I didn't want to go behind your back. I really hope you don't think too badly of me. I know the rest of your family want me to desist from asking any more questions.'

Eddie digested this for a moment or two before saying, 'So you haven't really pursued me to London because you can't bear to live another day without me? Ah well, I guessed as much. But at least you can dine with me this evening.'

'Oh no, I can't,' protested Fran. 'I'm still waiting for my decree absolute, you see. I can't just go about, dining with other men. Besides which, you must have plans already. Why are you in London?'

'I had proposed to meet a few friends for dinner and then go and listen to the new pianist at the Little Lotus Club in Soho. He's fresh over from Chicago and I haven't heard him yet. They say he's jolly good.'

'Then of course you must go and meet your friends.'

'Rubbish. I fully intend to cancel and have dinner with you.'

'But I've already explained that's out of the question.'

'Come now, do you want to go and meet my uncle and aunt this afternoon or not? As you admitted yourself, you need me to make the arrangements, but only a promise of dinner this evening is going to get you into their company.'

'But that's not fair.'

'I think you'll find that all's fair in love and war.'

Fran hesitated. If she went to dinner with Eddie, who could possibly know? Besides which, the prospect of his company was much more alluring than the thought of a lonely evening at her hotel.

'Come on,' he said, sensing her acquiescence. 'Let's go back inside and I'll use the club telephone to make sure that Charles and Dolly are at home.'

They took a cab to the modern block where Charles Edgerton and his wife had their apartment. An enclosed lift conveyed them to the third floor, where a uniformed maid answered their summons on the doorbell and showed them into a drawing room which had been furnished in the latest style, so that it looked more like a stage set than a room in which someone actually lived. The sole occupant of the room was a tall, middle-aged man, running to fat, who rose to greet them.

While Eddie performed the introductions, Fran took in the

fact that Dolly was not present. It was equally impossible not to notice that a faintly awkward air hung over the party. The two men initially did the talking, exchanging news of their various relatives with one very obvious exception, until Eddie said, 'And how is Dolly? Will she be joining us?'

'I'm afraid not.' Charles looked extremely uncomfortable.

Fran had also observed that Charles Edgerton appeared to be rather flushed, as if he were finding the room uncomfortably warm.

'Oh dear. Don't tell me she's unwell?'

'No. At least . . . not so far as I know.'

'Is she . . . out somewhere?'

'You could put it like that, I suppose. No point beating about the bush and I dare say it will soon get around. Dolly has left me.'

Eddie was momentarily silenced. After a moment, he said, 'Well, I'm most frightfully sorry to hear that.'

'No, you're not.' Charles Edgerton stood up abruptly and crossed the room to the sideboard, where he helped himself to a whisky from the decanter, without bothering to offer anyone else a drink. 'You all despised Dolly, you know you did.'

'Oh, now, Uncle Charles, that's not entirely fair,' Eddie protested, while Fran wished the ground would swallow her up. She had envisaged that her interview with Charles and Dolly might be awkward, but this far surpassed her expectations.

'And now I suppose you've come to announce your engagement.'

'Not at all. Why ever would you think that?'

'Since when have you been in the habit of paying social calls on me – and with a young lady in tow? What I am supposed to think? Well, you treat her properly if you want to hang on to her, that's my advice. These modern young women won't stand for the sort of nonsense which went on in the old days, I can tell you.'

'Uncle Charles, I really don't think this is a fit topic—'

'Nonsense, boy! *Mrs* Black, you said her name was. So she's not some innocent young flower maiden, is she?'

It had become apparent to Fran that this was by no means Charles Edgerton's first drink of the day.

Eddie was about to protest more forcibly, but his uncle gave him no time. 'It's my own fault,' he said, waving his glass in their direction. 'She was a good little woman, Dolly, my own good little girl, but I played fast and loose with her affections, you see. It's all my own fault,' he repeated. 'I'd do it all differently, given the chance. I want her back, but she won't listen to me. "No more chances," she said. Told me I'd humiliated her. Said she could put up with my toffee-nosed family, but she wouldn't put up with any more flings.' He gestured the glass in Eddie's direction again. 'Toffee-nosed, that's what she called you.'

'Well,' said Eddie. 'She's probably quite right. I say, Uncle Charles, I can't help feeling that you shouldn't have another drink just yet. You see, Mrs Black wants to ask you some questions.'

His uncle did not appear to have heard. Pivoting back towards the sideboard in a somewhat unsteady fashion, he picked up the glass stopper belonging to the decanter and regarded it uncertainly. 'Dear, sweet Dolly. I do miss her, you know.'

'Yes,' Eddie began, but Fran silenced him with a swift glance. Under the circumstances it felt pretty much impossible to frame any questions, not least because Charles Edgerton was becoming less coherent by the minute.

'If you were to give us Dolly's address,' she suggested, 'then we could go and tell her that you want her to come back and are promising to turn over a new leaf.'

'That's jolly civil of you. Go and see her, you say? The feminine touch, smoothing things over and all that?' A new idea seemed to strike him. 'D'you want a quick snifter, before you go? Bit of Dutch courage, eh?'

'No, that won't be necessary. But if you could just give us her address.'

'Address?' Charles glanced down at the glass stopper again, almost as if he was surprised to find it in his hand. 'Dolly's address? She's gone back to her brother's house: 23 Shenstone Hill in Croydon.'

'Thank you.' Fran rose to her feet and Eddie followed suit.

'I am so sorry,' he said, as soon as they had put the lift doors between themselves and Charles Edgerton. 'I knew Uncle Charles was fond of a drink, but I never imagined that he would be in such a state in the middle of the afternoon. He gave me no indication that there was any problem when I telephoned.'

'Please, don't think anything of it at all.'

'And you haven't had any chance to question him.'

'I think he was fast becoming too intoxicated to answer me sensibly, don't you?'

'Then you will need to return at some point, I suppose. You had better let me come with you. I don't want you being alone with such a boor.'

'I don't believe it will be necessary to question him. I'm much more interested in speaking with his wife.'

'Dolly? But surely my uncle was alone and unaccounted for, whereas Dolly was playing tennis with me?'

'Your uncle was not alone. I have good reason to believe that he spent most of the afternoon in bed with one of the housemaids.' There, it was out in the open. She felt a flush rise in her cheeks, as she avoided his eye, resolutely facing the lift doors as they slid apart.

Eddie swallowed hard. 'My word, but you do get to the bottom of things, don't you? How frightfully sordid.'

'It's the sort of conduct which explains why Dolly has left him.' Fran headed for the big swing doors which led into the street and Eddie skipped ahead to open them for her.

'What an absolute cad,' he said. 'I must say that I feel quite ashamed on behalf of my family.'

'Now,' she said briskly, 'I wonder which station we will need for a train out to Croydon.'

'That will take far too long,' Eddie said. 'I'll hail a cab.'

'Tell me,' he said, when they were installed in the back of a taxi and Eddie had given the driver Dolly's address. 'Do you intend to continue with your life as a lady detective, once you have remarried?'

'As I've already told you, I'm not a lady detective. It isn't as if I advertise my services in the newspapers. It's pure chance that your brother heard about what Tom and I had managed to find out last year in Durley Dean.'

'Tom? That would be Tom Dod?'

'Yes. The case involved his great aunt.'

'Oh, I see.'

In the short silence which followed, Fran wondered how much Eddie did see. She felt as if she ought to explain about her friendship with Tom, but it was complicated.

'Of course you're being far too modest as usual,' Eddie said cheerfully. 'When Roly contacted Mr Dod, he said at once that all the credit was yours. You were just the same over the discovery of the diamond, telling everyone that it was mainly down to Imogen that it was found.'

'No, really . . .' Fran began.

'The thing is,' Eddie continued, 'I wouldn't mind, you know, if you carried on your detective work, just so long as you let me drive you about and act as your faithful Passepartout. By the way, did you manage to get anything useful out of Monica?'

'I'm not sure. There were one or two things. You know, I think Henrietta may have been right about her being romantically involved with the Baddeleys' chauffeur at one stage, even though she denied it. She was . . . well . . . almost too emphatic.'

'Monica? Romantically involved? You do surprise me. I always thought she must be the sort who had a heart of stone.'

'I suppose he was questioned at the time and asked to confirm that they'd spent the afternoon together?'

'I'm pretty sure he was. I definitely remember something being said about the police checking that Monica had been seen at the hotel where she said they went for tea. I'm surprised that anyone would have enquired as far into it as that. It wasn't a full-blown murder enquiry, after all.'

'I suppose not,' Fran agreed. 'What mattered was that Monica was off the premises, not what she was doing, or who she was with – particularly as there's no question of seeing anyone else *on* the premises.'

'If anyone had wanted to harm Grandfather, Monica's afternoon off was just about the only time to do it.'

'That isn't quite true,' said Fran. 'She must often have left him alone for a few minutes, or even longer every day. I bet he had a nap in the afternoons and she didn't sleep in his room at night. There were other opportunities and it may be that someone had tried to hurt him on previous occasions, without the rest of the family realizing it.'

'Gosh! Are you saying that there was skulduggery afoot under our very noses and we just didn't see it?' Eddie sounded both excited and amused, but then his voice changed as he said, 'But you know, I can't really believe it. I mean, we're just not that sort of family.'

'Why look,' Fran interrupted. 'Isn't that Croydon clock tower? We must be almost there already.'

When they reached Shenstone Hill they found that it was a typical suburban street, lined with tall, thin terraced houses; respectable but slightly faded, where the arrival of a taxi was an unusual event. Dolly must have either seen or heard the car, for she swung the front door open before Eddie had time to apply the knocker. Recognizing one of her two visitors, she made no attempt to disguise her surprise.

'Hello, Dolly,' Eddie said. 'May I introduce my friend, Mrs Black? We would very much appreciate a few minutes of your time if it's not too much bother. Perhaps if we might come inside?'

Dolly looked momentarily doubtful, but then invited them into the front parlour. 'Please sit down,' she said. 'It isn't what you're used to, I don't suppose. My brother Albert works on the railways,' she added, as if this provided elucidation to an unasked question. 'He's on duty at the present time and his wife, Ellen, has taken the baby to the park. What was it you were wanting exactly?'

Eddie glanced at Fran, who said, 'We called at your flat, hoping to speak with yourself and your husband today, Mrs Edgerton, and your husband told us that you had left him. He was very anxious to get a message to you. He wants you to forgive him and says he will turn over a new leaf, if you will only return.'

'Dear me.' Dolly's face relaxed into a half smile. 'Poor old Charlie. I suppose I will go back then.'

'You will?' Fran was positively flabbergasted at the ease with which Dolly had capitulated.

'Well, I can't stay here, can I?' Dolly lifted her shoulders into an expressive shrug. 'He's a kind man really, and he's got a good heart, my Charlie, but he will keep panting after other girls. When he took up with that Edna from the bakery, well, that was just about the giddy limit and out I walked. It seems that it has taught him a lesson. I might manage to keep him on the leash a bit longer this time.'

Fran could not help noticing the way Dolly mangled her words, 'Hai can't stay he-ah, can hai?'

'So,' said Eddie. 'Happy ending all round, eh? Jolly good show.'

'What are you then?' Dolly turned to Fran. 'One of those new-fangled marriage counsellors, are you?'

'Nothing like that,' said Fran. 'The thing is that now we have passed on your husband's message, it would be splendid if you could do something for us in return.'

'And what would that be?' A hint of wariness appeared in Dolly's eyes. She was very pretty in a superficial sort of way, Fran thought, but behind the pretty face there was something much harder and more calculating.

'All I want is for you to think back to a couple of occasions when you and your husband were staying at Sunnyside House. First of all there was the day when – and I'm sorry to raise something so painful – when you saw your husband meeting a housemaid called Connie, in the garden. I think you'd followed him up from the beach, when he said he was going for a walk.'

'What of it?'

'I want you to tell me if you saw anyone else at all between leaving the beach and seeing your husband with the maid.'

Dolly looked puzzled. 'There was no one else there.'

'What about after you saw them?'

'What do you mean?'

'Can you tell me what you did after you'd seen them and who was the next person you saw after that?'

'I didn't do anything. I suppose I should have wanted to tear her eyes out, the little cat, but to tell you the truth I just felt humiliated. I wondered if all his la-di-da family knew what he was getting up to and whether they were all laughing at me.' She shot a swift look at Eddie. 'If you must know, I just stayed where I was. There was a little rustic bench, just to the side of the path and I sat down on it and had a bit of a cry. Then I thought I'd better go and show my face at the tennis court, otherwise someone might ask what I'd been doing and I wouldn't have known what to say.'

'And you didn't see anyone else at all in the garden?'

'No. Not until I got to the tennis court. Why? Is it important?'

'Probably not. You see, there was some slight suggestion of an intruder in the grounds, but you know nothing about that?' Fran tried to ignore Eddie's quizzical expression. He didn't know about the footsteps heard in the wood, or the car seen by Max.

Dolly shook her head.

'Now the other occasion was almost a year ago, when you were again staying at Sunnyside House and there was a fire, in old Mr Edgerton's room. Can you remember that?'

'I'm hardly likely to forget it,' said Dolly. 'Being woken up like that, people shouting and screaming and rushing along the corridor. And in the end it was only a bit of wood smouldering on the hearthrug, or so I believe.'

'You didn't think your father-in-law was ever in any great danger then?'

Dolly shrugged again. 'I didn't really think about it. I just supposed it to be an accident. But I think that you're hinting at something else, aren't you? Is it that you think someone tried to set fire to the house and when that didn't work, they pushed the old man over the edge of the cliffs?'

'It's only a remote possibility,' said Fran.

'That's how it would have happened in the flickers, isn't it?' Dolly nodded as much to herself as to her visitors. 'The villains would have crept into the house while the old fellow was asleep, tied him up and gagged him, so's he couldn't raise the alarm, then wheeled him out into the garden and shoved him over the cliff.'

'I suppose so,' said Fran. 'Anyway, thank you for your time.' She rose to her feet and appeared to stumble slightly. In reaching for the mantleshelf to steady herself, she contrived to knock an envelope, which had been propped there, on to the hearthrug. 'Oh dear, I'm so sorry. It's these wretched shoes. No please, let me . . .' She bent to retrieve the envelope as she spoke. It was evidently an item of unopened post, awaiting the return of the intended recipient. 'It was most generous of you to see us,' Fran went on, as she replaced the envelope in its former position. 'And I do hope things can be worked out between you and Mr Edgerton.'

TWENTY-SEVEN

E ddie picked Fran up from her hotel at 7.45. She had already protested about having 'nothing fancy' to wear, but he'd waved this aside. 'We won't go anywhere public or grand,' he assured her. 'I know just the place.'

He had made a reservation at a small French restaurant, which stood, at the end of a shadowy side street, just off the Strand. Here a waiter wearing a long white apron, escorted them into a booth which had candles on the table to supplement the very subdued electric lighting. 'No one will see us here,' Eddie said. 'So you can rest assured that your divorce proceedings will not be compromised.'

'I imagine you are right,' said Fran. 'Given that it's so dim in here, we can barely see each other.'

'Next time I take you to dinner in London, it will be sparkling chandeliers at the Savoy, I promise.'

Fran was prevented from making an answer by the arrival of the waiter, with menus and a wine list, over which Eddie ran a swift glance, before stating that they would have a bottle of the Chateau Margaux.

'You know,' he said, when the waiter had gone off to fetch the wine, leaving them to choose their food. 'This sleuthing business is fascinating, isn't it? The way you find out clues, just by talking to someone.'

'And what clues did you feel we got from Dolly?'

'Well, she made a jolly good point about Grandfather being tied up. I expect it had occurred to you ages ago, but I had never thought of it that way.'

'What do you mean?'

'Well, it's obvious, when you think about it, that Grandfather wouldn't have gone willingly. Or at least he would have done if he'd wanted to be taken out for a walk but suppose he didn't. If there was "a villain", as Dolly puts it, that person couldn't have risked Grandfather protesting when he was taken out of the house. I mean, we mightn't have heard him if he'd cried out at the very last minute, when he realized that he was going over the edge, but if he'd shouted out when he was inside the house, or very close to it, there's every chance that one of the servants would have heard him and come to see what was going on.'

'So you think the only sure way of pulling this off would have been to tie him up in order to prevent him from throwing himself out of the chair? And gagging him to prevent any noise?'

Eddie nodded enthusiastically. 'That's the ticket.'

'And when your grandfather's body was found,' Fran said gently, 'was his body tied to the wheelchair or a gag found around his mouth?'

Eddie sighed theatrically. 'I'm not cut out for this lark at all, am I? So what the circumstances really tell us is that Grandfather either went willing – perhaps even propelling himself – or else . . .'

'He either knew and trusted the person, or else when he was taken from the house, he was dead already,' Fran finished for him.

'Nothing had been disturbed in the library,' Eddie mused. 'There weren't any bloodstains. Of course, if you strangled someone, then I suppose . . .'

'Look out,' said Fran, 'the waiter is on his way back. He'll be expecting us to order and I haven't even looked at the menu yet.'

Once decisions had been made and the waiter had left them alone again, Eddie resumed his speculation. 'Dolly suggested a villain coming in from outside, but it would be quite difficult – and certainly pretty risky – to attempt to approach the house without being seen.'

'She probably thought it was an outsider, because I suggested to her that there might have been an intruder. I thought that was better than letting her think other members of the party were being investigated.'

'There isn't really any evidence of an intruder, is there?' Eddie sounded sober. 'If someone did murder Grandfather, then it must have been what the police would call "an inside job".'

'I'm afraid it does look that way.'

'You know, nothing much is ever said, but I reckon Uncle Charles is pretty short of the readies.' He allowed the comment to hang in the air before asking: 'Is that maid able to vouch for him the whole afternoon?'

'I'm afraid not. She left him in the bedroom and went back to her duties.'

'Oh dear,' said Eddie. 'That's not good. And I suppose there must be a few other members of the household with periods of the afternoon unaccounted for.'

'No one saw your mother all afternoon. Imogen went missing for a substantial period, and Miss Billington too, though it is hard to see Miss Billington's motive, unless she had intended to steal the diamond.' Fran decided it was better not to mention that the governess might have had her reasons for stealing the diamond. If Miss Roche was right, then Miss Billington could have grown to resent her employers. What was it Miss Roche had said? *Only a complete change of personal circumstances would facilitate her escape.*

'But why would she hide it in the grotto? That doesn't make any sense.'

'None of it seems to make any sense,' Fran said. 'That's the problem. There are also the other suspicious incidents. There was an occasion when your grandfather thought that his food tasted strange and then there was the fire in his room. I find it odd that no one mentioned that incident to me until Miss Roche did.'

'The poison episode was just Grandfather's fancy. There couldn't have been any problem with his food, because after he'd complained Monica tasted it and found nothing wrong at all. As for the fire, when you put it like this, well, of course, it sounds suspicious, but at the time everyone assumed it was a pure accident.'

'What do you remember about that night?'

'Let's see . . . We'd had some people to dinner, but they were all long gone. Everyone had gone up to bed and the house was completely quiet. I had put my light out, but I wasn't quite asleep, when I heard Grandfather suddenly yelling fit to bust. Naturally I jumped out of bed and ran out on to the landing at pretty much the same moment as Hen. Then everyone else started to appear and we all went dashing downstairs.

'I was one of the first down and of course we could smell the smoke even before anyone opened the library door. I seem to remember that there was a blazing fire in the grate and a part burned lump of wood had fallen from the fire and set alight the hearthrug. We were in the nick of time, I think. The armchair nearest the fire was starting to smoulder and in another minute or so it would have caught properly and the whole room – maybe the whole house – would have gone up. I grabbed Grandfather's wheelchair and helped him into it, while Roly yelled for people to fetch water and began to tackle the fire. When I got Grandfather out into the hall – which wasn't easy, as people were all scooting about, getting in one another's way – I remember Monica came to help and once she took over, I dashed along the passage and grabbed a bucket of water from Jamieson, who'd just brought it from the scullery.'

'Was there much damage?'

'We were jolly lucky. The library had to be repainted and the carpet replaced. The rug was a goner, but I think Mother managed to get the armchair reupholstered.'

'And did your grandfather explain what had happened?'

'According to him, he just woke up and found the place was burning.'

'And was there any investigation as to what had caused the fire?'

'Well, only among ourselves. One of the maids had lit the fire and she claimed that she hadn't banked it up overmuch and said that she'd left the guard in place, but there of course, she would say that, wouldn't she? Monica was a bit more honest. She said that she thought the guard was in front of the fire when she'd left the room, but she couldn't absolutely swear to it. I think she rather blamed herself for what had happened.'

'I suppose it would have been quite easy for someone to sneak downstairs and slip into the library after your grandfather had fallen asleep, in order to interfere with the fire?'

'I suppose so. It would have been easy enough to remove the fireguard, then use the poker or the fire tongs to drag the burning wood out on to the rug. Pretty risky strategy though. I mean, one could have gone back upstairs and ended up trapped in the fire.'

'I doubt it,' said Fran. 'If I were plotting something like that, I'd just give it a little while to allow time for my victim to be overcome by the smoke and then if no one else raised the alarm, I would go out on to the landing and do it myself, claiming that I'd smelled smoke or heard something.'

'Of course. It's obvious when you put it like that.'

'And I believe your uncle Charles was staying in the house on the night of the fire.'

Eddie nodded.

'Tell me, do you happen to know what Dolly's name was, before she and Charles were married?'

'No. The wedding took place abroad. They only wrote and told us about it once the deed had been done, so to speak.'

'And the occasion when your grandfather thought someone had tried to poison him – were your uncle Charles and his wife staying then too?'

'Oh no, it was just the usual household.'

Their own food, when it came, was excellent. By unspoken mutual consent, speculations about violent death were suspended in favour of more cheerful topics. Eddie was disappointed to discover that Fran was returning home the following day and remained deaf to his pleading that she stay on.

'We could have gone to the theatre. There's a fearfully jolly show on at the Criterion. And I know a very nice place for a late supper afterwards.'

'I have to go home,' Fran said firmly, though a voice in her head asked her why. There was nothing pressing which could not be put off.

Eddie refrained from any further imprecations or remotely romantic utterances until they had been served with tiny cups of strong coffee accompanied by little tots of brandy. After Fran had taken an initial sip of coffee, she rested her hand momentarily on the starched white tablecloth and Eddie reached across and took it in his.

'Darling Fran, I promise not to put you under any pressure. I know you must have had a terrible time and that your heart has probably been broken. But you see, I keep imagining us standing under the stars together. In the garden at Innominate House, or perhaps on the deck of that ocean liner, which is taking us all around the world. It would make me the happiest man alive if you would say "yes" – and I would do my best to make you very happy in return. Only tell me that you are still thinking it over . . . at least tell me that.'

'I am . . . still thinking it over.'

He continued to hold her hand as they sat for a moment or two in silence, only relinquishing it when the waiter approached to see whether they required anything more.

On the short walk back to her hotel, Fran steered the conversation to more general topics, telling him about the time last year when she and Mo had come down to London and seen the Astaires in *Funny Face* at the Winter Garden. Apart from commenting that rumours of Miss Astaire's engagement to one famous person after another seemed to be ever present in the newspapers, Eddie made no further attempt to raise the subject of matrimony and he bid her goodnight in the hotel foyer in such an entirely platonic fashion that even her mother could have found nothing to disapprove of.

It had been very tempting to tell him about the name on the envelope she had contrived to knock off the shelf at Dolly's brother's house – an envelope addressed to Mr Albert de la Tour, a surname which Mrs Headingham might easily have confused with a fellow seventeenth-century French artist – but she decided that she needed to think things through herself first.

TWENTY-EIGHT

F ran faced a long, slow journey home the next day. She was unlucky at Euston, for having initially gained sole occupancy of a compartment, she was joined before the train pulled out, by a woman who was carrying a large basket on one arm and a fractious baby in the other, while trying, but failing, to keep a small lively boy under her control. Fran did her best to help by attempting to distract the boy, offering games of I Spy and similar pursuits, but the boy was not for being distracted from alternately racing from one side of the compartment to the other, while yelling loudly, or else crawling about the floor, pretending to be a roaring lion. By the time the little party left the train at Rugby, Fran's nerves felt so frayed that she began to wonder if Mo quite realized what she was letting herself in for.

After this unfortunate episode travellers came and went with considerably less fuss, keeping themselves to themselves and leaving her in peace with her thoughts. As the train approached Birmingham, she found herself considering the fact that just a few weeks earlier, she had been standing at a chilly bus stop, resolving that she must make a new life for herself and now, as if conjured up by a fairy godmother, there was a charming, handsome man, offering her a home and marriage. She wondered what her mother would say, if she announced that she intended to marry again – and to a man that she had scarcely known for more than a couple of weeks. (Well, she had known Michael for at least a year before he proposed and how much good had that done her?) And what would her mother make of an announcement that she intended to live in Devon? That was a big stumbling block, for as the only surviving child, she couldn't just abandon her mother, and go off to live hundreds of miles away. It was most unlikely that her mother would agree to move down to Devon . . . No, let's be honest, it wasn't just *unlikely* . . . her mother would never agree to it. In fact, she would put every possible emotional obstacle in the way.

Fran turned to look out of the window. Now that spring had properly arrived, everything was turning green, though it was mostly a pale, watery green today as the train passed through rain showers interwoven with occasional patches of sunshine. They would be coming into New Street station soon. There would be no meeting with Tom today. No chance to discuss the case.

A vision of Tom was replaced by Eddie. 'We're just not that sort of family,' he had said. A statement with which, on the face of it, she could not disagree. The exception was perhaps their uncle Charles, with his fondness for drink, his womanizing and hints of uncertainty regarding his finances. Well, every family had its black sheep. Charles Edgerton would not have needed to bind and gag his father – he could have walked into the room and suggested going for a stroll in the grounds. But suppose his father had declined? That would have messed up the plan to be sure. And what about the diamond? Where did that fit in?

Out of nowhere she remembered Eddie again, saying that in a novel one of the descendants of Georges Poussin would have married into the family. Dolly did not sound French, but it seemed likely that she had a French maiden name. Suppose her family had brought her to England at a young age and raised her here, while they continued to search for the person who had purloined their most valuable possession?

Miss Billington, on the other hand, spoke French like a native. Moreover, Miss Roche had spoken as if Miss Billington had cause to hate the Edgertons and felt trapped into remaining in their service. Was Billington her real name? She was surely too young to have been Poussin's daughter, but if his daughter had married an Englishman called Billington . . . How very useful it would be to have access to her birth certificate.

Her thoughts returned to Dolly. Dolly who would return to Charles Edgerton, because she essentially had no better place to go. The family had rated her a gold-digger, but perhaps in Charles Edgerton, she had picked a gold mine, which was yielding less and less. Dolly would surely have guessed that her husband stood to inherit something on his father's death and with no love lost between her and the other Edgertons, she might have taken considerable satisfaction in dumping the head of the family over the edge of the cliffs.

Fran had initially pitied Dolly, for she understood only too well the humiliation of discovering that one's husband had been unfaithful. She herself had been fortunate enough to inherit sufficient money to provide her with a degree of autonomy. (Thank you, Great-Aunt Rachel!) Without her legacy she might have been forced to return home and live with her mother, whereas Dolly was trapped between two fires. On the one hand, she could stay with Charles, whose philandering would no doubt continue in spite of his periods of remorse and the regular turning over of new leaves. On the other, she could lodge with her brother, Albert de La Tour and his wife, perhaps returning to work as a waitress, relying on a pittance in wages and the charity of her family. However, if Dolly had managed to secretly acquire a valuable jewel, it would have enabled her to embark on a new life of financial independence.

Suppose Dolly had stolen the diamond that afternoon? Having taken her father-in-law on his last walk along the cliff path, she would then have been left with the question of where to put the diamond. She could hardly have introduced it into the room she shared with her husband. Even if she had hidden it in her suitcase, the maids would have come across it when packing Charles and Dolly's things for them, in readiness for their departure. Keeping the diamond on her person or among her things would have been fraught with risk. It would perhaps have entailed a constant need to transfer the stone from one place to another in order to avoid discovery. However, if after pushing poor old Mr Edgerton off the cliff, she had turned back towards the house, walked up on to the higher path and secreted the stone in grotto, she could then have slipped back to retrieve it just before she and Charles left for London. If she had placed it in her handbag, there would have been no reason for her husband to have looked inside it during their journey, and once back at home she no doubt had a suitable hiding place in readiness to keep her newly acquired treasure, until she was able to turn the stone into cash. It was a perfect plan – or would have been, if Imogen had not decided to go treasure hunting on that very same afternoon.

Fran considered the problem from various angles, unconsciously nodding to herself as she did so. Then she sighed. If she had a likely solution to the problem, there remained the seemingly impossible task of proving it.

TWENTY-NINE

'Eddie? Is that you?'

'Yes, it is. Fran, what a delightful surprise. I wasn't expecting to hear from you so soon.'

'No . . . yes. The thing is that I need to talk to you. It's about the death of your grandfather and I'd rather talk face-to-face, if that's all right.'

'Of course. Anything to spend an hour or two in your company, you know that. Do you want me to drive north within the hour?'

'No. I'm not in the north. I'm in Torquay. I'm staying at the Palace Hotel.'

'You truly love to spring a surprise on a chap, I must say. It was only two – no three – days ago that I saw you on to the train in London and now here you are, back in Devon. What on earth are you up to?'

Fran lowered her voice. 'I believe I'm on the trail of a murderer. That's why I need to talk with you.'

'I see.' Eddie's voice sounded unusually grave. 'Well, in that case, I'd better come at once.'

Eddie was as good as his word and must have driven like the wind, for within less than forty minutes, he was walking into the hotel lounge.

'The thing is,' Fran said, after outlining her theory, to which Eddie had listened in silence, punctuated only by gasps and occasional disbelieving shakes of his head, 'that your family has to decide. If this were to lead to an arrest and a trial, then the whole story becomes public and that's exactly the kind of scandal that you all wanted to avoid. In fact, it's the whole reason why you called on myself and Mr Dod rather than sharing your concerns with the police in the first place.'

'What do you think we ought to do?'

'I think that someone who has committed a cold-blooded murder needs to be brought to justice. But I don't always see things in the same way as say Mellie or your mother would.'

Eddie digested this briefly before asking, 'What is to prevent you from taking this story to the police yourself?'

'I don't believe it would do any good. You see, I don't have any actual proof. The only way I can see of getting that proof would need the full cooperation of your family.'

'So you need me to intercede on your behalf, is that it?' Eddie gave a chuckle. 'I'm not much of a diplomat, you know. It would probably be far better coming from you.'

'I don't think so. You can tell them my ideas and they will be able to discuss it openly, between themselves, without an outsider present.'

'Don't be an outsider then. Wouldn't it be much better if we drove back over there now, walked into the drawing room and announced our engagement? Then you could tack all this business about unmasking a murderer on at the end while Jamieson cracked open a few bottles of champagne. It would help them get used to what it will be like, having a lady detective in the family.'

'Eddie, this really isn't a joking matter.'

'Dear thing, I wasn't entirely joking.'

'It is far better for you to tell them and for me to stay out of it. Don't forget that the rest of your family doesn't even think I'm still detecting – if you must call it that – they think I've found the diamond for them and left it at that.' Fran did not add, though it was certainly in her mind, that they might turn out to be jolly angry on learning that instead of leaving well alone, she had continued to poke around in their family mystery until she had unearthed a solution.

Eddie pondered again for a short while, then said, 'So you want me to persuade them. That's it, isn't it? I have to persuade my family to do the right thing. I'm sort of riding into battle, as your Sir Galahad. Well, I undertake your commission, but in return, I—'

Fran did not let him get any further. 'I'm not making any bargains or any promises.'

'Very well then, let right prevail. But there's one thing I'm not at all clear about. You say that you can only prove this with the help and cooperation of the family. I don't quite see how any of us can help with that.'

'What I mean is that we can only catch the killer by setting a trap – and for that I need your family's help.'

'A trap, eh? That sounds pretty exciting, I must say. Do I get to hear the details before I go off and do my Sir Galahad bit, or only if my mission succeeds?'

'You need to hear about it now, because it's something else that you are going to have to explain, in order that everyone understands what it is they are agreeing to do.'

Eddie listened carefully again, without interruption. When he had digested what she had to say, he rose to his feet and, bowing slightly, lifted her hand from where it had been resting on the arm of the chair and kissed it. 'Madam,' he said, adopting a grave, theatrical tone, which much to Fran's embarrassment caused the heads of some card players at a nearby table to turn, 'consider your commission accepted.' Straightening to his full height, he turned to leave, but he had only taken a step before he turned back and said in an entirely different tone, 'I always knew you'd solve it. What a girl!'

THIRTY

With Roly's agreement, Fran used the typewriter in the estate office to produce the letter, using cheap, plain white stationery which she had acquired from the post office in Frencombe. Naturally she included no signature or return address.

You did not see her, but Imogen saw you in the woods that day. She saw you pushing the old man along the path and she followed you to the grotto. That's how she found the diamond. I can see to it that the child doesn't breathe a word to anyone else, but I would need to be sure of avoiding financial hardship. £500 should do the trick. That's a lot of money, but I could accept small instalments. Perhaps we should discuss terms? I will be waiting in the grotto at ten o'clock on Thursday evening.

THIRTY-ONE

'On reflection, perhaps we needn't have made it so late,' Fran said. 'Any time after dark would have worked equally well and it will be dark by nine.'

'We should have made it midnight,' said Henrietta. 'That's the traditional hour for assignations in all the best novels.'

'I do hope it doesn't start to rain,' said Eddie.

'It isn't going to. The barometer is absolutely steady.' This from Roly.

'I'm going to wrap up jolly warm,' Henrietta said. 'It's darned chilly out there tonight.'

'No use complaining about catching a chill now,' said Eddie. 'When all's said and done, you're the one who insisted on coming.'

'Your mother will have a conniption fit if she finds out that you're going with them,' said Mellie. 'You had far better stay here, with me.'

'Mellie, this is the most exciting thing that's ever happened at Sunnyside House. You can hardly expect me to skulk about back here at the house and miss it.'

'I hope you're not suggesting that I'm skulking?'

'Of course not, dear, we all know you would be coming too if you weren't in a delicate condition.'

'You mustn't even think of coming,' Roly put in, giving his wife's shoulder a reassuring pat, while Fran reflected yet again that making babies was all the fashion in 1930.

'Never mind about Mother, I'm not too happy about you girls having any part of this. We're dealing with a dangerous individual here. Someone who has already killed once,' said Eddie.

'And happens to be a woman,' said Henrietta. 'Besides which, you need us. Fran has to sit inside the grotto and I will be helping to keep watch and listen outside.'

'Roly and I can do that. In fact, one of us could lie in wait inside and the other could be outside. It only needs one person to have the conversation and the other to be a witness. Even the fact of her turning up is incriminating.'

'Well, I'm coming with you and that's that.' Henrietta was emphatic.

At that moment they were all surprised to hear the distant peal of the front doorbell.

'Who on earth can that be?' asked Henrietta.

'Heaven only knows. We're not expecting anyone.'

'Well, whoever it is, we must get rid of them in plenty of time if we're going to get ourselves into place early enough.'

A tense silence was hanging over the drawing room when Jamieson opened the double doors and announced, 'Miss Mabel Trenchard.'

As Mabel entered the room and the Edgertons all rose to greet her with apparent enthusiasm, Fran decided that every one of them could easily have made a career on the stage. Not for a moment would Mabel have detected the consternation which her arrival had provoked.

'So sorry to interrupt everyone's evening, but I've got a flat tyre I'm afraid. I've had to leave the car on the main road and walk down. I've got a spare, of course, but I can't manage to change it by myself.' As she spoke, Mabel was divesting herself of her heavyweight motoring mackintosh, gloves, scarf and bright red beret, which she handed item by item to the waiting butler.

'Poor Mabel, you must be frozen,' said Mellie. 'Jamieson, please bring in some hot coffee for Miss Trenchard at once.'

'Actually, I'm pretty warm from the walk, but coffee would be jolly nice all the same. Oh, hello, Mrs Black. I wasn't expecting to see you back here so soon.'

Though Mabel smiled and extended a hand, Fran felt sure that she was actually not at all pleased to see her.

'I'm just passing through,' Fran said, returning the smile while wondering how long it might take for someone to escort Miss Trenchard back to her car, help her change the wheel and get her back on her way.

As if he had picked up on Fran's thought, Eddie said, 'I'll get Jamieson to roust out Jennings and his lad from the top cottages. They can walk up to the main road and get the tyre changed while you're having your coffee, Mabel.'

'Oh, thank you. But there's really no rush. I mean, I could do it myself if someone could walk back with me and give me a hand.'

'Not at all. Wouldn't hear of your having to mess about with it.' Eddie positively scooted out of the room without giving Mabel any further opportunity to object.

While Eddie was gone, Mellie asked Mabel about the health of her parents and sisters and then Mabel, who gave every appearance of settling in for the rest of the evening, volunteered that Cecil Truscott was rumoured to have asked Evangeline Bicknell to marry him and wasn't it a scream, what with her being forty if she was a day. Fran and Henrietta covertly exchanged agonized looks.

'I say, Mabel,' Eddie said on his return, 'I've had an even better idea. My car is being brought down from the garage so that I can run you back up to the main road as soon as you are ready.'

'But there's absolutely no need. It barely takes a quarter of an hour to walk it. Anyone would think you were eager to get rid of me.'

'Of course we're not,' said Roly. 'It's just that we don't want them getting anxious about you back at home.'

'Oh, good point,' said Mabel. 'Why don't I use your telephone and call to say where I am? That way no one will worry for hours yet.'

While Mabel was out in the hall, using the telephone, there was a hasty conference in the drawing room.

'I suppose we could come clean, swear Mabel to secrecy and let her in on what's afoot. Mabel's a jolly good sport and up for anything, you know.'

'Don't be ridiculous, Hen,' said her older brother. 'We can't possibly involve Mabel in something which is top secret, could easily go wrong and may be dangerous.'

'Anyway, Mabel can't keep a secret to save her life. She would blab across the entire neighbourhood,' protested Mellie. 'And suppose your plan doesn't work? Suppose no one turns up? We would be the laughing stock of the district.'

'We have to keep Mabel out of it,' said Fran. 'Eddie will have to take her back to her car as soon as possible. If he doesn't get back in time, then we'll have to go without him. That still leaves three of us.'

'Oh, I say! I'm not at all happy about that.'

'Hush, don't shout, Eddie, she's probably on her way back. You have to do as Fran says. We can't afford to have someone blundering about after we ought to be in position. If you were seen that would completely put paid to the plan.'

The discussion was brought to a close by the return of Mabel, who settled herself back into an armchair and announced, 'There now, no one is in the least worried and I can stay out as long as I like.'

Poor Mabel, Fran thought, as the young woman made her farewells less than half an hour later, while Eddie held open the drawing room door for her and Jamieson impassively helped her into her outdoor clothes. It could not possibly have escaped her notice that her hosts were in a hurry to see the back of her.

In the end it was a close-run thing. Fran, Henrietta and Roly were gathered at the door which led out on to the terrace, and on the point of departure when they heard the roar of Eddie's returning Riley and in no more than a minute he had raced through the house to join them.

'Make sure that top button is fastened,' his sister chided him. 'You don't want to leave a great swathe of pale shirt showing.'

'Listen to my sister, a veteran of undercover operations,' Eddie laughed, but there was a nervous edge to his voice and he did up the button as instructed.

'Now remember,' said Roly, with his hand on the door-knob, 'although there's still almost an hour to go, we don't do any talking and we don't put on our torches unless we absolutely have to.'

'Just be careful on these paths,' hissed his sister, already dropping her voice to a whisper, though there was as yet no need. 'We don't want anyone to end up missing the edge of the path and breaking an ankle.'

'Teach your grandmother,' retorted Roly. 'I know these paths like the back of my hand.'

The conduct of their mission had been planned in detail. Firstly Eddie (who was nearest the switch) turned out the light to avoid their exit being easily observed in the unlikely event that anyone was watching the house from the garden. Then, after a few seconds standing in the dark passageway, Roly opened the door and the others followed him on to the terrace, sticking to the previously agreed order: Roly, Henrietta then Fran, with Eddie bringing up the rear.

Roly led them along the terrace and round the side of the house, where lights still shone from behind the curtains of the servants hall. The path which skirted the rockery benefitted from some of this light, but the steep steps beyond it were in darkness and Fran was glad to grasp Henrietta's outstretched hand and to hear her whispered count of, 'One, two, three, four, five, six and that's the top.'

As Roly began to lead them along the narrow path in single file, Fran realized that she would have to put her trust in him and walk blindly, for there was no chance of seeing where she was going. Gradually, however, as they left the artificial brightness of the house behind them and she followed the tall, slim shape of Henrietta, which moved steadily no more than half a yard ahead of her, Fran began to make out the shapes of trees and bushes. She had grown up in the countryside and knew that it was never truly dark – or quiet – though it seemed eerily so tonight, with the sound of their feet as audible as if they had been deliberately stomping, rather than attempting to remain unheard.

The route to the grotto seemed twice as long as it had been when they'd visited it that morning to finalize their plans, but just when Fran thought they must have taken a wrong turn, she realized that they had arrived on the edge of the little clearing at last. Henrietta turned and gestured silently in the direction of the dark mound which represented the grotto, and Fran responded with a series of exaggerated nods. She stood for a moment to get her bearings as the others melted away into their predetermined hiding places among the surrounding trees. It was, she estimated, at least half an hour before the rendezvous was due. They had done well, arriving in plenty of time in spite of the unscheduled interruption from Mabel

Trenchard, and during their cautious approach they had done nothing to betray their presence. All that remained was for her to take up her own position in the grotto and wait.

She stepped forward with an arm outstretched until her fingertips came into contact with the rough stones from which the little folly was built. Feeling her way along, she sidestepped around the outside of the building until her fingers encountered the rough wooden post which framed the left-hand side of the door. The grotto was inky black inside and she wondered whether she dared risk her torch for a second, just to get her bearings, but decided against. Even the smallest light escaping from the opening at the front might be visible for a long way into the woods. Instead she raised her hands again, in order to avoid walking into anything, took another exploratory step forward and in so doing, collided with a solid object.

The hands came at her so fast that there was no time to cry out. One clamped across her face, almost immediately finding and silencing her mouth, while the other brought something hard and startlingly cold against her neck. The voice in her ear was so low that she could scarcely make out the words. 'I have a knife. If you struggle or make one sound, I'll use it to cut your throat.'

THIRTY-TWO

'Move.' The voice in her ear was accompanied by a shove which took her whole body in the direction of the doorway.

Only too keen to cooperate, Fran stumbled forward, kept upright by the force of the body pressed against hers, her direction of movement mostly determined by the arm clamped around her head and mouth. The voice in her ear was unrecognizable, so low that it could have belonged to a person of either sex, but she knew that her captor must be Monica Roche, the woman she had lured here with her anonymous note. A dangerous woman she had thought to outwit. What a stupid, stupid thing to do!

What, if anything, she wondered, could the others see as she and Miss Roche emerged from the grotto and into the clearing? A light breeze had begun to rustle through the trees, masking the sound of their feet. Would any of the others even be watching the entrance to the grotto at that particular moment and, if they were, how much would they be able to make out of the two dark figures against an even darker background?

They were out in the open now, moving unsteadily across the clearing, with not a sign that any of her companions in tomfoolery had noticed them. But perhaps that was a good thing? One shout or sudden move from anyone and Monica could make good her threat, without greatly delaying her subsequent escape into the woods.

Though she had only passed that way a handful of times, Fran recognized the gentle downward incline of the track they were taking. Soon they would reach the wider path which ran between the terrace and the clifftop shelter. The path along which Monica had pushed old Mr Edgerton to his death. With a sickening sense of certainty, she understood what her captor intended. Miss Roche must have assumed, just as she had intended, that the blackmail note had come from Miss

Billington. She had made her way to the rendezvous early – had perhaps been waiting there for hours – ready to seize the governess the instant she walked in. *And she still thinks that I'm Miss Billington*, thought Fran. *It's too dark for her to see, otherwise and she never gave me a chance to say anything, which would have given the game away at once. She thinks that getting rid of Miss Billington will put her in the clear. Imogen may know something but no one ever takes any notice of Imogen. Miss Roche thinks that if Miss Billington has an accident – just like old Mr Edgerton – and there are no witnesses and no apparent suspicious circumstances, then she will still be in the clear.*

The plan to trap Monica Roche had seemed so clever and the Edgertons had fostered her vanity in it, all of them convinced that she had some sort of genius for solving mysteries and therefore willingly embracing her ideas for providing the evidence that was needed. (The very fact that Monica Roche had answered the anonymous summons was compromising, but Fran had also hoped to involve her in an incriminating conversation in the hearing of her hidden witnesses.) Only now, when it was far too late, did Fran appreciate the degree to which the whole enterprise had been fraught with personal risk. Hadn't Tom and Mo both warned her repeatedly about getting herself into dangerous situations? Well, in a very few minutes, she would be literally poised between the devil and the deep blue sea, and she couldn't see any possible way out. As the sound of the breakers at the foot of the cliff grew louder she vainly strained her ears for any sign of the rest of the party, who were presumably still staking out the grotto, in the mistaken belief that she was safely waiting inside.

If only she could get Miss Roche talking, she might be able to persuade her of the pointlessness of shoving another individual off the edge of the cliff by explaining that as the individual in question was but one of half a dozen people who now knew the truth, it would be far better to spare herself the trouble of a second murder and focus instead on making good an escape; but her captor's hand still silenced her and she was afraid that any attempt to struggle would lead to Miss Roche fulfilling her threat. Cutting her intended victim's throat on the path would be messy, and the discovery of a murdered governess would lead to a great many more questions than another death from a fall, but even so Miss Roche had no way of knowing that she would be suspected. So far as she was concerned, the meeting in the grotto was a secret known to herself and Miss Billington alone.

Fran's eyes had long since grown accustomed to the dark, so she was aware that they had joined the main path from the terrace. To her right she could make out the shapes of the trees which grew in the garden below, and ahead of her she became aware of the pale nothingness where the land ended in a drop of perhaps eighty to a hundred feet. The sound of the water washing over the unforgiving rocks at the foot of the cliffs was growing louder. She knew she had to do something before they reached the edge, for Monica Roche was a tall, strongly built woman. In a pushing and shoving contest, which relied on physical strength, the smaller woman would inevitably come off second best.

Fran began to inch her hand towards her coat pocket. Her small torch was a puny sort of weapon, but perhaps it was better than nothing.

'Stop! Who's there?'

A figure seemed to rear up out of nowhere on the path ahead of them. Fran was so startled that she let out a muffled squeak of shock. Monica Roche seemed equally at a loss, jerking to a halt and in the next moment shoving Fran forward so hard that she cannoned into Henrietta Edgerton and sent them both flailing to the ground. Miss Roche took the opportunity to turn tail and race headlong back the way she had come, but within seconds the sound of her progress came to an abrupt halt and was replaced by muffled cries and the sounds of a struggle.

'Look out!' Fran cried. 'She's got a knife.'

'Never fear.' Hen's voice was remarkably calm under the circumstances. 'She'll be no match for Eddie and Roly. Come on, let me help you up. Are you all right? You know,' she added as she reached out a hand and hauled Fran to her feet, 'it sounds like quite a scrap. I think we might be needed after all.'

Henrietta set off at a sprint to cover the twenty yards or so which separated them from her brothers, while Fran – who had never run towards 'a scrap' in her life – hastened after her. They arrived to find a dark jumble of figures scuffled on the ground and it did indeed require the effort of all of them to subdue Nurse Roche, who had already been forcibly disarmed, though not before she had managed to strike a couple of blows at Roly, which were fortunately mitigated by his tweed jacket and thick Aran knit jersey. Matters were eventually brought to a halt when, having been comprehensively pinned down, the woman on the ground simply stopped struggling.

'Now then,' said Roly, 'you may as well come back willingly with us and wait at the house for the police. Otherwise we'll just have to keep you out here in the cold until reinforcements arrive.'

'Very well. Kindly stop shining that torch in my face and I'll do as you say and come quietly.' Fran was astonished to note that Miss Roche spoke in the same dispassionate tone she had employed in the teashop. Apart from being a little out of breath, no one could have guessed that she had just been involved in a life-and-death struggle.

Henrietta, who had switched on her torch, obediently swung the beam away from their captive and in doing so, saw a red stain on Roly's sleeve. 'You're bleeding,' she said.

'It's only a scratch,' said Roly. 'But someone had better go on ahead to telephone for Dr Deacon, as well as the police. You never know, it might need stitching.'

'To the charge sheet of murder and attempted arson, we'd better add malicious wounding,' commented Eddie, as he and Roly cautiously relinquished their holds enough to allow Monica Roche to get to her feet.

'What I don't understand,' Fran said, turning to Henrietta, 'is how you managed to get ahead of me on the path?'

'Oh, that was easy. As soon as I spotted you coming out of the grotto, I knew that something must have gone wrong. Then I realized that it wasn't one person, but two, very close together, and I guessed that whoever had hold of you might be armed, so I signalled to the boys to follow at a distance. Once I saw

that you were definitely headed for the edge of the cliffs, I
knew I had to risk intervening. Don't forget that we grew up
in these woods, stalking and tracking one another. We often
played here after dark. I know all the short cuts.'

'In addition to which,' Eddie put in, 'Hen won the cup for
the hundred-yard sprint at her school three years in a row, so
she can easily outflank anyone if she puts her mind to it.'

The brothers had positioned themselves one to either side
of Miss Roche, taking her arms in readiness to frogmarch her
back to the house.

'One moment,' Miss Roche said. 'I think my shoe has half
come off. Let me straighten it.'

She moved with surprising agility for such a large woman,
twisting away from her captors as soon as they relaxed their
restraint on her and dashing back the way they had come. The
benefit of surprise had given her a yard or two on them, but
not for nothing had Henrietta won that silver cup. She drew
level with Miss Roche within a few strides and attempted to
arrest her progress, while the other woman forged on towards
the cliff edge, dragging Henrietta with her like a terrier clinging
to a rag.

'Hen, be careful!' Roly's warning rang out in the same
moment as Monica Roche shrieked and disappeared, leaving
a single slim figure silhouetted against the sky.

Fran was the first to reach the place. She put out a hand
and realized that Henrietta was shaking.

'Oh my God,' Henrietta whispered. 'I didn't mean to push
her over.'

'That isn't what happened,' Fran said firmly. 'If you hadn't
let go and pushed her away, you would have gone over too.
She meant to take you with her.'

'But . . .'

'There is no but. I believe that she fully intended to jump.
She knew the other alternative was the hangman's rope. When
you caught up with her, she thought she would take one more
Edgerton with her – a final act of revenge.'

THIRTY-THREE

'I bet it all took some explaining to the police.'

Fran had taken advantage of the weather to set up a couple of deckchairs in the garden of Beehive Cottage and Mo was reclining in one of them, using her bump to balance a cup and saucer in a singularly unladylike manner.

'It took hours. Shall I make some more tea? Or would you rather have some lemonade? Ada has just made her first batch of the year and it's jolly nice. Gosh, but it's good to have you home.'

'It's good to be home. The voyage back wasn't half so much fun as going out. I couldn't even enjoy a few cocktails. Do you know, it's the strangest thing, but I just cannot abide the taste of alcohol, since I've been preggers. I do hope the effect isn't permanent.'

'I'm sure it won't be. Once you've had the baby, the local wines and spirits merchants will be able to breathe more easily again.'

'Well, I sincerely hope so. In the meantime, I will try some of Ada's most excellent lemonade and just have to *imagine* that there's some gin in it.'

While Fran disappeared into the kitchen, Mo idly watched a butterfly negotiate the canes which had been erected in readiness for runner beans to climb them. By the time Fran emerged, bearing a tray containing a jug full of misty yellow liquid and two tumblers, the butterfly had finished its investigation of a couple of stray stinging nettles which were growing against the dry stone wall and fluttered away out of sight.

'So I can see how you lured her back to Sunnyside House,' Mo said, seamlessly continuing an earlier conversation. 'What I don't understand is how you worked out that the murderer was Monica Roche.'

'I was on the train when I finally realized the truth. There's nothing to beat a long train journey for thinking things out,

always providing you don't have to share a compartment with
. . .' Fran reigned back what could have been a tactless remark
and continued, '. . . with anyone kicking up a row. As you
know, I had gradually convinced myself that the culprit was
Dolly Edgerton. She had a motive and she didn't have an alibi
for part of the afternoon. She had also been staying at
Sunnyside House when a fire had started in old Mr Edgerton's
room and I could see how easy it would have been for any
member of the household to slip downstairs and use the poker
to drag a log out of the fireplace and on to the hearthrug, then
head back up to bed.'

'That's a pretty risk strategy, surely? I mean the whole house
might have burned down. How close is the nearest fire engine?'

'It is risky,' Fran agreed. 'But I assumed that the culprit
would lie in bed long enough for the old man's room to fill
up with smoke and then pretend that something had woken
them up just in time to give the alarm, which would ensure
that everyone else got out safely and the fire could be
contained.'

'I still say you'd be taking a terrible risk.'

'Oh, undoubtedly. Of course, the risk of the plan going
wrong would have been significantly reduced, if you had taken
the precaution of removing yourself – and the diamond – from
the building in advance. Monica claimed that she'd gone out
on the terrace for a breath of fresh air, but I think what she
had really been doing was concealing the diamond. Her plan
had probably been to hide the diamond somewhere outside,
then let herself back into the house and raise the alarm,
pretending that she'd gone downstairs to get a drink or something, and seen the smoke coming under the door, but as it
was Mr Edgerton started yelling, so she had to come up with
a rather weak explanation for what she was doing outside.

'The trouble was that I tended to overlook Monica, because
it seemed to be impossible for her to have been the killer, as
she had an alibi. It appeared that Monica couldn't possibly
have committed the murder, because she was collected by car
and driven to Torquay. Jamieson had seen the victim alive
after she had left the house and by the time she came back,
the old man was already gone, so we all knew that the murder

must have been accomplished while she was away. The hotel staff vouched for the fact that she and her friend had taken tea there and although that didn't account for the entire afternoon, her companion, Mr Moncrieff, appeared to be a thoroughly trustworthy and reliable witness, who had worked at Baddeley Court for years and years and had no motive to lie for her.

'Lots of clues pointed to Monica Roche. First of all, her name is originally French, though it's quite common in England too. In France they pronounce it "rosh", I believe, but over here we say "roach" like the fish.'

'Or the cockroach. Thanks,' said Mo, as Fran handed her a glass of lemonade and then poured one for herself.

'So I'd noticed the possibility presented by her having a French name, but then I dismissed that because she seemed to be so completely English, and besides which we thought we were looking for a completely different French name.'

'Well, that was the fault of the old woman in Sidmouth,' said Mo.

'Not really. At least it was as much our fault as it was hers. Mrs Headingham couldn't remember the name of the Frenchman, but she told us that the word which came into her head reminded her of poison. That led to Poussin, and we all latched on to that, but we were heading down completely the wrong track. She originally said that the name sounded like poison, which is very similar to Poussin, but it's even closer to *poisson*, which is French for fish. Roche – roach – fish – *poisson* – poison.'

'Good heavens, that's all a bit cryptic. How strangely some people's minds seem to work.'

'And it also happened to be the case that Dolly's family name turned out to be shared with another French artist, which coincidentally suggested Poussin as well.'

'But in that case the only fish was a red herring.'

Fran ignored the lame jest. 'Even Eddie's funny idea about a burglar gagging his grandfather and tying him to the chair was a clue in its way.'

'Go on.' Mo laughed. 'Don't keep me in suspense.'

'Well, you see, Eddie was quite right. Suppose you'd laid

your plans, checked that the coast was clear, gone into the library and offered to wheel old Mr Edgerton as far as the cliffs and he'd simply said thank you but he didn't want to go?'

'I suppose you'd try to persuade him.'

'And what if he didn't want to be persuaded? If you attempted to force him into coming with you, he might kick up a regular shindig and alert one of the servants.'

'Quite so. But you said he wasn't tied up or gagged.'

'He wasn't. But he was probably drugged. It would have been easy for Monica Roche to have given him some sleeping pills with his lunch. When Jamieson collected his lunch tray, he was fast asleep in the wheelchair.'

'So he couldn't call out because he wouldn't have realized what was happening. I suppose that was probably a blessing. So again and again, things pointed to the nurse.'

'Exactly,' said Fran. 'When it came to hiding the diamond in the grotto, I'd thought out the reason why Dolly might have hidden it there, but what I hadn't initially realized was that the same thing applied to Monica in spades. You see, Monica couldn't be sure that the diamond wouldn't be missed right away. For all she knew, a member of the family might have looked in the safe on the very first day after Frederick Edgerton died and spotted that it was missing, but in order to alleviate any suspicion she had to stay and work out her notice. It's a well-known fact that if valuables go missing, the servants' things will be thoroughly searched, so Monica needed to hide that diamond somewhere no one was likely to look for it. It was no use putting it in the house. It needed to be somewhere she could return to unseen and retrieve it after she'd officially left. By putting it in the grotto, she knew that even if her belongings were checked on the very day she left, no one would find the diamond on her.'

'But instead the noisy child, what's-her-name, went and found it.'

'Imogen found it within less than half an hour of its being hidden.' Fran gave a chuckle. 'I bet Monica Roche was furious when she went back and discovered that the stone had gone.'

'How soon do you suppose she checked that it was still there?'

'I doubt if she would have returned to the grotto until she came back to actually collect the diamond. She wouldn't have wanted to risk being seen there in the immediate aftermath of old Mr Edgerton's death, just in case anyone got interested in what she was doing there and started snooping around. On the face of it, the grotto represented a really safe hiding place because the family was hardly going to start organizing a treasure hunt with the chief instigator of treasure hunts barely cold in his grave. It must have seemed safer than handing it to her accomplice, because he was in service too, and might have come under suspicion by simply having been on the premises when he picked her up and dropped her off that day, so he too risked the possibility of being searched if the theft had been discovered immediately.'

'Her accomplice? This is the first I've heard of an accomplice.' Mo sounded rather as if she thought she had been short-changed.

'Mr Moncrieff, the Baddeleys' chauffeur. Though he's pleading not guilty to accessory to murder, he's admitted everything else to the police, which has helped fill in some of the gaps in the story. He claims that he was only ever party to the theft and has always believed that Mr Edgerton's death was an accident.'

'So Moncrieff was in on it! The nurse inveigled her way into his affections and persuaded him to help her. There was a love affair after all.'

'Not a love affair. A completely different relationship, in fact. Moncrieff is Monica Roche's half-brother.'

'But hold on – surely Moncrieff is a Scottish name?'

'It is, but the thing is that you can be born in England but still have a French father . . . and a Scottish mother. If Monica Roche had been born today, there would have been an even bigger clue, because since 1911 the index to English births provides the mother's maiden name, but of course Monica Roche's birth was registered long before that.'

'I'm not sure that I follow what you're getting at there,' said Mo.

'Not to worry, I'll come back to that in a minute. You see, Eddie and I had assumed that the address Georges Roche gave

to Frederick Edgerton was in France, but it's now emerged
that Monica Roche's father had lived in London for quite a
while before he went to South Africa. That's probably why
he and Frederick Edgerton hit it off so well. Georges Roche
would have spoken fluent English and been used to British
ways because he'd married a British girl called Mary Moncrieff.
That was what I meant about being able to see the mother's
maiden names in the birth registrations index. I had to get
copies of the actual birth certificates to be sure of the connection. Mary already had an illegitimate son before she married
Georges Roche. His name was George Moncrieff.

'Soon after she married Georges Roche, he went off to seek
his fortune, and not long after he left, Mary found out that
she was expecting his child. She named the girl Monica and
waited for her husband. In the fullness of time, he wrote to
say that he was coming back, but unfortunately he didn't make
it. For some reason he came back via Morocco. He'd lost or
been fleeced of his money and he died of typhoid in a doss
house in Tangiers, but in his last letter to his wife he'd told
her not to worry because a friend and business associate called
Freddie Edgerton had been keeping a valuable jewel safe for
him and would bring it to her when he returned to England.'

'But somehow or other, the diamond was never handed
over,' Mo finished for her. 'Do you think it was an accident?
Could Frederick Edgerton not have found them, if he'd tried
a bit harder?'

'I don't know. I suppose it wasn't easy to track people down
in the London slums, back in the 1880s. Mary Roche may have
been moving from place to place, especially if she owed the
rent, and in those circumstances, she's unlikely to have left a
forwarding address. Perhaps Frederick Edgerton didn't try as
hard as he might have done. Perhaps he thought his friend had
taken his wife back to France. Who knows? The important point
is that the Roche family didn't get their diamond back, so the
widowed Mrs Roche had a struggle to bring up her children
and those children had to work hard for their living.

'According to what Moncrieff told the police, they never
seriously tried to track down this man who was supposed to
be bringing them a diamond. I'm not sure that Mary Roche,

or her son, were entirely convinced of the diamond's existence and even if they believed in the story of the diamond and the man who was supposed to be bringing it for them, they had no idea where he might be, or even whether he had made it back to Britain. In time Moncrieff left school and went into service. He got his post at Baddeley Court when Colonel Baddeley first bought a motor car, back in 1907, so of course he was already there when Frederick Edgerton bought the land to build Sunnyside House, but according to Moncrieff, he had long since forgotten the name of the man who was supposed to have been bringing back a diamond for them. However, his stepsister, Monica, had not forgotten and when her half-brother happened to mention the new family who had moved into the district, she put two and two together and realized that it might be the same man. She became obsessed – in Moncrieff's words – with finding out the truth and when the vacancy for a trained nurse came up, she applied for the post.'

'But surely, when she was taken on as his nurse, the old man must have realized that she was his old friend's daughter?' protested Mo.

'Apparently not. If he noticed the name at all, then he must have assumed that it was a coincidence. There's more than one family called Roche and he probably wasn't aware that there had ever been a daughter. According to Moncrieff, the fact that her surname didn't create so much as a flicker of interest with the old man just made Monica all the more bitter and she decided to take back the diamond. "The way Monica put it, it didn't seem like stealing," Moncrieff said, "because it had been our property all along."'

Mo shifted in her deck chair and wedged a cushion more firmly behind the small of her back. 'Hmm,' she said. 'I'm not so sure about that.'

'The irony is that if Monica had actually told him who she was, Frederick Edgerton might have given her the stone. I know he didn't appear to have made much effort to find his friend's wife, but at the same time, he'd never sold the diamond, or given it to anyone else either.'

'Goodness, why didn't the stupid woman just confront him with the truth about who she was?'

'She wasn't going to risk it,' Fran said. 'Think about it. Suppose she had revealed her connection with the diamond and Frederick Edgerton had refused to hand it over and told the family who she was. If she'd tried to take the diamond after that, suspicion would have fallen on her at once. Besides which, she had developed a real hatred of Frederick Edgerton, imagining that it was entirely due to him that she and her half-brother had endured such hardships throughout their lives. You can imagine how life at Sunnyside House would have fuelled that resentment. Here was this big, happy family, living in the lap of luxury, while she and her brother had worked so hard all their lives and ended up with next to nothing.'

'So at some point,' said Mo, 'she decided that getting the diamond back wasn't enough. She wanted revenge.'

'It may have been more complicated than that. Don't forget that she couldn't just make off with the diamond because sooner or later it would have been missed and she would naturally have come under suspicion as a person who enjoyed almost constant access to the room where the safe was. She had to hatch a scheme which would deflect suspicion away from herself, and she must have realized that Mr Edgerton's death would remove the one person who might have been able to say with any certainty when the diamond had definitely last been in the safe. Everyone knew that Mr Edgerton liked to get the diamond out and look at it from time to time. The family all knew that Mr Edgerton was becoming a little bit confused, so Monica played up to that, encouraging them to believe that he was getting worse. It worked too, because after his death it was suggested that he might have hidden the diamond some-where, which was extremely useful from the point of view of a thief, because it threw up an element of doubt as to whether there had actually been a theft at all.

'Remember that he claimed his food had been tampered with? Well, I don't believe that was an attempt on his life. If he'd died suddenly and poison was found, that would have immediately aroused suspicion and Monica Roche was far too clever for that. I think it was just another means of drawing attention to his supposed eccentricities. It would have been very simple for Monica to have added something bitter to his food then thrown it away, claiming to have tasted it and found nothing wrong with it herself.'

'What an evil woman,' said Mo. 'She must have planned and schemed for months.'

'From the moment she first took up the post, she was probably working out the lie of the land. It wouldn't have taken her long to discover where the diamond was kept. She would have kept her relationship with Moncrieff a secret, just in case anyone became overly interested in their background and started to ask questions, besides which, I don't think she had originally planned to involve him at all. If I'm right, then her first plan had been to arrange for her employer to die accidentally in the fire. I expect that's when she first hit on the idea of hiding the diamond safely in the grotto, but of course the fire came to nothing, because Mr Edgerton woke up and gave the alarm. That experience probably taught her that when the time came to attempt something else, she would need to ensure that her charge *didn't* wake up. The other problem on that occasion was that when the old man gave the alarm, she must have had to smuggle the diamond back into the safe at the first opportunity, before it was missed.

'After that she revised her plans, setting up a supposedly accidental meeting with her half-brother so it could appear that they developed a friendship which would make it natural for her to go out for trips with him in the Baddeley's car. Trips which would eventually provide her with an alibi. The idea was that on the day of the murder, Moncrieff would collect her from the house, then take the lane which ran along the perimeter of the Sunnyside grounds and park the car in a secluded spot. He was to wait in the car while she went through the woods to steal the diamond, and after that they would drive into Torquay and create an alibi by being seen in the Palace Hotel. With Frederick Edgerton dead, it would be natural for her to give in her notice, then a few days after she had officially left, Moncrieff would borrow the car again, meet her off the train somewhere well up the line, drive her back to that same place and she would slip through the woods and collect the diamond from the grotto.'

'But when she got there, it had already been removed. She

must have been furious,' said Mo, as if she found the prospect distinctly pleasing.

'She had been biding her time for months, waiting for the moment to send Mr Edgerton over the cliffs, because all the conditions had to be just right for it to work.'

'What conditions do you mean?'

'Well, she could hardly just push him out of the house and up the path in full view of everyone, could she? It had to happen on a day when Moncrieff had use of the car, so she would appear to have a solid alibi. The day had to be warm enough for it to be credible that her victim had been tempted to take himself out into the garden. Most important of all – and this was potentially the most difficult thing of all – it had to be done during a period when there was no one within sight of the terrace.

'Joe, the young apprentice gardener, mentioned that the car, which he'd assumed belonged to a courting couple, had been seen parked in that same spot before. It had probably been there on quite a few other occasions, but there hadn't always been anyone in the right place to see it. There must have been several false starts, when Moncrieff collected her from the house, parked in the lane and waited while she doubled back through the woods to see whether the coast was clear. She would be able to get in among the trees which overlook the terrace and if she saw anyone sitting there, or hanging about nearby, she simply slipped back to the car without being seen.'

'But eventually there was an afternoon when there was no one to see her.'

They were both silent for a few seconds until Mo spoke again. 'The other thing you still haven't told me – and it is of course, the most important question of all – is whether or not you have decided to accept Eddie Edgerton?'

'I've told him that I'm not going to marry him. Oh yes, I know, he's awfully nice and I've grown to be quite fond of him, even in the short time that I have known him, but . . . but I'm not in love with him, you see.' Fran had turned away and was looking far beyond the garden wall, towards some distant treetops, as if she had discovered something of immense interest there. 'And that wouldn't be fair.'

'Lots of things aren't fair,' Mo said quietly. 'Does Tom know?'

'Does Tom know what?'

'That you have turned down a proposal from an extremely eligible young man?'

'I've mentioned it, yes.'

'Mentioned it how? I thought there had to be an absolute wall of silence between the two of you.'

'I've spoken to him on the telephone. I don't believe that one call bringing him up to date on the resolution of the Sunnyside House affair can be deemed particularly suspicious. Besides which, my decree nisi came through, in spite of someone sending a very silly anonymous letter to the court, suggesting that there was something going on between myself and Tom.'

'Any idea who was responsible?'

'I think Tom has worked out who was behind it. When he went to the Robert Barnaby Society annual weekend at Furnival Towers, he happened to have a minute alone with a rather spiteful woman called Sarah Ingoldsby, and he commented, apropos of nothing in particular, of course, that it was quite appalling the way some people sent letters containing slanderous allegations in respect of other people's divorce proceedings, and that people who lived in glass houses shouldn't throw stones, unless they wanted a few house bricks to land on their own doormats.'

'Strong stuff,' said Mo. 'Isn't she the woman who was so obstructive when you were investigating your first case?'

'She is. She's also been having a long-term affair with the Barnaby Society chairman.'

'Ahh . . . And what did she have to say in return?'

'Nothing at all. But Tom said it was obvious his arrow had hit the mark from the expression on her face, so I'm fairly confident there will be no more letters. I think it's just a question of time before the rest of the paperwork goes through and it becomes final.'

'Not that it will make any difference to your situation with Tom.'

'As I keep on telling you, Mo, there is no situation between myself and Tom.'

'As you keep on telling me.'

'But it does mean that we can resume our friendship. Which is just as well.'

'What do you mean "just as well"? And stop looking so arch.'

'It seems that word of the Sunnyside House affair has spread as far as Wiltshire, where another family mystery awaits resolution.'

'Excellent!' exclaimed Mo. 'I can see that I've got back in the very nick of time . . . well someone has to keep an eye on you and regularly remind you not to fall into the hands of homicidal maniacs. Now do tell me all about it . . .'